D0469920

Back to Life

By Kristin Billerbeck

THE TROPHY WIVES CLUB

Back to Life

a trophy wives club novel

with faith and friends
there's always a light at the end of the tunnel

Kristin Billerbeck

AVON
INSPIRE
An Imprint of HarperCollins*Publishers*

HarperCollins books may be purchased for educational, business, or sales promotional use. For information please write: Special Markets Department, HarperCollins Publishers Inc., 10 East 53rd Street, New York, NY 10022.

Designed by Diahann Sturge

Library of Congress Cataloging-in-Publication Data
Billerbeck, Kristin.
    Back to life: a Trophy Wives Club novel / Kristin Billerbeck. — 1st ed.
        p. cm.
    ISBN 978-0-06-137877-5
    1. Widows—Fiction.   2. Female friendship—Fiction.   3. Divorced women—
Fiction.   4. Executors and administrators—Fiction.   5. Family secrets—Fiction.
6. Los Angeles (Calif.)—Fiction.   I. Title.

PS3602.I44B33   2008
813'.6—dc22   2008013054

08 09 10 11 12 OV/RRD 10 9 8 7 6 5 4 3 2

Chapter 1

"Lindsay, come on, we're going to be late!" Haley pounds on my front door like there's a fire. Haley does most things in life like there's a fire these days. I'm certain it has something to do with her chocolate frosting fetish, but I have no proof. While I slide my last earring in, I unlatch the door and let it creep open.

"Calm down. Everyone here is eighty; do you want to wake the devil?"

"It's nine-thirty." She rolls her eyes, acting more like—well, more like me than her. "His minions are already up, eating their cat chow or chicken livers or whatever disgusting things that smell up your open-air hallways. This place reminds me of the lion house at the San Francisco Zoo! It's a vegan's nightmare."

"All right. Must you be so dramatic? Get in here." I grab her by the arm and pull her inside.

"It's not like I'll wake them, you know." She drops her purse on the entry table. "It's daylight. Everyone's going to bed, probably closing the top on their caskets as we speak." Haley takes her sweater and drapes it across her face like Dracula.

After living here for a year and a half, Haley doesn't have a lot of heart for my neighbors. I can't say I blame her. The old women (former actresses, most of them) are the very definition of curmudgeon, as if life has done nothing but kick them and all they can do now is kick back.

Personally, I admire them. It must be absolutely freeing to say and do as you please. And at the expense of their good name, they live the lives they want. Granted, it's a little lonely for my taste, but that doesn't mean I can't see the value in it.

I step out of the foyer to pick up a newspaper. I notice a few eyes peering at me from behind slit curtains: The only sign of life in this place, other than the nine million cats, is the sliding window coverings. It's like there's always an imaginary puppet show and I'm the star.

I slam the door, shuddering as I do so. "Maury must be on commercial. I'm obviously the only entertainment."

"Look at it this way. It's like having your own security firm. As long as they can still dial 911, you're safe."

"No, it's like living in a costume shop. The blinking red eyes follow me everywhere . . . when my back is turned, I know their eyes follow me . . . And just when I get that cold, prickly feeling on the back of my neck, one of those blasted cats will rub up against my leg and scare the life out of me!"

Haley laughs. "Now who is being dramatic? They have a sixth sense. Instead of dead people, cats see cat-hating people. Your hatred of them is like a call of affection. Sort of like a signal to that special guy you do not want to date. Maybe you should try to pet one."

It's eerie living here since Ron died. I suppose part of it is my own *Tell-Tale Heart*, throbbing with guilt. Maybe that's why I'm so aware of the neighbors. Chances are they've done some regrettable things in their long lives, but it doesn't seem to bother them. But I'd love to know the actual odds. What are the chances that these guiltless women would all move here? Or that I'd be in their midst? My unfortunate providence knows no bounds. If indeed it is providence, and not divine penance. They say what goes around, comes around—and it certainly doesn't leave.

"No, thank you. Who knows where those cats have been?"

"You're just spending too much time here, and your life is paralleling theirs a tad too closely, which would be fine if you were fifty years older."

"You cannot really think that." I stop applying lipgloss and look at her. "My life isn't like theirs. I'm not that pathetic. Not yet."

She bites her bottom lip and shrugs.

"Haley, no." I beg of her to tell me something different. "Come on—these women are like one of those sad faces you see in the depression ads. You don't really think I'm like them. I'm young. My hair is still blonde. Well, it would be if it were really blonde. I'm happy, see?" I give her a broad grin.

"Their faces are still beautiful, too. They may not talk to us, but they clearly communicate well with their plastic surgeon. Back in the day, they probably only had to talk to their colorist, too."

"My life is not like theirs."

"It's not. You have your whole life in front of you. More places to see, people to meet. So what does that mean to you? What's next?" She starts tapping her toe, and it's as though I can hear the *Jeopardy!* music.

"I've been busy, Haley." I roll my eyes. "I did lose my husband. One doesn't just move on like you've lost a favorite sweater."

"Of course they don't, but I've always thought of you as a person who really experienced life. I'm the one who was content to watch it play out on TV. But you . . . well, you sulk all the time now. *They* sulk all the time. It's this great mass of sulking energy you feel whenever you enter this place. I suddenly have the urge to nap. It's depressing."

As is my life. "I don't sulk! And you're feeling cat energy, not mine. It wasn't depressing when you lived here."

"That's because you weren't depressing. You were always the life of the party. The person who stirred people up into some great debate. Where is that, Lindsay? At some point, you have to come back to us."

"You don't have to keep saying that to me, Haley. I know he's gone. They say not to make any important changes for a year."

"And we're past that mark."

I search my mind to think of something to justify why I need more time but nothing comes. I've turned into a slug, and my friends know it. Which bothers me more than actually being a slug—that people know it. "Why can't you let me take my time? People react to circumstances differently. I shouldn't be faulted for listening to the experts."

"You're not reacting. You're not doing anything. You've become like a murky fish tank and you, the lone fish, are presently floating at the top. It's time for some action!"

"That's not true. I'm . . . I'm waiting for the California real estate market to turn around."

I live in Bel Air! An address doesn't get much more high-end than that. A virtual real estate mogul I thought I'd become, buying and remodeling this place while new neighbors did the same—except the old neighbors never actually moved or died, which I suppose was a necessary and diabolical part of my plan. The only turnover going on is down the street at the local bakery. The rest of the units look like Mrs. Roper could appear at any moment. With her cat.

"Then what? Will you remodel another condo in here, the morgue? That's your plan?"

"It's not all bad here. There's the garden," I say with realtor enthusiasm. The center courtyard has a myriad of greenery that's almost tropical in its feel. With a small waterfall splashing gently into a man-made river, it would seem like heaven, were it not for the slow stalking of birds by an abundant feline population.

Haley raises her brows. "Are you forgetting the headless birds?"

"All right. Maybe it is all bad. " But work with me here. While Haley plans the wedding of the century to the man she adores, I spend my days trying to prove that my husband is truly dead. Haley's best friend is tall, dark, and handsome, and mine has an official death certificate.

"You just have to focus on what's right in your life again. You've got the Trophy Wives Club, church, me, money to travel with and any number of opportunities. I just think you need some direction."

Can you give me one? My eyes plead. I look around the room. "I just need more time. After selling Ron's business, I wasn't exactly ready to start one up right away. Are you telling me to get another job in the meantime?"

Haley sighs. "This is pointless. You're like the friend who is going to start her diet on Monday."

"What? Am I looking like I need to diet?" I try to contort my body to get a look at my backside.

She sighs again. "I was making a point."

"Not very well. Not if you have to call me fat to do so." I snicker.

"You call me cheap all the time!" Haley accuses.

"You are cheap," I remind her.

"I'm frugal. We're very wasteful here in L.A. I learned how much money my ex wasted when I had to stay in that seedy motel. You really don't need that much to get by. I simply love thinking about every penny that goes out. It makes me feel powerful."

"It makes you look cheap."

"Whatever. You won't be laughing when I leave you something fabulous in my will."

"You have to actually *buy* something fabulous to leave it to me. Maybe I'll point a few things out while we shop." I wink at her. It's really easy to forget your joy in life when things suddenly go fantastically bad. And you're alone. The Bible says man was not meant to be alone—well, neither was I. I'm terrible at being alone and yet afraid to get back out in the world. A terrible mixture of issues—leave it to me to make life complicated. "Why don't you move back in until your wedding, Haley, and you can remind me how great my life is?"

Haley stopped renting from me to buy her own condo near her work. Just as I was about to put it back on the market, Ron passed away, and the thought of being in our big house alone got the best of me. I moved back in and when I felt up to it, wiped the Pacific Palisades house clean of our memories. Most of them, anyway. Now that probate is almost up, the mansion and its mix of memories, good and bad, will be sold to the highest bidder.

Haley picks up my wedding photo from the table in the foyer. "Lindsay, I'm not kidding. I think you should get out of here or make some kind of effort to spend less time here. You bought this place when Ron and you were separated—that can't remind you of the best of times. It won't be long before you have a cat. You mark my words."

"Where would I go? The big house is still in the trust, and I hate that palace, anyway. It makes me feel guilty."

"Why would you feel guilty?"

My eyes go wide. "I don't know. I just do. A lot of things happened there that I'd just as soon forget. It's where Ron and I started our lives together, but it's where we ended it, too. The house feels alive to me. And not in a good way."

"Now you're just freaking me out. You could sell this place and buy something else. Maybe in a younger part of town."

I shake my head to yet another one of her perky suggestions. I know she means well. I couldn't sell this place, even if I held the deed in my hot, little hand, along with a real estate license. "This place is the only thing I own by myself that's not in Ron's name. Until probate clears, this is all I have and without an income . . . well . . ."

"So why don't you get your CPA license and start up another accounting firm? You knew how to do all the work. It should be a cakewalk."

"I just don't have the patience to get the degree. And it won't help me in what I want to do . . . Either way, I can't sell this house."

"So go on a vacation."

"I don't like to travel alone."

"Maybe you should get a job. You could work part-time. It worked wonders for me. You could go back to Nordstrom."

"The last thing I want to do is fit men who have no business in a double-breasted suits, in double-breasted suits."

"They're out of style anyway," she says hopefully. "Maybe you could be a stylist?" She presses her finger to her chin. "An interior decorator? I know—a stager! The world is your oyster. You're so good at all that artistic stuff, and Ron left you enough to start any business you wanted."

I shrug. "I don't know."

"I'm worried you're finding excuses. For all we know, the will could go on for years. Wherever there's money and lawyers involved, you might as well sit back and wait it out. What better way than to keep yourself busy?"

"Must I remind you that you're marrying a lawyer?"

"I'm marrying him *despite* the fact that he's a lawyer." She smiles. She gets that mournful look again as she stares at me. "Lindsay, you don't have to go dress shopping with me. You seem so down today. Maybe we should just get a pedicure instead."

"No, we're going to shop. Let's go!" I say, clapping my hands together. Haley clearly needs to see some enthusiasm on my part, and who can blame her? No one wants to be around Eeyore for long, and I've been a complete downer for more than a year now. She wants to shop for her wedding gown, not hear about my pathetic life.

It's not like I should have been surprised. I knew this would happen with my husband being so much older than me. It's part of the Trophy Wife syndrome. I simply didn't think it would happen so soon. Ron was young. Fifty-three is far too early to cash in—we had our whole lives in front of us. We had travel, a family—a whole world set before us—and he had to go and die on me. I clench my teeth and smile. "When the going gets tough, the tough go shopping. Am I right?"

Haley throws open the curtains. "Sheesh, you're even starting to live like them. Afraid of the light. Let's get out of here before you vant to suck my blood."

I blink against the sun's rays. "I just don't like how my neighbors peer in here all the time. It's like I'm being watched, my place surrounded by little, furry sentinels. You remember the flying monkeys in *Wizard of Oz*?"

"I hated that movie. Except for the ruby slippers, of course." Haley grins.

"Of course."

She finishes pulling the curtains wide open and walks back to the foyer. She adjusts a painting, so that it's lopsided on the wall. She shrugs. "I'm trying to show you can let things go. It's too neat in here. Don't you miss me living here and making it feel like a home?"

"In a word? No." But of course, I miss her terribly. I miss her tales about what star she'd met that day at her agenting office, about the young actors' pathetic attempts to get a meeting with her boss, her cooking . . . but all these nice thoughts disappear as I speak. "I don't miss your empty tubs of frosting! I don't think you ever threw one away or realized where the garbage can was—or the dishwasher. Did you know that it opens?" I straighten the picture. "How you stay so thin with all that frosting, I'll never know. One day it's going to catch up with you."

"No, I have a system. One tub equals ten miles. I have to run ten miles and then I get to start on a tub of frosting. The faster I run, the faster I eat. As for cleaning up, have you ever eaten a tub of frosting? The last thing you want to do is clean afterwards."

"How can you be anal-retentive about chowing down a tub of frosting? You're after me for wanting to clean?"

"It's a gift." Haley motions toward the window. "Like the gift you have for organizing things and wanting to clean is different from having your shoes thrown on your closet floor. We're all dichotomies."

"That's all I've done for the last year is organize things. Organize the funeral, organize the bank statements, organize Ron's closet, organize charities to pick up his things. I'm sick of organizing."

"That's a start. Quit organizing things."

"Spoken by the woman who is having *me* organize her groom's gift and wedding favors."

"Well, but that's fun organizing."

"All organizing is fun organizing."

Her lighthearted tone changes. "So if you had one wish, Lindsay. One dream. What would it be?"

I think about the monumental moments of my life and I'm filled with regret. A Christian shouldn't be filled with regrets, but focused on the heavenly realms and what lies ahead. Which is why I feel so horribly guilty over my answer. "I wish I could start over. I wish I could take everything I've done wrong back and have a do-over."

"So do it. Erase your history and start again. Jesus gives you a do-over in heaven. Why not start here?"

I feel hope well up inside me for the first time in years. A do-over. That's exactly what I need. "Where would I start?"

"Maybe something as simple as changing the routines you've become stuck in."

"What's wrong with my routines?" I cross my arms, thinking about scrubbing down the showers on Monday. How does one simply change that to Tuesday without a domino effect? When would I vacuum the living room if not on Tuesday?

Haley shakes her head. "You can't change anything if you keep the same routines."

She's got a point. "I scrub the showers on Monday."

"Showers? Lindsay, you're one person. Why do you need to scrub all the showers on Monday?"

"It's what my mother always did."

"It's a good start. Scrub your shower only on Monday. Let the other ones go."

"One day, you're not scrubbing the shower; the next day, the short-sleeved shirts are hanging with the long-sleeved ones and it's absolute chaos!" I'm only half-kidding.

Haley opens her mouth. "No, I'm not even going to respond to that. The very fact that you said that scares me. So let's shop now—otherwise you'll be polishing the silver before we go."

Haley peeks out the window. "They're fascinated by you, you know. Your neighbors and their cats. That clean aroma coming from here probably makes them uncomfortable. Like garlic." She giggles. "Maybe if you wore little spray cans of Lysol around your neck, they'd want to move. WAALAAH! Instant turnover."

"Would you cut it out? It's *voilà!* It's French."

"Whatever. I'm Haley, have we met? I'm American, and I shop at Old Navy and watch bad television. My French is a little rusty."

I sigh. Haley is not as simple as she thinks. She was married to one of Hollywood's richest producers and ran his soirées with little trouble—that is, until she turned of age (twenty-eight). Like a leased Mercedes, he turned her in for a new model. Haley only pretends to be simple when it suits her. She remembers the neighbors even if she plays innocent. "The women here are not that bad, you know. You just have to get to know them. Mrs. Davenport was just telling me last night that—"

"Mrs. Davenport? You talk to them? They would scurry in their places at the very sight of me when I lived here."

I shrug. "Sometimes I talk to them. They're my neighbors."

"She was married? Which one is she? The one with the brunette wig that doesn't fit?" Haley cups her eyes at the window and peers outside, but she quickly backs away. No doubt, she found someone peering back at her.

"See? I told you it was creepy."

Haley closes the curtains and turns around. "You must live a more interesting life. They didn't do that when I was here. Let's get out of here already."

I am not having this conversation. "Where are we going for dresses?"

Haley lowers her voice. "Remember, Linds—there's a difference between organizing and controlling. I want you to help me find a dress. I don't want you to bulldoze me. I am not spending a fortune on a gown."

"I'm not controlling you! I just want you to get the best. You deserve the best." I can understand though. Haley has an ex-husband who would make Cinderella think twice about marriage.

"I'm still buying off the rack," she deadpans, as though she's winning something for herself.

"Fine. Maybe we can find a flour sack at Whole Foods and add sequins."

"You think?"

I grab my sweater out of the closet and reach for the doorknob when the bell rings. "Who could that be?" I ask.

"Maybe someone needs a cup of gizzards."

Opening the door, there's a middle-aged woman standing on my stoop. She's pretty, but in that funky, Berkeley kind of way, with a multicolored tunic and flowing, crushed-cotton slacks. Definitely not from around here, because she looks her age, which I would guestimate as near fifty. She's standing beside a very large suitcase and a cat carrier. I bend over and see there's a cat inside. Just what this complex needs.

"Can I help you?" *The mother ship? Your cat people?*

She looks down at an envelope and then back up at me. She has bright, blue eyes and perfect cheekbones, although her face is lined from the sun and she definitely comes from a place with a serious lack of sunscreen. "Lindsay Brindle?"

"That's me. Am I being served with something? Because I've never actually seen a lawsuit arrive with a kitty cat." I try to keep my voice light, but her presence brings a foreboding that I can't put my finger on—and I don't believe the cat is a good omen.

She laughs. "Heavens, no. I'm . . ." She clutches the envelope and sucks in a deep breath. "I'm Jane Dawson." She shoves the envelope into an oversized (read: cheap) canvas bag and reaches her hand out toward me. "Jane *Brindle* Dawson."

I feel my head sway from side to side. And I'm dizzy. *It can't be.* I hold my hand up to the doorjamb to steady myself and let my eyes take her in fully. Now that I know her identity, Jane appears more beautiful than she was five minutes ago, more worldly and intelligent. Capable and self-reliant. Jealously surges through me.

Suddenly, her appearance at my door is beginning to make sense. "You're the unnamed executor of the will?"

She nods slowly. The one woman with the ability to unravel my life, and she's here on my doorstep with a cat. It's a sign, I tell you. At least now I have proof. There can be no question that this is divine penance. The cats are God's vultures, circling and waiting for my time to come.

I married for security. Now, my husband is gone, and so is any hope I had in being secure—and to make matters worse, this message comes to me courtesy of yet another cat.

A do-over. *As if.*

Chapter 2

Jane

She's barely more than a waif, and I ponder if there's enough meat on her bones to allow her to float in a swimming pool, or would she sink like a lithe pebble. I never doubted that Ron would find someone easy to maneuver—someone he might rein in with a simple tug—but I did have faith he'd try to make more of an effort to withstand appearances. This girl is barely grown. She's shaky and nervous and on those itty-bitty, lanky legs. She's like a shivering Chihuahua, yapping at my heels with all her ineffective might. I'm certain she was everything Ron wanted her to be. Everything it wasn't possible for me to be. Or *any* woman over thirty to be. Ron always did see women like a fine, grapevine—train them as they grow.

He purchased her allegiance, and it was money well-spent, as her adherence to his rules seems unflappable. He said she was tall, and she is that, but her length is lost in the fact that she's so insanely skinny. *Muy flaco*, as we would say at home. In Mexico, the men like their women with a little meat on their bones. A little junk in the trunk, as my friends would say. This emaciated look is unknown, unless someone has a tapeworm, and it's certainly not celebrated like here in Los Angeles. It's funny how times change. A suntan used to be the sign of a field hand; now it's a sign of leisure. The bony look was used to advertise feeding the hungry; today, it's hard to tell the difference between a World Vision ad and a copy of *Vogue*.

The last time my thighs were as small as hers . . . scratch that, I don't think my thighs were ever that small. The last time my *arms* were as slender as her thighs was back sometime near the era of John Travolta's *Stayin' Alive*.

I don't know what Lindsay has to be upset about. She's the one who looks like a million and probably inherited many more with Ron's estate. So she had to wait a year for me to get here. No doubt she can postpone her spa treatments and shopping as we get this taken care of. I'm just the ex doing all the work so she won't get her precious, manicured hands dirty and if she were more than a child, she could appreciate that fact. But I refuse to sink to her adolescent ways. It's clear I'm going to have to be the adult here.

"I'm the resident artist in Campeche." She looks at me questioningly. "Campeche, Mexico."

"I don't understand. They don't have mail in Mexico?"

"I've been on sabbatical. I take tourists on hiking and painting excursions. Somehow, this information and I kept missing each other. You have a right to question my presence, but I can assure you, I barely understand it myself."

"We had to hire an investigator to find you." She thins her eyes warily. It's like having Shirley Temple stare threateningly, and the desired effect is lost.

I can't help myself as a snicker bubbles over. I never was good in decent society, and apparently that hasn't changed. Being an artist, I'm loved for being quirky in Mexico. Here, it's viewed as a transmittable disease.

"Like I said, I'd been on sabbatical."

"From what? I thought you lived in the middle of nowhere. Is something funny?" Lindsay asks.

I flatten my lips and bite on them to keep another inappropriate grin from growing. "Nervous energy. Terribly sorry. It's been a long trip and—"

Ron Brindle made half my life miserable by "rescuing" me, and now he's determined to put a serious crimp in the second half. These are supposed to be my golden years—the self-indulgent, lacking-in-serious-responsibility age. Executor of a trust is a serious responsibility, especially when there's a nipping, yappy widow at my heels. I rub my temples, not really having the energy to explain my presence in full to this blond child. I never understood Ron in life—why would death make him more reasonable to me?

Lindsay knows a different Ron than I did, and I have to be careful how I frame this, so as not to harm his carefully constructed legacy. No sense in ruining her memories of a man she clearly adores and is now dead, but whoever said, "Dead men tell no tales," didn't know my ex-husband. Ron took a lot with him to the grave, and it's up to me to keep it buried, I would guess. Otherwise, why leave me with the burden of his will?

"I shouldn't be in California but maybe two weeks, Lindsay. That should give me time to clear everything up, and then you can move forward with life. It's just my signature needed on a few things, I'm certain." But as I think about the bulging envelope given to me by the lawyer's office, I'm sure Ron probably made things more difficult than they needed to be. He had his motive, after all.

Saving his brother from life's consequences probably seemed a good idea at the time, as did rescuing his current wife from doing the hard work. Neither rescue attempt worked—that's the irony of it all. *Ron and his Superman complex.*

Lindsay blinks those wide, blue eyes at me, giving me more power than I deserve. I'm telling you, I could kill him. It's a good thing he's already dead.

"Hamilton told you I was coming, I assume?" I ask her.

"Hamilton?" the other blonde perks up.

"Haley is marrying Hamilton," Lindsay explains. "We were just on our way out to shop for her wedding dress. Another two minutes and you might have missed us."

Interesting. I've been gone for nearly two decades and not a thing changes. There's an endless supply of new blondes and lots of tired, old men waiting to rescue them. Although I've never met Hamilton in person, maybe he's an exception. I highly doubt that, though.

"In any event," Lindsay says with a set chin, as if she's channeling her mature self, "Hamilton didn't tell me you were coming. He told me only that he'd made contact with the executor through the investigator, and now, here you are with a suitcase. And a *cat.*" She says the last word with an emphasis on the vowel. A long emphasis that makes no bones about her thoughts on felines. "I'll just call him." She whips out a cell phone and hands it to Haley, who punches in the number. Old moves from their cheerleading days obviously coming in handy.

"Hamilton? Hi, baby, it's me. Lindsay has a question for you . . . I know, I love you, too, sweetie . . . Yes, we're going shopping soon. I will. I'll pick the most beautiful dress ever . . ."

Lindsay grabs the phone, and I think she's more perturbed by the sickening conversation than I am. "Hamilton, there's someone here saying they're the executor of Ron's will . . . yes . . . uh-huh . . . no . . .

all right, thanks." She narrows her eyes again, not unlike a Gila monster back home. "He says you were expected, and his secretary gave you what you needed. He got busy on a case and forgot to call." She looks down and then back up to meet my eyes. "Do what you have to do. Haley and I are going shopping."

No doubt what they do best.

I feel the walls closing in on me. Being in America is hard enough. Being in L.A. is enough to drive anyone insane. "I take it you're not a big fan?"

"Of you or the cat?" she asks, and I see a little of her claws. She probably held herself fairly well against Ron, but she's got no beef with me. I wish I could make her understand that. I want out of here probably worse than she wants me out of here.

"I'll just go straight to the hotel."

"Just stay here. Honestly, what hotel in L.A. is going to take the cat, anyway?" Lindsay offers and I can tell there isn't a sincere syllable in her invitation, but she's obviously been taught her role of hostess and does as she is supposed to, without regards for her true feelings. I remember when I was just like her.

"Lindsay, that's very sweet of you, but I'm perfectly comfortable in a hotel, and there are many that are animal-friendly these days."

"They're dog-friendly," Lindsay says. "No one likes cats."

"Perhaps you'll let me peruse a phone book then, and I'll find her a kitty hotel. Many vets have them on-site."

She rolls her eyes and walks to the kitchen. Soon, she comes back with a telephone book the size of a Mayan temple. She slams it on the table, but as I reach for it, she picks it up again.

"No. I can't let you stay in a hotel. Ron wouldn't have appreciated that. The guest bedroom is down the hall, and the quicker this is over, the better."

"I know my presence can't be the best way to start your day and

I appreciate not having to schlep around for a hotel." I smile at her. She's too young and naïve to know the gift she's been given—the second chance at life. I want to gift wrap her future, tie it with a nice, pretty bow, and push her out onto the doorstep: *Off with you now. Fly. Be free!* "My goal is to get out of your way as soon as possible and let you move on with your future. It's open to you now."

She plunks a fist where her hip should be. "I'm a thirty-five-year-old widow. I live with eighty-year-old women and four hundred cats. My future isn't looking extremely bright at the moment. You'll forgive me if I lack enthusiasm," she snaps.

"No, of course it isn't." I offer gently, but inwardly, I think, *Great, a drama queen.* Just what I need to make things easy. Is it really possible for a man's first wife to say something that the second wife will be happy with? Women are odd creatures. I imagine that's why I spent most of my life around men. She's determined to get into some competitive battle with me, and there's no making her see I'm not even in the race. I pull in my suitcase and the cat into the foyer. "This is Kulkucan." The both stare at me open-eyed, obviously unfamiliar with Mexican history. "He's named after the Mayan god." Again with the empty stares. *This city has absolutely no culture beyond what* Entertainment Tonight *features.* "Quetzalcoatl?" I ask, hoping to see something register.

Lindsay shakes her head. "Whatever. It's a cat. It can stay in the laundry room down the hall. Your room is that way, too, though I haven't made the beds. I wasn't expecting houseguests."

"That's fine. Before you go, I just need a few things from Ron's desk. If you'll just point me in the right direction." I pull out the folder. "It says here in the attic storage above his office."

"His office was at the other house, but the desk isn't there."

"Ron said in his letter he has something to leave to Ron Jr. in his desk. If you'll just tell me where that is, I'll be out of here when I have all the paperwork in one place." I hold up the key that Hamilton's office sent with the letter.

"Ron Jr.?" Lindsay sputters.

Uh-oh. Open mouth, insert foot. "It's not what you think." Both of them start to walk toward me, and I feel the hair on the back of my neck bristle.

She blanches as easily as white asparagus. "It sounds like Ron had a son I never knew about. Is that what you're telling me?"

"No, that's not what I'm telling you. It's a complicated story, but it's not what you think." I say nothing more. I could kill Ron for his stupid suggestion, and why I didn't change my son's name in Mexico is beyond me. I suppose because he's not a cat—once his name was set, I could hardly go calling him Barney now, could I? Hindsight is, in fact, twenty-twenty. Ron did have a powerful way of getting exactly what he wanted, and—here's the beauty part—he made you believe it was your idea all along. He wore charm like a silk shirt.

Lindsay's face contorts, and it's clear her loyalty to Ron is more tentative than she lets on. "Then who is Ron Jr.?" She doesn't even try to hide the animosity from me. There is so much venom, I fear she might snap at me like a provoked, eyelash pit viper. Incidentally, they don't need much provocation.

"He's my son," I repeat. "Just let it lie."

"Your son alone? How is that possible, exactly, that another man lets you name his son after someone else?"

"Ron protected my son and me. You haven't heard this story?"

She shakes her head.

I let my eyes wither shut at the admission. How could I just blurt that out? I've spent thirty years hiding this secret with absolutely no issues. I come in here, and it's as though I'm in a Catholic confessional, looking for absolution. "I'd appreciate it, Lindsay, if we could respect each other's privacy. You don't have to know everything. This isn't about you. I'm sure you have secrets of your own that you'd just as soon keep to yourself."

Haley walks toward me, giving me her best, tough-blond look—which is more comical than Lindsay's. "Listen, this is hard on Lindsay, and I don't want her hurt anymore. Where is your son?"

Their blue-eyed gazes would bore a hole in me if I stayed put, so I start to pace. "He's my son." I look up to see a well of tears in Lindsay's eyes. "*Only* my son. I've given you more explanation than anyone else in my life has ever asked for, including my mother! He lives here in L.A. and he's comfortable with the notion that his father isn't in his life." They both want more, but what am I supposed to say? *Oh, back in the day . . . it was after the sixties, what can I say? Free love—and then, the harsh realization that there ain't no such thing.* "Ron Jr. just assumes his father and I did what was best for him. Which I did, so if you ever meet Ron Jr., I would appreciate it if you allowed him to—"

"You want me to lie for you?" Lindsay asks.

Already, I am stone-cold tired of how much work a conversation in this forsaken place is. No one takes you at your word; no one thinks anything about barging into your personal business. This is a town raised on tabloids, and it shows!

"No, let's forget we had this conversation. You two run along and go about your business. I've probably upset your whole day. If you direct me to the desk, I'll be out of your way." She's right, of course. Pixie thing that she is. She knows it's wrong to lie for a stranger. She's not stupid, but then I guess she thinks I have some kind of power over her, and she's going to do her best to exert what she's got. But asking a complete stranger to lie for me in the first five minutes I've met her—it's just not like me, and I add one more reason I can't stand the States. I am someone else here. Someone

I don't like at all. But there's one thing I did right in my life and that's Ron Jr. and he is worth every continuous battle. I'll just have to make certain that Lindsay and Ron, Jr. never meet.

"The desk is gone."

"Gone?"

"I gave it to an after-school club."

"Where is it?"

"It's on the south side."

"You gave Ron's desk to a southside after-school club?" Couldn't she have just gone to Ikea and donated three hundred desks for the price of Ron's? "It was an antique, wasn't it? He had that desk before either of us."

"It's not for the after-school club. They are going to auction it off for cash."

"Lindsay," I say calmly. "I need to find that desk."

"I'll give you the number of the club when I get back. We're shopping for a wedding gown today, and we're in sort of a hurry. If you'd called and said you were coming . . ."

He found a way to control me beyond the grave. Somehow, I knew he would. "Did he ask you to give away the desk?"

"I didn't have any use for it, so I got rid of it, Jane. It was my way of telling myself he wasn't coming back, and it didn't go with the decor he'd picked for his own office. Now, here you are looking for it. Why didn't he tell me to keep it?"

"I don't know. Maybe he thought you'd respect it and keep it in his house?" I feel my heart pounding and try to remain cool, but the tension between the two of us fills me with angst. I try to take a few deep breaths and focus on the sound of my exhaling to find a centering place. "I'm sorry, you're right. It's my fault for being lost in the mountains so long."

It's hard to have pity for Lindsay. She can haul her size-zero frame out and find herself a new Ron. One who will support her very expensive shopping habits and lead her like a horse with reins. I'm haunted by the old Ron for the rest of my days. Him and his constant quest for me to forgive. *"It will free you, Jane. You must do this!"* he would say. I wouldn't even be here if her dead husband— *our* dead husband—hadn't had to be such a martyr. *Why couldn't he just let things be?* I screwed up, yes, but I moved on. Isn't that what we're supposed to do in life? Not wallow in the old cesspool that is your past?

Lindsay straightens up, and her hard expression melts into a smile. She's suddenly insanely unruffled, which naturally makes me nervous.

"So you may as well make yourself comfortable. It sounds like there's a lot of unfinished business to be done," she coos. "I'll find the receipt for the desk when I get back. Hopefully, they haven't sold it yet, or Hamilton has a copy of what you need."

Nice Lindsay is far more frightening than Threatening Lindsay, but this condo offers me the best hope of an escape route. I have access to the lawyer through the other blonde and access to Ron's quest through the papers in the house—if she didn't get rid of them all.

"His filing cabinet is in the guest room. You should be able to find it all there." Her voice is wearing with fatigue.

"If you'll just let me know where the sheets are, I'll make up the bed myself and get started. You two go on about your business. I'll be fine." But that's a lie. One mistake and it seems as though there is no end in sight. I can't ever seem to get past it. Not even after thirty years of trying to bury it.

Lindsay blinks quickly but can't stop a single tear that escapes down her cheek. She's softer than the schemer I originally took her for, but this is why I fell for Ron in the first place—the mother in me wants to embrace her and tell her it will be all right. I'm a caretaker. Always did think I could fix whatever was broken. Had to get the house that needed the most work, the man who needed the most coddling. I've tried to shake this personality downfall, but it bobs to the surface continuously. It's all that Catholic guilt.

"I don't understand," she squeaks. "Why didn't Ron let me handle it? I was a good wife to him, Jane."

Ron, how could you do this to me? You marry someone young enough to be your daughter and leave me to mother her? Life isn't fair.

I rub her shoulder. "I know you were, Lindsay. Ron had only wonderful things to say about you. He worshipped you, really."

"Why you? Why are *you* here?" A touch of the sharpness in her voice returns. "If he didn't trust me, he could have found anyone to have done this. Hamilton could have done this."

"I'm here for me. I left unfinished business the first time, and Ron wants me to finish it. He wasn't a man to let sleeping dogs lie, and you know how he felt about his newfound religion. He wrote to me before his death, but you have to understand, I had no idea he was anywhere near the end. I just thought it was more nagging on his part to get me to come back here."

"It wasn't all that new. His religion," she tells me. "What did Ron write to you? May I see it?"

I clutch the blue envelope from the manila packet and extend my arm to Lindsay. "I hope this answers some questions for you. Let's just get through this, all right?"

She nods.

"If you read the letter, I think you'll see where his loyalties were." I wink at her and take the cat out of his cage. Haley retreats to the kitchen like I've just let loose a rattlesnake.

"Lindsay's allergic to cats."

"I thought it was you who was allergic to cats."

"We're both allergic."

"Not liking them is not an allergy."

"It's not?" Haley asks.

The two of them make me feel so old. Don't get me wrong, I wouldn't go back to being worried about my image for all the gold in the Sierra Madre, but neither one of them is old enough to be nursing the wounds of a deceased husband. Naturally, Ron made sure Lindsay wouldn't be burdened with the reality of a widow. He left all that red tape for me.

To have their bodies with my brain—I'd be unstoppable. But as they say, youth is wasted on the young. I'm an artist, a gypsy by nature. To be in civilization is bad enough, but to be in L.A. with my former life barreling down on me is like an Aztec sacrifice. Maybe it is time I faced the music. The thought flitters only briefly before I realize running is the only life I know. The faster I move, the happier I am.

I lift Kulkucan from the tile floor and cuddle my cheek into his fur. He purrs and for the moment, all is right in the world.

"Go ahead—you two were going out, weren't you?" I ask.

They look to one another, clearly mistrusting my presence, but decide they're more anxious to get away from me. "I'll leave my cell phone number in case you need anything while we're out." Lindsay scribbles down her number, and Haley has to tug at her to get toward the door. They finally leave, and I collapse onto the couch with Kuku on my lap.

Once again, Ron's left a giant mess for me to clean up. And this time, someone is bound to get hurt.

Chapter 3

Lindsay

Haley and I crawl into her car without a word. I feel numb, if that's possible when you've just been bludgeoned by a painful reality. I look back at the complex, thinking that someone else is in my place—physically and emotionally. I feel betrayed by my husband, and he's not here to reassure me, which makes me want to scream. I need reassurance. I want proof that my life with Ron was not a lie. That he did this because it was best for me.

I know Haley wants to soothe me, and she's searching for words, but every time she opens her mouth, she snaps it shut again and keeps driving. And it's just as well. What's she going to say? *I'm sure Ron meant nothing by avoiding the topic of a Ron Jr. Or that he put his ex-wife in charge of all his major investment assets. How serious could it be? Someone else bearing his name means nothing. Someone else closing out the rest of his assets—nothing. Nothing, I tell you.*

My heart is in my throat, and I question the last ten years of my life. "Why on earth wouldn't he have mentioned Ron Jr., Haley? I mean, even if it wasn't his son. *Especially* if it wasn't his son!"

"You're worrying over nothing, Linds. Ron loved you. I suppose we all have our secrets."

"Are we supposed to? Within marriage?"

"You're asking me?"

"I have the letter."

"What letter?"

"The one Jane is looking for in the desk. I have it. Obviously, I emptied his desk before I gave it away. I thought the letter to Ron Jr. meant Ron hoped that I was pregnant. I thought he was writing a letter to our unborn son, hoping I'd name him Ron Jr. Now I find out, the name was already taken. What if I'd been pregnant, Haley?"

"You weren't. And the world would survive two Ron Jr.'s. I once knew a guy who named his five sons Oscar."

I just stare at her. "And?"

"That's it. Just a guy who named his five sons Oscar and without middle names. So I'm saying there could be two Ron Jrs."

"But there aren't!"

"Well, yeah. Unless you've got some DNA in a cryogenics lab somewhere."

"Okay, I know you are trying to help me, but could you relent on the bad soap opera ideas?"

"Suit yourself."

"I just realized that he left the Pacific Palisades house to Ron Jr. We'd discussed it, and I said I didn't want the house, but I never thought he'd leave it to some stranger, bearing his name."

"He must not have wanted to hurt you."

"Well, obviously, I was going to find out, Haley. I mean, he left our house to the boy."

"The boy? How old is he?"

"Haley! You're not helping I don't know how old he is!"

"I just meant that it's not like he's a small child. Couldn't you tell that from the letter? I trust you opened it."

"I opened it. I thought it was so sweet that Ron would write a letter to his future son."

"Future. Past. What's the difference? You didn't want the house, and Ron got rid of it."

"I'm not even going to dignify that with an answer."

"Probably for the best," Haley says.

"I'm telling you, Ron just wouldn't have abandoned his son. Even if it wasn't his biological child, he was named after him, and I know Ron. He loved duty. Lived by it. Stonewall Brindle, you might have called him."

"But you also knew he would have told you that he had a child named after him."

"I know you didn't just say that."

"You're telling me you kept nothing from Ron?"

"Whose side are you on?"

"Lindsay, we don't have to go wedding dress shopping." Haley announces in the sacrificial way that seems to come so easy to her. "You can't possibly be in the mood, and I completely understand."

"I'm always in the mood to shop!" I say brightly. "Especially with you. I consider it my civic duty. My ministry, if you will. You've only got six months before this wedding. That's an unacceptable amount of time to plan, and I want to keep the rhinestones to a minimum." The words come out as confident as ever, but they're hollow. "I have to have something to do."

"You seem really shaken. I'm not used to seeing you this way. You're always the one who handles everything."

We stop at a stoplight, and I stare at her. She has way more faith in me than I'm worthy of and I feel another rush of guilt. Whatever strength I pretended to have was nothing more than false bravado. When I first met her at our Trophy Wives Club's Bible Study, she was like a female Clint Eastwood, bent on revenge, but that, too, was only false bravado. "Haley, I don't handle everything. I never did."

"Ron probably didn't want to hurt you, or he would have told you the whole truth. You've been through so much in the last year. And now this. An ex-wife and a mystery son who is inheriting the house. That's shocking by Hollywood's standards." Haley shakes her head. "It's not like that wouldn't rattle someone, no matter how faithful. One thing I'm certain of: Ron loved your life together and everything you both planned for the future. You didn't have an easy marriage, Lindsay, but you had a good marriage. Ron having Jane back now doesn't negate that. He had to have a reason for bringing her here."

I nod.

"Maybe he thought you two would have something in common, Lindsay."

"Maybe."

"Let's get a coffee before we get started. We're in no hurry." Haley pats my hand on the center console. I stare at my wedding ring, wondering when it's appropriate to take it off. Is it ever appropriate, considering?

"I thought you said there was a sale on seconds? Everything will be gone if we're late. People may have camped out." I inform her.

Haley shrugs. "They probably did. No biggie. I'll find something."

The fact is, she will. Haley is charmed. If I went to find a wedding dress, there would be nothing but strapless, size-zeros in pink satin. But Haley? She'll find the perfect designer gown in her size without any effort at all, and most likely, she'll get it for half-off. If I could just get her to improve her taste, she'd be set. She pulls her

Mini into a parking place right in front of the Coffee Bean & Tea Leaf. See? A parking place on the street in Bel Air. *Charmed.*

I, on the other hand . . .

"Haley, I really think we should head to the wedding shop," I prompt. The last thing I want is any girl talk. I need time to process all of this. I *need* to read this letter.

"I'm not doing anything without caffeine. Without it, I might let you talk me into some simple sheath with no sparkle to it whatsoever and be a *Glamour* "do" and that scares the life out of me. If I want to sparkle like a pink party bulb on my big day, by golly, I'm going to. You'll put me in something a Kennedy might wear. Oh no, we need to stop because I have to get me some power. I have to be able to stand firm against the natural-born stylist that is my best friend."

"Haley, I want you to be married in what you want to be married in. I'm not going to try to talk you out of anything." Even as I say it, I wonder if I can keep my opinions to myself. What a burden to be saddled with my mouth!

She flattens her smile. "Do I look like I'm a natural blonde? Born yesterday? You may have good intentions, but I know you." She gets out of the car, and buttons up her white seersucker jacket (with red rhinestones on the lapels—I'm sorry to report they match her sandals.)

"Do you really need a jacket? It's eighty degrees out."

"The air-conditioning always gets me. Oh, but you're right. It's February. The air won't be on too high." She slinks out of the sleeves and tosses the short, springy blazer into the car. She straightens her shirt collar. *Her rhinestone-studded shirt collar.*

I drop my chin to my chest. "Just because you're not married to Jay anymore, does that mean *everything* has to sparkle? You're like a walking fishing lure. Restraint, Haley. A little restraint."

"How else am I supposed to get noticed, standing next to your statuesque self?" she asks me.

"Good shoes?" I suggest. "And please. Don't think I'm fooled by the compliment. You're changing the subject." I grin. If anyone can make me forget my circumstances, it's good-natured Haley, under the constant sunbeam that brightens her path.

I grab a table while Haley stands in line for our order. We have a system. Whoever drives, pays. The passenger gets the table. It sounds strange, maybe slightly anal, but our choreography works for us. This is California, after all, and good espresso is a hard-won entity—even if there is a coffee shop on every corner. When you add in the ratio of espresso drinkers, it negates itself.

I drop my purse on Haley's chair. I peruse the table tent, advertising all the fattening chocolate creations posing as coffee drinks, and mentally calculate how many miles Haley'd have to run to enjoy one, guilt-free. I wonder what the ratio is to one of Haley's tubs o' frosting. Is it more miles or fewer?

Looking up toward the window, I see him. It's been years. Nine? Ten? Every muscle in my body goes lax, while the butterflies in my stomach soar to new heights. He looks exactly the same. He makes me feel exactly the same. Not a thing has changed. My heart aches to run out of my loneliness and into his arms, but reality hits me like a sledgehammer. I remain firmly planted in my chair, sliding the table tent and my handbag in front of me, while I peer around them, like I practiced as a hallway-stalking schoolgirl. For a moment, I'm lost in his rugged profile—his slightly crooked nose, the solid, angled jaw and that perfect chin. It's amazing how seeing an old flame when you're fresh from pain can negate every reason you broke up with him in the first place.

He watches Haley for a moment of unbridled narcissism. I wonder if he doesn't recognize the similarity between us with our long, blond hair. He looks down at his work boots, as though he's avoiding the view, and my hope sinks that he's forgotten what happened. Why would God allow my house of cards to fall today? Besides God and my mother, Jake is the only person who knows what I did. All of it—the whole sordid tale. The butterflies quickly morph into something more like bats.

"Linds? You okay?" Haley puts my iced soy latte in front of me. "You're as white as a sheet."

I can't bring myself to stop looking, but I close my eyes and capture it in my memory. I will remember this moment and be glad for it. *What would my life have been like with him?* I mouth my words of thankfulness.

"Do you know him?" Haley asks, looking toward the line where Jake is still waiting for his coffee.

I tear my gaze away and nod. "I think he's someone I went to high school with. You know, back in the day." I try to laugh.

"No way. He looks too old. Either that, or he can't afford La Mer."

"He's hardly the type to smear moisturizing cream on his face. You've been out of the real world too long."

"Simmer down; it was a joke. I'm only saying you don't look like you could have gone to high school with him. It's a compliment. Maybe he just looks like someone." She slides into her chair, hanging her handbag over the back.

"He's not wearing a wedding ring. My mother said he got married."

"I thought you didn't talk to your mother?"

"She mailed me that little tidbit. Another nail in my coffin, if you will."

"What a peach your mother must be. Maybe he's divorced. Or did you ever date him? Maybe he's sworn off women for good now." Haley giggles.

"Not funny."

"Why don't you go talk to him? Do you have a reunion coming up? I must say, he's a hot ticket. Dark hair, brown eyes . . . you are single, you know?"

"They're blue." I inhale a long sip of my iced coffee. "Blue-green. His father had them, too."

"You seem to know a lot about him for just being a classmate." She leans in. "Are you holding out on me?"

"It's not juicy. Not in a good way, anyway. Haley, I have a confession to make." I move my seat over, so she's blocking my view of Jake.

"This sounds serious."

His cell phone trills, and I hear his deep voice answer. I close my eyes again and concentrate on his voice for a moment, before looking at Haley again.

"You're killing me. What did you do already?"

"I did something terrible when I was younger."

"Terrible, as in you killed someone and stuffed him in a closet? Or terrible as in you said you'd go to prom with someone and then dumped him? There was no pig's blood involved, right?"

"It's somewhere in the middle, and I think that Ron—"

Haley is looking at Jake when he suddenly heads toward us. "Shh! He's coming over here!" Haley sits back in her chair, like she's about to watch a romantic movie unfold. If only she knew that it was probably more of a horror flick in the making.

He sidles toward us, talking into his phone, and then he sees me. Our eyes meet, and once again, the past dissipates and I am not so very naïve, not so very worn down. I am me. *Today's me*. I know what I want and I tell him so, and we laugh about all the mistakes, all the misunderstandings, and he's over it. He understands me.

Or not.

He stops walking, and I look down at the work boots he wears, the length of his jeans spilling over the top of them. I lift my eyes back to his, and he offers a warm smile, that charming dimple on the left side appearing as he looks to Haley. My smile wavers. I stand up, and I meet his Ceylon sapphire gaze.

"Lindsay," he says coolly as he nods his chin, steps around me, and saunters right out the door.

Haley watches him slam the door, and my confession hardly matters now, does it? "It wasn't him, I guess."

She giggles at me. "He just knew your name and gave you a dirty look?"

I shrug. "Weird, isn't it?"

"We have got to get you back on the market before you go completely nuts."

Lord have mercy. Lindsay Brindle on the market is more than L.A. needs.

Chapter 4

Jane

My head just aches with all this paperwork. Ron hid money everywhere, like a human, banking pack rat. I can almost see him sniveling as he said, "Let's see if she can find this account." Now it's me who is the rat, lost in the maze that is his will. The lawyer's work is done, and now it's a matter of approving everything. Ron easily could have hired yet another lawyer to do this, but when I see the blue envelope stashed among the information, I know I have my answer as to why he didn't. I slice open the envelope with his engraved letter opener and sit back in his brown leather office chair. Honestly, when did he have time to do all this? He might have been around in Victorian days when the written letter was still the dispatch of choice. I get married once in life, and I had to find a Shakespearean accountant whose legacy is determined to be in script.

"Ron, if only you had been this interesting when you were alive, I might have never left."

Dear Jane,

If you are reading this, I am dead and gone, and you, you are in California, where you belong. You will have met Lindsay by now, as this was my plan. As a man who got very little he wanted in life, I made sure I'd be fulfilled in death, and if I am capable, I am smiling from above. This is why I hid everything in the condominium. (Aren't I clever?) Isn't my Lindsay a dream? She made my years so happy, saw me through thick and thin—even the drink, when I had another bout with it. Don't let her frail appearance fool you; she's tough as a wolverine and smart, too. I had a good life with her, and I hope that gives you some comfort.

All is forgiven, dear Jane. I realize you most likely believe that I brought you here to punish you, but I assure you, I did not. I brought you here to force reconciliation, and I know you will be blessed for your efforts. A man needs to be known by his father, and Ron Jr. needs to know the truth. I have left him a considerable amount of money, here in these bonds. Bonds I purchased when he was a baby and I thought I'd raise him as my own. Naturally, you broke my heart when you left with him, but I imagine the fault was as much my own for interceding where I probably should not have. Over the years, I have prayed over my actions many times, and I am sorry if I took advantage of the situation. To possess a woman like you—and yes, as a young man I thought possession was my right—was more joy than I could hope for.

*You were right to leave, and I paid for you going, but so
has Ron Jr. No matter what kind of life you gave him, you
need to give him a father, no matter how awful the truth.
A man has a hole there, where his father should be, and
you have no right to say it doesn't exist. I beg of you, Jane.
Humble yourself before God and do the right thing.*

With everlasting love,
Ron

"I'm not telling him a thing, Ron, and you're not here to control any longer. I'll go to my grave with it." I crumple up the blue
missive and shove it in my pocket. If Ron meant for me to tell the
truth, he did himself a disservice giving Ron Jr. the bonds. It only
builds my case. Proof that he was my son's father.

I feel sick to my stomach, pondering more lies. It doesn't bother
me, except when I have to do it directly to Ronnie. His big, green
eyes and their tenderness are something any mother would be
proud of. He has learned a great deal from living out my mistakes
and grown into the man I'd hoped he'd become. One mistake
ruined the course of my life, but it's the many lies since that have
made his more difficult. Some days, I wish I could be free of it. I
only ever thought of myself, and who wants to look back and see
the shambles they've made of their life? I'll do what I can to spare
Ronnie more pain. If I can swallow the pain for some thirty-plus
years, I can certainly gulp down whatever I have remaining.

The doorbell rings and I try to well up enough rage about being
here to forget all of this busy work ahead of me. I throw the papers
back into its bulging, brown folder, along with yet another blue
letter, and cinch the rust-colored string around the button.

Running down the circular staircase, I skid through the blue, glass-tiled foyer, which is something like that children's book *The Rainbow Fish* come to life, and I reach the door. Kuku wraps around my legs and vibrates with happiness. I open the door and practically explode.

"Ronnie!" He embraces me tightly in his muscular arms before I pull back. "Let me look at you. You're just more gorgeous with every year on you!" I grab him up again.

"Hey, Mama! Betcha didn't expect to run into me here."

"You bad boy." I whack his arm. "You told me you'd be away! Shame on you. How did you—"

"Hamilton Lowe called me and told me the will was finally getting processed. I knew that meant you got my message. Smart man, that Hamilton, to have tracked me down like he did. He knew I'd lead him to you." He smiles, and everything within me feels like Kuku purring at my feet. Ron Jr. is by far, the best thing I ever did.

"How did you know how to find me?"

"I knew where Daddy lived," he says with sarcasm in his voice.

"Don't call him that!"

"He shares my name. We live ten miles apart. It was ridiculous to act like he didn't exist. Besides, I wanted to see what he'd made of his life. Wouldn't you be curious?"

"Did you . . . did you ever speak to him?"

"Never got the chance. I did go to his funeral, though. People at his church had fantastic things to say about him. Of course, he was dead; what else are they gonna say?"

I feel the weight of the world pressing down on me. "I need to sit down. Would you like something to drink? I don't know if Lindsay has anything besides wheatgrass, but it's worth offering. I can always get you a water."

"So this is where the little woman lives, huh?"

"She made your father very happy."

"I'm sure she did! What hot blonde in her twenties wouldn't make an old, shriveled-up man happy?" Ron's momentarily hard expression turns back into a smile. "I'm sorry, Mama. I'm not talking like a good, Christian man, am I? Every time I think I've made peace with the past, something else happens, and I go right back into the same old thoughts. I want to lay it on the altar and be done with it once and for all. Maybe having this all over with is my answer." He walks into the foyer, studying the rooms where Ron's young wife lives. He looks so much like his father, and I know there might not be much time left. I need to tell him the truth. I owe him that much.

Christian. I swear that was Ron's legacy on the boy, praying him into a religion that keeps women in their place. The investigator found proof of Ron Jr., and that's how they finally found me. Interesting that Hamilton didn't let the truth out to Lindsay. One has to love that client privilege!

I lead him to the couch. "It seems Ron left you a great deal of money in bonds. He's also left you the big house in Pacific Palisades, from what I can tell. It's going to be a much bigger responsibility than we'd planned for."

My son laughs. "What am I going to do with a house in Pacific Palisades? As if I could pay the water bill, much less the taxes on it. I thought you said most of it was left to his alma mater."

"That's what he'd told me before I saw the actual will, but darling, he was like a human pack rat. He stashed money everywhere. When it comes to diversifying, Ron Brindle was his own stock exchange. He did think of you. Very generously, it seems. You can always sell the house and buy something appropriate for a teacher. You can put the rest in your retirement or into the school down in Mexico. It's really a nice gift for you."

"Well, if he's trying to dissuade his guilt, I want no part of it."

"Spoken like the proud son I raised, but not a very practical one. You live in California, remember? Something about the million-dollar fixer-uppers ring a bell?" I make light of his comment, but I know my son could easily turn his back on this money, on every-thing Ron may have left to him. I'd chalk his religious beliefs up to genetics, if he were truly Ron's son—as it is, I have no idea where he gets this deep-seated religion of his. If he only knew how hard I worked to make sure he had his future set before him, he would never turn his back on this inheritance.

"My father made his thoughts of me quite clear during his life-time. It's too late now. Besides, I'm not here to talk about him. I came to catch up. And to tell you that I've met a woman."

I shiver and wrap my arms about me. Something about this lie gets harder now that Ron is gone and not here to defend himself. He came up with the deception. He sought to protect everyone from natural consequences, but now as the chips fall, Ron is long gone and the rest of us are left to deal with the crimes of thirty years ago.

"Did you say a woman?" I'm pulled back into the present.

My heart bursts with joy. I can only hope she's good enough for him and she'll give my baby everything he could want in a future. I promised myself early on that I would be a good mother-in-law. Not the sort who offered unsolicited advice about parenting or meddled where it wasn't their place.

He grins. "Yes, Mom. A woman. Does that surprise you?"

"Is it serious?" I ask, which shows incredible self-control. What I want to ask is when are my grandbabies coming? I picture myself being the picture of contentment with my grandchildren around my feet. It's the dream that I will finally be settled.

Ron shrugs. "It might be. We've only been seeing each other for four months, but Mom, she's just beautiful. She's got long, dark hair and a perfect, petite figure. She runs, she bike rides, and she does Pilates twice a week. I'm not sure what that is, but it keeps her in great shape, and she loves the Lord."

"And her personality?" I ask.

"She's a sweet, gentle, Christian woman."

"Ron." I smile in my most motherly fashion. "I asked about her, and you've given me the best résumé for a personal trainer I can imagine. I haven't heard much about her being wife material. The mother of my grandchildren . . ."

"Well," he pauses, his face scrunched in thought. "We like to do the same sorts of things. We're both very active. Isn't that important?"

"It's important, but it's not everything. I just want to make sure you don't—"

"When I get married, Mom, it's going to be for good."

Ouch.

"It's just that—well, it's hard to be married, Ronnie, and I want to make sure you're going about this in the right way. You're still young, and I haven't given you much in the way of a role model there."

"Mom, I'm thirty-six. That's ancient in the church, just so you know." He places his hand on my shoulder. "Don't worry. We're not planning the wedding just yet. We're still getting to know each other, but I'm anxious for you to meet her. It's not everyday you're in Los Angeles." He grins. "It's not even every decade."

"You could have stayed in Mexico," I remind him.

"I practically am. Many of my students are just learning English. I'm where I belong. You can't hold me back. I wonder where I get that trait from."

"I want to see you happy, that's all."

I look at the clock on the wall and suddenly panic. I have no idea when Lindsay is due home, and I do not dare let her and Ronnie meet. The last thing I need is to offer more explanations. "Son, it was really great seeing you. I cannot wait to take you and this very special woman to dinner. You name the evening, and we will have a night to remember." I pat him on the shoulders. "As soon as I'm done with the will's details, I am all yours. The lawyers took care of most everything. It's dotting the i's from here on out." I start to close the door, feeling desperate to tell him the truth and have this whole sordid thing behind me, but the truth would kill him.

"Mom, what are you doing?" He pushes back on the door. "I haven't seen you in a year! That paperwork can wait. You don't have to do it all today. It's me, Ronnie!"

"Ronnie, I know it's you, darling. There's not a person on earth I'd rather be with, but I don't want to lose my train of thought. You know how flighty your mother is. I just want to get all this work done so you can claim your rightful inheritance. Incidentally, you might want to keep it under wraps from this special lady that you've inherited a mansion until you have some sort of commitment."

"Mom, Kipling's not like that."

"Kipling?" *I hate this place.*

"Isn't that a great name? It inspires adventure and the arts, don't you think? I knew you'd love it."

"As long as my grandson isn't named Mowgli, it's a fine name." I let the door close a little farther.

"Mom," he presses his palm to the door. "Why are you trying to get rid of me?" He pushes the door back open and steps into the foyer. "Do you have a man in there?" He looks at all the glass tiles and subtle shades of sparkling blue. "What happened in here? The little wife dating a tile guy? I don't even want to know what the house I inherited looks like. A Peter Pan motif? Yet another reason not to claim it. Imagine the work to sell the place."

"Don't talk crazy." I grab his wrist and look him straight in the eyes. "Ron is gone, Ronnie, and he left you the house. There's no strings attached now, and you can do whatever you want with that money."

"I see money every day, Mom. It never seems to do anyone an ounce of good. Come on—let's go get dinner, I'll bet you're famished. You never did eat properly when traveling."

"I ate already." I stay right beside the doorway. He stares at me in disbelief. "Really. I ate."

"Mom, what is up with you? You practically tackle me when I come to Mexico, and now you're acting like I'm not even your son."

I exhale. "I'm not sure when Lindsay is coming home, all right? I'd just as soon we not make ourselves too comfortable until the details of the will are all on the table. Let's plan on dinner tomorrow night after work. Would that work for you?"

"Would that work for me? What am I, a business associate?" He looks down at me and winks. "All right, but you're taking this job far too seriously." He bends over and kisses my forehead. *Kipling better take care of him, or I'll come after her like no jungle cat she's ever seen.*

"Only because I want you to get everything coming to you." *Everything I stole from you.* When I think about how comfortable his childhood could have been.

"Hi," Lindsay appears on the porch. She's alone and as she appears, Kuku races out the door.

"Kuku!" I yell. I don't dare run after him for fear Lindsay will spill everything to Ron Jr. So I try to act casually as I see my cat headed toward the street, and though I'm not a praying woman, I shoot up a request. "You better run and get the cat!" I say to Ronnie.

He feels slightly more enthusiastic about my cat than Lindsay does. Slightly.

"He'll be back, Mom. He's got it too good here." I see him smile at Lindsay in a way that stirs every fear within me. He's talking about the cat, but his eyes never stray from Lindsay. She, on the other hand, doesn't seem to notice him, not even in a casual glance other than a conciliatory greeting.

"Mom?" Lindsay repeats. "This is Ron Jr.?" Now, instead of looking straight through him, she takes the time to stare at his features, probably to take notes if there's a resemblance to her own precious Ron.

He nods eagerly as he waits for an introduction. I fear I didn't give that boy enough birds-and-the-bees information, because in this, he couldn't be more Ron Brindle's son. He's like a second grader in the body of a young Mel Gibson. Women like Lindsay will chew him up and spit him out. It's times like these that I wish I owned a cage to lock him up in until the danger passed.

She presses her small hand into his palm. "It's really nice to finally meet you. Do make yourself at home. I'll be upstairs if either of you need anything." Lindsay walks through us and up the stairs in some sort of zombie state. She never looks back. Her hips don't sway, and she wasn't the least bit moved by my gorgeous son! *What is wrong with that girl?* I must admit, though, I'm thankful for the slight.

Ron watches her all the way to the top of the stairs, and his jaw is significantly lower than it was a moment ago. "Ronnie?"

"Huh?" He pulls his eyes away. "That's her?"

"That's her."

"She didn't look that good the day of the funeral."

"No, I imagine she wouldn't." I clear my throat. "So, you were saying about Kipling?"

"It's nothing. I'm not even sure if I'm ready for you two to meet, but you'll like her. She's a nice girl."

"I'm sure I will, if you do, sweetheart. Four months is a long time these days."

"How old is she? Lindsay, I mean? I didn't realize she was so—"

"She's younger than you, darling. I think a year younger. Thirty-five, thirty-six, somewhere in there. Your father must have charmed her with the gifts! Or she was easily purchased." Granted, that was slightly catty, but Ronnie needs a reality check. I should be grateful for Lindsay's quick exit, which saves me at least a panic attack or two.

"You think? She doesn't seem like that type of girl. She seems like a sweet girl."

"Precisely. She's a girl, who was married to your father." I remind him. "I hope Kipling has no such baggage."

"Why is she here, do you think? This place isn't so great, and it smells like cat pee out here in the halls. I assume Ron left her something, too."

"She probably can't afford living in Pacific Palisades. I think she worked as a salesgirl in retail before she married your father. I don't know what she was left with until the will clears. She's got to be maintaining on some sort of stipend."

"Nothing wrong with honest work, and she has to have title on the house still. Wouldn't you think?"

His answer makes me want to swat him on the behind, as I might have done when he talked back to me as a child.

"She still wears her wedding ring. Did you notice?"

"I didn't. She probably will until the will is complete."

"Mom! She looked upset. Maybe you should go check on her."

I step outside and pull the door shut behind me. "I'd like to, but I have to find the cat. She'll be fine. She's a strong girl." I cup my mouth with my hands and start to shout. "Kuku! Kuku!" I notice all the neighbors snap their curtains and stare, but my heart is pounding. Ronnie remains fascinated with the door, and I'm assuming who's behind it. If I didn't know better, I'd say Ron planned this, as well. "Come help me, Ronnie!" I snap back at him, and his trance is shattered.

He lifts his hand to the doorknob, and I barricade myself in front of the entry. The last thing Ronnie needs is to play nursemaid to Ron Brindle's trophy wife. "Come on, you can tell me more about Kipling while we look."

Chapter 5

Lindsay

Nothing ever truly changes. In biblical times, I'd have a father with no dowry to offer. In Victorian times, I'd be standing against the wall in my best gown, grasping an empty dance card. Presently, I am seated in the back row of my church's singles' group, wondering why on earth I came and how I let Haley talk me into this. Even though we're in the back, we might as well be onstage, for all the attention we're receiving. People are milling about—correction, *women* are milling about—and so far, not a one of them has come to welcome the new faces into the room.

"I feel stupid," I say through my clenched teeth. "I'm a widow. I don't belong here, Haley."

"You'll get over it," Haley says with all the compassion of a meter maid on Santa Monica Boulevard. "It might help you feel more comfortable if you took off your wedding ring."

"That would imply I'm on the market, and I'm not on the market. And you say I'm controlling?"

"You don't have to be on the market to attend a singles' group. You're single. You don't have to fill out a form telling how you're single. The Trophy Wives Club is dealing with so much angst right now. With Bette getting married and Helena's divorce finalized, you don't need all that added stress."

"I can handle the stress of friends. It's the stress of strangers that bothers me. Really. I think we should go." I add, in my best ventriloquist, "This is for young people."

"You're young."

"Young people without a history."

"Everyone has a history."

"But most of them in here could get the PG-rating. PG-13, at the very worst. Seriously, Haley, I don't belong here. I'm an old woman in mind and spirit. These people have their whole lives in front of them."

"This, too, shall pass, Lindsay. Sit down. You only have yourself to blame for being forced into this. You're the one who sat around for a year. Did you think Bette was going to let that go unheeded?"

"Don't try to blame this on Bette. You're the one who brought me here." I can't meet a man in the church. Is she kidding me? Jesus may forgive me of my sins, but the church—well, it keeps a long account.

"You were really no help on my shopping trip. I thought this would get you in a better mood. Besides, if you chose to get out, you might have chosen where you went." Haley presses me back onto the hard, metal chair.

"You used to be the nice one," I tell her. "'Oh, that Haley is so sweet!' people would say. I'm only staying because I'm worried about too many sequins on my bridesmaid gown. Is that clear?"

"Would you stop fidgeting? No one would notice us, if you'd just sit still."

This is a complete lie. We're members of the Trophy Wives Club—a diverse, yet strangely similar Bible study of women whose sins have been made public. Most of us come with the title Divorced. I came a more circuitous route, marrying a man much older than myself, but the fact is, we might as well wear the scarlet letter. Everyone knows who we are, and their hushed whispers and stolen glances only confirm my fears.

"I'm not single, and they all know it. Why else has no one said hello?"

"You *are* single. Your husband is gone, and last time I checked the Bible, young widows were allowed to remarry. Remember? So they didn't burn with passion." Haley giggles.

"There's little chance of that." Being in this large group of women brings out all my fears and insecurities. It's like being in junior high school when every other girl was wearing Nordstrom's Brass Plum clothes, and I was sporting elastic-waist polyester. I may have learned fashion and appropriate responses, but in this scenario, the old insecurities rise to the surface effortlessly. I am not one of them.

I settle into the chair, my plastered smile greeting every woman as they enter the Sunday school room, hoping they won't remember where they've seen me before. "This is like being the new kid in school . . . only chillier." I lean over to Haley and whisper into her ear, "Where are the men? I thought the point of a singles' group was to meet others of the opposite sex."

"No. The point, Lindsay, is to meet people who are in the same life situation that you are. Bonding. Fellowship."

"Oh, trust me, none of these people are in my situation. We're the visiting circus people, come to Mayberry. We could probably charge a quarter for a viewing. Should I get a tattoo, maybe?" I lift up my bicep. "Hang from a rope by my teeth?"

"Lindsay." Haley says with her serious, are you kidding me? look. "Focus on being quiet. You don't have to fill every second with verbiage or fight every activity. We're here at the singles' group because Bette thinks you need to be around younger people. It's time to move forward."

"You're still a Trophy Wife," I say with so much whine, it has cheese on the side. The Trophy Wives Club is my Bible study. It's where I belong and no matter what they say, throwing me back into the singles' scene is simply not going to work.

"You'll always be a Trophy Wife, Lindsay. No one is kicking you out. We're simply saying, explore your options. Start living again. Now quit talking unless you're going to meet someone new and talk to them."

"I talk when I'm nervous."

"You talk when you're hungry, happy, depressed, and most probably in your sleep, too, because—here's the thing—you talk constantly."

I shrug. "Ron's not there to listen anymore. I still have things to say."

"I'll take you to breakfast. Save it all up for then. We're here to meet people. Why don't you use a little of that verbiage on meeting a new friend?"

"I'd rather get a cat."

"Now you're just being rude. Lindsay, you have never been shy a day in your life. Come on, do you really want to be with the Trophy Wives forever?"

"I do. They're my homeys. They took me in and loved me when no one else would. Bette accepted me from the start and so did the rest of them. I stayed with them when I separated from Ron. I stayed with them when we got back together. Why can't I stay with them when I'm single?"

"Ron was twenty years older than you. You didn't exactly fit in with the young couples' group. They were having babies; you were managing retirement accounts. But now . . . now you could meet a man in the same life circumstances as you."

"Fanning about a death certificate?"

"You belong here. It's the truth." I can tell Haley feels guilty for saying it, though, and she gets that teary look she has. "I'm sorry, Lindsay. Ron was a good man, but he's been gone more than a year and you can't live the next sixty years as a mourning widow. At some point—"

"Don't say it. Just don't say it."

"Mingle a little, why don't you?"

"Mingle? Did you notice no one has talked to us yet?"

I look around the room, which really is all female—I'm not just saying that for effect. There's not a set of Dockers in the place. *Whoops, I stand corrected—but it's just a bad fashion choice, not a man.*

I'm not in the market for a boyfriend, and forgive me if this is wrong to think, but this . . . this situation cannot be good for the churchgoing women of the greater L.A. basin. Did God put a female elephant on the ark without a male elephant? He did not. And He most certainly did not put forty female elephants with only one male. I don't care if you're a gambling sort or not, these odds stink. Perhaps, the men are waiting to make their dramatic entrance. Or maybe they're just not good at waking up in the morning, but as far as a singles' group goes, this is looking like a marked deck, and the last thing these gamblers want is another player.

Finally, at four minutes past the hour, the first man walks in. All heads shoot up and gaze at him. He's not a handsome man. How can I say this nicely? He's chinless and has a beer belly. I'm not exactly sure how a church boy gets one of those guts . . . french fries, maybe? Too many Doritos? *Ewww. Maybe he has bad breath, too.* But we're talking about the only man in this room. Here, my chinless friend is Bond. I can almost hear the sucking sound as the women surround him, latching onto him with their eyelashes batting. I roll my eyes. "Oh, brother. Haley, please. I'm begging you— can we go?"

"Shh!" Haley says.

"Do you see that?" I point to chinless Bond.

"Maybe he's a really nice guy."

"Maybe he's just a guy. Maybe that's all you need to be around here. Oh my gosh, we have to go out recruiting." I grab her arm. "These women need men. Come on, let's go to The Grove and pick up some men and bring them back! We can evangelize and everything! You're good at that."

"I do think recruiting men might be illegal, or at the very least, cultlike. Don't be so pessimistic. Maybe it's the guys' camping weekend or something."

"I'm a pessimist? I'm watching Sunday morning roller derby played out with women with Bibles. It could get violent at any moment. That's not enough to make you a cynic? This is worse than an open casting call for a Spielberg flick. You don't think this is where they got the idea that mud-wrestling on *The Bachelor* would be a feasible option?"

"Lindsay, you did things differently last time, marrying older. Do you want to do them the same way?"

I give up. I cross my arms and lean back in the chair. If I were a betting woman, I'd lay odds that the pink, pleather Bible could take down the old-fashioned study Bible in a fight to the finish.

Sitting in the back row is like being, once we're sized up, invisible, and I thoroughly enjoy the dance of the singles before me. More men have entered the room, which makes for a human version of bumper cars, where friends seem to break off into groups and commune.

As I'm watching, I don't notice that chinless Bond has just noticed us and separates the gaggle of women to approach Haley and I. Neither my wedding ring nor Haley's engagement ring seem to deter him.

"Haven't seen you two around here before."

"We attend a different group, normally."

"So we all go out to eat when we're done here. You girls up for it?"

Girls? There's a reason I like older men. "We are going to get breakfast after this," I say, unwilling to let Haley out of her offer of pancakes and certainly not wanting to extend this pain any longer than I have to. Chinless Bond belongs to the women of this Bible study, and whether he realizes it or not, I'm not incurring their wrath while he discovers this truth.

One of the women comes up and cups Bond's ear with her hand to whisper. Apparently, her mother forgot to tell her how rude it is to tell secrets. She points at me. Another nicety her mother clearly failed to mention.

"Haley!"

She pats me on the wrist. "You can handle this, Lindsay. You've got to get past this part of it. We're new. They'll get used to you."

Chinless Bond backs away from us and so many emotions well up—emotions I could kill Haley for making me battle.

"It looks like we're about to get started. Glad to have you both join us." Something about his casual dismissal of me enrages me.

I stand and meet his gaze. "We didn't actually meet. I'm Lindsay

Brindle, and this is my friend, Haley. We're from the Trophy Wives Club down the hall, as you probably heard." I stare at Miss Bible who forgot her manners and stick my hand toward her. "And you are?"

"April," she stammers. "April Endicott."

"April, it's nice to be with you this morning. Thanks for welcoming us to your Bible study." Granted, I put a little extra emphasis on the word Bible. Who could blame me?

"Sure." She nods, unsure of herself—which makes me feel guilty.

"Have you two known each other a long time? You seem like such good friends."

"Tim and I?" She looks to our Dockers-clad 007. "Since high school."

"So not very long then."

She grins. "Longer than I'd like." Her eyes widen as she looks at Tim. "I meant since high school, not that I've known you too long."

They share a laugh, and I notice Tim lets his gaze linger so long that April has to look away.

"I lost my husband last year."

"I'm so sorry," April says with true sincerity.

I shrug. "You just don't want to take things for granted. Things like good friends."

The two of them smile at me and take a seat together in the front row. "You're such a romantic," Haley whispers.

"I have my moments. Can we go now? I'm not ready to date. Even if I were, none of these men would want me. These men want fresh, young, virginal brides who haven't ever been on a date."

"These men want women with a good heart, and that's you, Lindsay. You loved Ron well when he was alive. You took care of him. That's a great track record, and any man in here would be lucky to have you."

"Is the pep talk over now? You promised pancakes." I gaze around the room, and I feel like I'm cheating on Ron. You don't just get used to the fact that it's all right to see other people. It seems so dishonoring to his memory—as though our love were nothing more than a vapor.

"We haven't listened to the sermon. Sit down and be respectful."

"Couldn't we start somewhere simpler? Like maybe nursery duty?"

"Bette said to be here."

Bette is older. The church is into that whole respect-your-elders thing. I appreciate that, but in this case, I think Bette might have been premature. "It's only been a year!" I protest.

Haley puts her hand on mine. "He wouldn't have wanted you to stay holed up in that condominium, Lindsay. He was a good man. Without Ron, I never would have understood that I could live on the money I had. I might never have moved out of that motel or on with my life. But don't you think if he wanted me to move on, he'd want the woman he loved to move on?"

At the sound of Ron's name, I shiver. "It's hard for me to see what moving on has to do with being here." The entire singles' group has now huddled into the front corner, surrounding Tim and April. I'd like to think it's my imagination and paranoia, that they're not up there discussing my presence, but just as I give them the benefit of the doubt, the sea of faces turns toward me and I quickly turn around.

"I've heard the singles' leader is really good. Don't think about dating, Lindsay. Think about making new friends, gaining new spiritual insight."

"He's late, this spiritual guru of yours, and I don't know how much longer I can stay here and be whispered about without standing my ground. It's stifling in here." I pull at my collar. "No wonder there are few men in here. It's like open season. Answer me this: would you feel safe letting Hamilton run loose in this group?"

"Excuse me, I am marrying the man! Of course I would!"

"Tell them that." I nod my chin toward all the women surrounding Hamilton, who have appeared in the doorway.

"This is a desperate group." Haley stands to go stake her claim. "I trust him implicitly, of course. It's the women I have issues with."

I watch Hamilton smile gently at one of the women. It's a friendly smile, not one of flirtatiousness at all, but she doesn't know that. She only knows what she sees—what she wants. Haley walks over, and like the Red Sea, the group parts as Hamilton lays eyes on Haley. It's obvious to everyone what they have. What they don't have. What I don't have.

"I'm going back to the Trophy Wives Group," I say aloud, not that there's anyone to hear. I sneak out the back door and lean up against the wall, trying to settle my rapid pulse. Ron is gone and he's not coming back. He took a part of me with him, and I don't know that I'm coming back, either. I'm not ready to commit—not even to a sickly goldfish at this point. I didn't even get any pancakes for my trouble.

I wander down the hall to where the Trophy Wives meet on Sunday mornings. I open the door a crack and peer in to see the women I'd call my group. Bette is there. She's older, the leader of the group. Her husband died years ago and she never fit in with the married groups with her kids, so she started this collection of misfits. Women come and go as life circumstances change, but Bette never has. She spots me and excuses herself from the circle of familiar women.

"What happened?" she asks me. "You're supposed to be in the singles' group today. Where's Haley?"

"Bette, don't make me go back there. You know I don't fit in with those young, innocent women." I clutch the edge of the door with more desperation than I care to show.

"You're always welcome here, Lindsay," Bette says, while keeping a tight grip on the door, subtly battling me.

"Just not today?"

"You have to at least try, Lindsay. You can't go on forever clinging to the mistakes you made, not allowing God to cover them. I know you've had issues with your mother, but this feeling of failure seems to follow you. You always go back to it."

"So you're not letting me in?"

"No." She shakes her head, looking down. "No, I'm not." She pulls the door shut, and I stare at the doorknob, feeling like a lost puppy with nowhere to call home.

Chapter 6

Jane

I'm done." I exhale with vigor into the phone. If I have stress in my life, I definitely want Hamilton Lowe to know it. "When can you come by and pick it up?" I ask. I keep my voice low, to hide my disdain for the man whose job I'm doing. He knows as well as me, he'll have to check everything I've done anyway—nothing more than a useless step to slow down the process and keep me locked away in California. Away from my art, away from my freedom, and closer still to my secrets being exposed.

I suppose I always did love living dangerously.

"I'm having dinner with my fiancée," tequila-worm lawyer says. "I'm afraid I don't work on Sunday."

"Some of us should have that luxury." Definitely didn't hide the disdain that time. "In case you weren't aware, I'm anxious to get back to my home. I do believe I've done my part." I gaze down at the stack of paperwork understanding instinctively that Ron had no idea how quickly I'd get through it, or he wouldn't have bothered.

"Not quite. We did start probate months back after Ron's death, but we will need to allow for any creditors to come forward on certain accounts. I need to have access to you in case anyone questions the will during this last phase of probate. You'd be the one to answer those. We can meet first thing in the morning to discuss the details. Say, my office at nine? Did you need a ride?"

That's a lot of words for someone telling me to take a hike. *I can see from previous billing, Ron paid the man well enough to make house calls.* "I'll take a cab." I relent. It's not like being in the girl-wife's condominium is uplifting. I long to go back to the comfort of my home. Something about L.A. puts me into feeling I need to accomplish everything within a small time frame, as though I've entered a different plane where life is on warp speed.

"While I have you," Hamilton continues. "I'll need your son's decision on the Pacific Palisades home. He will be taxed as soon as the transaction is complete, as the house is worth over one million, which is California's inheritance limit before taxes must be paid. The house wasn't included in the trust. Ron Jr. can pay the house taxes at the rate which Ron did, being his son, but the inheritance tax is separate."

"He's a teacher."

"So he won't be keeping the house?"

I stare at the receiver, wondering if Hamilton really does think the world can afford luxury living. "Yes, well, right now he's not interested in the house, it seems."

"My best guess on what it's worth now is about three and a half, maybe four million. So that leaves taxes on approximately two and a half million to three million. I'll need his decision on putting it on the market."

People in California rattle off these numbers like they're simple math. They have no clue that the rest of the world is lucky to get enough water or rice for their day. They're too busy buying expensive clothes with someone else's name sewn in the collar and diversifying capital—Ron's favorite pastime and the reason his will was such a bear.

All this money and not a speck of common sense about living the good life.

"I'll speak with him tonight, but he's a schoolteacher, so my best guess is the obvious. He won't be able to pay the taxes, so I think the house will need to go on the market."

"I'll just need his signature to verify that. See you in the morning, then."

I hang up, disgusted Mr. Lowe has a date so I'm stuck here even longer—perhaps probate is the official reason, but the lawyer having a date is not improving my attitude.

There are pictures of Ron everywhere in the house. Pictures of him in front of the Eiffel Tower. Pictures of him on a gondola in Italy—or maybe Las Vegas, one can never tell these days. In every shot, he smiles at Lindsay and she beams at him. "Good for you Ron. You managed to find your happiness."

The amount Ron left us with was more than generous. More than his waifish wife ended up with, surprisingly, but she probably doesn't need much to survive. Maybe six hundred dollars a year or so for food, and that much a week for shoes, judging by her closet. Yes, I riffled through her closet. It's human nature to know what makes another person tick—maybe not something we're infinitely proud of, but the curiosity is there, all the same.

Lindsay doesn't seem to want the mansion, and I can't begin to understand why. I would think the closet space alone was enough to call her name, but according to all the paperwork I've been through, she asked that the house not be left to her. She married for money after all, why wouldn't she take it? I mean, at ten years of marriage, she did pretty well, considering. Asking questions will only prolong my departure, so I'll keep my secrets, and she can keep hers. We generally pass each other casually in the house, offering a smile and move quickly on to our destination. We're two people who would have never met in life, and yet we were married to the same man. Life has a funny way about showing irony.

The phone rings. I secretly hope it's Hamilton Lowe, and he's been ditched by his lovely fiancée. "Hello, Lindsay Brindle's residence."

"That you, Jane?"

My throat tightens. His voice. He hasn't changed an iota. He still thinks all his problems stem from other people, and in those two words, I hear the accusations in the role he's placed me—the villain to his innocent victim. Some people never take hold of the damage they cause. The truth, when it gets close to touching them, must be taken out and destroyed. The lie protects him.

"Jane, I know you're here," he says. The man has the consistency of snot, but when he speaks with all the charm of a luxury-car dealer, I can't help but question my perspective. Maybe I have it all wrong—never mind that he's been in jail for most of his natural-born life. I hold onto these facts before my heart softens even a smidgen.

His voice doesn't bring the fear it once did, but I'm worried that, though all these years have passed, he's still nursing the same wounds. I slam the phone down just as Lindsay walks in the front door and I wander out of the kitchen. She pulls her key from the door and looks down at Kuku on the cool tile at the entry. I know she wants to say something about her precious condo, but she doesn't. She simply steps over him, and the cat mews his annoyance.

The phone rings again, but I don't make a move to press the button on the cordless sitting right in front of me. Lindsay runs for the kitchen phone, and I panic. "Don't answer that!"

"Why not?"

"Just don't." It's is the only explanation I can think of.

She looks at the phone. "California Department of Corrections?"

Stellar. She has caller ID. What does one say about getting a call from your local jail? *I have a pen pal?*

She puts the phone back in its cradle and shrugs. "Whoever this is . . . He doesn't know where I live, I hope?"

I shake my head. "I don't think so. Unless you're listed. Besides he and the California Department of Corrections have a long-standing relationship that isn't about to end soon. They do give them a dime here and again to spread their joy."

She nods. "Any other friends you plan to look up while here?"

"Lindsay, I—"

"It was a joke. Maybe a bad one, but I've had a bad day. I'm sorry, all right? My address isn't in the book, only the telephone number. How does he know to find you here? No, don't answer that. I don't want to know. Did you eat yet?"

"I did. I walked down to the bakery."

"That place is a lifesaver when I haven't been shopping."

Which, judging by her pantry and waist size must be every waking moment.

She drops her purse on the kitchen counter. "I have to plan a wedding shower. Could there be a worse person for that? What do they think, I'm Snow White and there are birds singing at my feet?" she asks. "It took me six months to sell Ron's car; how organized can I be?" She looks me straight in the eye. "Everyone on the planet has to see his death certificate. My life's work has become proving he's dead—it doesn't exactly make me want to whistle a happy tune, you know?"

We look at each other and start to laugh.

"Sorry," she says. "Bad day."

"You don't owe me an explanation. I worked on the will every day this week—me, who only has to worry if I have enough yellow ocher to get through a sunset painting. Finding names and addresses from years ago . . . are they kidding me?"

"I'm too old to plan a bridal shower," Lindsay says.

"Well, I don't know. You seem very organized. I thought I might eat off your floor when I first got here. Of course, with the dust around my front door, a clean floor isn't really a viable option unless someone mopped it continuously. Don't worry—I'm sure you'll plan a lovely shower."

She hovers over the phone. "I'm a widow. What do I know about romance and party games? Besides, of course, how to put a quick end to both?"

"You planned a funeral. It can't be that different. Food, flowers—just change the color scheme."

Lindsay starts to giggle. "Did you just tell me to change the color scheme?"

"Black to pink. It can't be that much trouble." I wink at her. As young as she is, Lindsay possesses a fire in her belly, and I don't believe there's much in life she couldn't accomplish.

She shakes her finger at me. "You have a wicked sense of humor, Jane. I do like that in a person."

The doorbell rings, and Kuku decides to move himself. He's not used to all this activity.

Lindsay opens the door. It's my son. Again. I don't know that I saw this much of him when he lived with me. All six-foot-four inches of him, and he's wearing a suit. *Why on earth would my son even own a suit?*

"You planning my funeral?" I ask him from across the room.

He pulls flowers from behind his back, and I rise with a smile on my face before I watch in horror as he hands them to Lindsay. "For giving my mother a place to stay while she's here. She wouldn't last a day in my place. Not that it isn't clean—just small."

"She's no trouble." She looks back at me. "Ron would have wanted it that way."

I notice she doesn't call him, "your father," and my stomach plummets with the knowledge she could ruin me at any moment. But I catch her gaze, and something's there. Something that says we understand each other. I look at a rattlesnake on my path in the same way—with mutual respect. Lindsay is deeper than I first gave her credit for. Unfortunately, my son didn't miss this insight either.

"What are you doing here, Ronnie?" I look to my watch. "It's late, isn't it? You'll be having to get up early to get to the classroom." I look at Lindsay. "He's a teacher." *Couldn't afford one of your shoes on his salary, much less a pair. No matter what Ron left him, he'll never live like this.*

"Come on in. I'll put these in some water, and then I'm going to go upstairs with the phone book so you two can have the place to yourselves. I have a wedding shower to plan."

"You're getting married?" Ron asks, his voice higher pitched than normal. I'm sure he's just worried about his father's memory. At least that's what I tell myself.

Lindsay rolls her eyes. "Um, no. I tried marriage once, remember? My best friend is getting married."

"She's marrying the lawyer I'm meeting with tomorrow about the will." I add, "It's all one big, happy family around here." I half expect Kuku to meow after what I've said, but if my comments are catty, no one seems to notice.

"Does Lindsay know about the Pacific Palisades house being left to me?"

My heart sinks. Did I teach this boy nothing? One good game of poker, and he might learn to keep things to himself, instead of offering up information like it's candy.

Lindsay smiles. "Don't worry, Ron told me he'd put it in another trust. We discussed it, and besides, it's none of my business where he leaves his money now, is it?" She lays the flowers on the island counter, pulls the phonebook toward her chest, and starts for the stairs. I watch her every move, wondering why she doesn't tell Ronnie that she asked specifically to be left off the will for the Pacific Palisades house. What could she be hiding?

I pick up the flowers and hunt for a vase. Lindsey turns around and finally meets my son's eyes, focusing on him as though he's an actual person. "You look like him." Then she looks at me, and I shrug. "He was bald by your age, though, so I guess you didn't inherit that."

He rakes his hand through his thick brown hair. "I guess not."

"It has been nice meeting both of you. I'm only sorry it didn't happen when Ron was here. He would have loved to see you both. I know he would have." Lindsay sees the newspaper on the console table and places it on top of the phone book. "I should look for a job, too. Have a nice time and make yourself at home."

"About the house—"

Ronnie, shut up, son!

Lindsay's expression softens. "Ron left his money where he wanted it left. I have no right to question a thing. I mean, no plans. I have no plans to question anything."

"You weren't after his money, then?" He steps closer to her, and my own heart pounds at their proximity. "You really loved him?"

She swallows visibly. "Ron lived a good life, Ronnie. It's been a very trying day. If you'll excuse me." She makes like a chased cat, scurrying up the stairs.

"I guess I shouldn't have said that," Ron mutters under his breath. I swallow my guilt. He's a man now, and still, the hole where his father should have been leaves its mark. He wants to know more about the myth I created. That Ron and I created. How can I say I love him and lie to him every day of his life?

"No, sweetheart. She did have a hard day, and I think Lindsay has secrets of her own. But look at the pictures around here. She's right—Ron had a good life."

He watches the stairs, as though she's still there, an apparition in his head. "She's undeniably the most beautiful woman I've ever seen. I can't find my tongue when she's in the room." He slaps his forehead. "She must think I'm a complete idiot."

"I never noticed. I'm sure she didn't." My stomach roils at his obvious lack of understanding. "What about Xena, Warrior Princess?"

"You mean Kipling, Mom." He shakes his head. "*This*. This is how a man should feel about a woman. This is what was missing." He places a palm to his chest.

"No, this is the feeling that got your father into trouble. This is why Samson lost his strength!"

He studies me carefully. "You know a Bible story?"

"I know a lot of things. One does not get to be my age without learning a few tricks of the trade. A thinking man looks at all aspects of who he wants to spend his life with; he doesn't let his hormones do the talking. Ron, she was married to your father. You don't find that, I don't know . . . unsavory?"

"There's something about her," he says staring at the circular staircase. "I can't explain it."

"There certainly is, and it got your father into trouble, thinking only with his . . . with his heart. Don't repeat his mistakes." *And definitely don't repeat mine.* If I knew then what I know now, I definitely would have researched DNA before considering my child's father.

He tears his gaze from her shadow. "I didn't mean that, Mother. Not everything is hormonally related. Her secrets intrigue me, that's all. If she married for money, why isn't she taking as much of it as she can?"

"A good question, but one we'll never have the answer to. It's Lindsay's business, and it doesn't concern us."

"I'd better get home."

"That's it? I thought you came to see me!"

"I was downtown for a computer class. I thought I'd stop by before I went home."

With flowers. For Lindsay. "Before you go, Ronnie, the lawyer's asking if there's any way you'll keep the house."

Ron laughs. "With what? My good looks?"

I look at my son's tall, handsome appearance. "If anyone could . . ."

"Mom—"

He turns and opens the door, and a there's a man on the small porch. His presence catches us both by surprise. He's tall, not quite as tall as Ron, but he's dark and handsome in that trademarked, rugged way. I can tell he's for real, because his teeth aren't the shade of Chiclet white of all actors. He looks us both over. "Is this Lindsay's house?"

"This is Lindsay's house," I croak, my voice still hammered by Ronnie's desire to know about his father's wife.

"Is she here?"

"Who's asking?" Ronnie says in a protective way that makes me bristle.

"Would you tell her Jake is here? I have business to discuss. It's about her house in Pacific Palisades."

My son starts to speak, and I talk over him. Definitely need to get the boy to Vegas and teach him a poker face. "I'll run up and get her." I kiss my son's cheek and he flinches. "Bye, Ronnie." I give him a gentle nudge out the door, but he stands firm.

"You better go get Lindsay, Mom. I'll let myself out." He crosses his arms and stares at Lindsay's guest.

I have trouble catching my breath as I start for the stairs. *I did what I had to do*, I remind myself, but the accusing voices become louder, and I know that I can't keep this lie up forever. At some point, I have to come clean with my son, but the fear of losing him always brings the clarity that made the lie tolerable in the first place.

Chapter 7

Lindsay

Time flies when you're having fun. Or so, the infamous "they" say. It apparently flies when you're not having fun, as well, because the date of Haley's wedding is suddenly sneaking up on me like one of the cats in the hallway.

I wanted to make everything perfect for her. To be the kind of matron of honor that left her nothing to worry about except enjoying her big day. Instead, I've turned into the flake who forgets to plan a wedding shower, who doesn't go for the dress fitting on deadline.

Worse yet, when Haley asked about the details, I sort of stretched the truth. More precisely, I lied, but I didn't want her to think I didn't care, and I definitely didn't want her to worry. I do care. I've just been too wrapped up in my own morbid life to be a good friend. That has to stop here and now.

I hear voices downstairs and force myself to focus on the task at hand. I'm sure Jane will say her good-byes expediently. She's made herself quite at home, and I've grown accustomed to being a guest in my own condo. She moves about with such an air of confidence, one can't help but get out of the way. With all this action, my neighbors must be worn out from all the curtain swinging. It's like the curmudgeon Olympics.

There's a soft rap at my bedroom door, and I open it to see a flash of black pass my feet.

"I'm sorry to disturb you," Jane says, quietly ignoring the obvious furry intruder.

Yeah, um, can you get this cat out of here? "The cat's in here."

"I'll get him." She watches him run and jump up on my bed and stretch his claws and pick at the bedspread, pulling up loops of threads before settling near the pillows. Jane acts as though I should be touched.

Yeah, um, the cat?

"You have someone to see you downstairs. He says his name is Jake, and he has to speak with you about the Pacific Palisades house. Is this something I should be concerned with? You know, in regards to the will?"

"Jake is here?"

"That's what I just said," Jane snaps.

"Is something the matter, Jane?"

She sighs. "No, nothing's the matter. I'm just not interested in your love life, and I want to go home."

"My love life?"

She shakes her head as she walks toward the stairs.

"No, wait a minute, Jane. I have no love life. I was married faithfully to Ron for ten years." I shake my head. "That didn't come out right. I was faithful to our marriage even if we didn't live together."

"Like I said, it really doesn't interest me."

What happened? We could go around like this for ages, but Jake is downstairs, and the thought sends flutters through my stomach. I've wanted this chance to tell him what happened—to explain myself—but reality sends shivers through my limbs. Jake never was a very forgiving man, and he probably views my sin as the unforgivable. At least that's what I told myself years ago when he refused to acknowledge Ron or my apology.

Extreme's *More than Words* tune fills the romantic void in my head and takes me back to a simpler time. Flashes of innocence flicker before my eyes. Dreamily, I realize Jake's being here offers hope of forgiveness, and I've become a sucker for hope. I left this powerful emotion in the past with too much life in front of me.

"Tell him I'll be right down," I say to Jane's back. I shut the door, trapping the stupid cat, who has made himself at home on my bed. I cross my arms and stare at it. "I'm not averse to seeing if cats can really survive a jump out of a two-story window, you know?"

He melts into my bedspread, thoroughly unscathed. I look into the mirror and recoil. Stress is not good for me. "I was meant for pampering. Like you, Kuku." I look at the cat in the mirror.

When I speak, the cat doesn't even open its eyes. This is my life—I'm not even interesting enough to lure a cat out of its nap. I pound Jane Iredale mineral foundation on and revel in what a miracle it is, taking away the day's shine in an instant. I wish I'd invented it. My life would have been so different if I'd realized I could have made my own money. I swish some blush at the apples of my cheek, but I don't like what I see. I look angry, and as if I tried too hard—hopeful for an invitation that will never come.

I stare into the mirror, pondering my options, then shimmy out of my slacks and throw on my home pants (read: sweats). I roll them up at the knees, wiggle into an oversized T-shirt and now I look like I'm not repentant. Too casual. It says, "I don't think you're important, Jake, and I don't regret a thing." So I try again with jeans and a bright pink C&C Tee. I ignore the call for lipgloss and open the door with a heaving, cleansing breath. In with the new, out with the old.

I halt at the door. Jake is at the bottom of the stairs, parading back and forth. I back up to the wall and watch him for a moment. He is here. In my house. I lean back against the doorframe and pray for strength. Jake is the only person who knows I married Ron for money besides my mother. I'm certain there are plenty of people who assumed that I married for money, but they are the only two who know it for certain. I pray he doesn't mention that fact in front of Jane, or I might find myself alone *and* out on the street.

As I glide down the stairs, thinking of each and every step, Jake's eyes meet mine. *I know him.* In his soul, I know what he's thinking, and his disappointment in me swallows any hope I had of this being a joyous reunion. I let him down, and he still can't believe it. Just like I let my mother down, and I let Ron down, or Jane wouldn't be here to finish his business. I am one, ginormous disappointment.

My body is drained of its humanity, and for the first time in a great while, I question my faith. Did I ever really have any? Maybe I've just been making myself feel worthy, hanging out with church folk. Could a Christian really do the things I've done and move forward? Zaccheus gave back four times what he stole, but how would that be translated for me? I stole someone's heart and trust.

Could a real Christian abandon the man she loved for something as ordinary as money? I put so much stock in security, and there is no such thing. God can take it anytime He pleases; then you're left with nothing—neither the love you've forsaken nor the mansion built on false expectations.

I've practiced this moment, but have nothing when I greet Jake at the bottom of the stairs. Jane stands alongside him in the foyer. "Did you meet Jane?" I ask him.

He nods.

"I'll just be going to bed. Did you want me to get the cat, Lindsay?"

"He's fine. He's sleeping on my bed."

"That won't be good for your allergies," she says with raised brows.

"No, it won't."

"It was nice to meet you, Jake. I'll be in my room if you need anything."

It feels like an eternity before the door down the hallway closes with a quiet click.

"May I offer you some coffee?"

He chuckles. "Ten years and that's what you have to offer me?"

I feel the temperature rise in the room. "I haven't been shopping. Is there something else you want?" Why is my mouth being so rude? It's not what I want to say at all. I close my eyes and ask God to speak the words of my heart.

"Am I boring you?" he asks.

"I'm trying to think, Jake. There's so much I want to say to you, and I haven't a clue where to start. Just let me think for a moment, will you?"

"Why don't you start with why you married him? I figure I've waited long enough for that answer."

I sigh. "You know why I married him. If you want to hear me say I married him for love, it's not going to happen. I'm not going to lie or pretend. Everything you thought about me was right on the money. No pun intended. I married Ron for his money, and I left you because you had none. Happy?"

I hear a footstep and turn to see Jane tiptoeing up the stairs, most likely to rescue Kuku from an early feline death. The look in her eyes makes me feel about an inch tall, and it feels like I can never recover from my sins so many years ago. As they both stand here judging me, I know they have every right to do so.

"Jane, I can explain—"

"You and Ron had yourselves a deal, it's none of my business. It surprises me to hear you admit it so readily. Is this your next target?"

I ignore her dig. "Ron must not have trusted me completely. That's why I assumed you were here. You can stay up on your perch, Jane."

"He saw only what you showed him. That's to your credit." She starts down the hallway again and enters her room, obviously giving up on Kuku.

"Yes, I suppose it is to your credit." Jake agrees. "You were an excellent actress. No one would have ever guessed. Least of all the fiancé, but they always are the last to know."

"Jake, don't look at me like that. I learned to love Ron. I did what I did. I paid for it. Trust me, I paid for it. I didn't get my Cinderella ending, so you can gloat all you want. He was never cruel to me— only to himself."

"You were cruel to yourself, Lindsay. I would have given you the world."

"I deserved what I'd created. We had a good life together. We found Jesus together, and we learned to understand each other in the end. A marriage that starts off as a business arrangement doesn't often get its happy ending, but Ron is happy now, and I'm done with the romantic notions of youth." My faith couldn't seem anymore shallow if it were a Hollywood princess on her sixteenth birthday.

Jake's jaw is tight as he looks at the pictures on every table. "You always were too hard on yourself, but I understood better than you think. I was living with my mom at twenty-five, and she washed my underwear. Maybe I wasn't ready to offer you that kind of security. Maybe I didn't try hard enough."

"Don't do this. Don't make me feel worse."

"I only ever wanted you to be happy," Jake says, bringing my chin up with his thumb. "I thought Ron made you happy. That was good enough for me."

"He made me feel safe. I wanted to feel safe and protected."

"You never had children," Jake states.

"No."

"You would have made a terrific mother. I always told my mother that you would have been an overachiever as a mother."

"I would have made a terrible mother! Jake Evans, do you remember nothing of the past?"

"On the contrary. I remember everything." His words make me dare to hope that he doesn't remember only the bad about me. I find this important, because one day, I hope to truly forgive myself.

"Jake, sit down. I'm going to get this out before you tell me what you came here to tell me."

He walks to the sofa and sits, crossing his foot onto his other knee. "I'm all ears."

"I've thought about what I did to you every single day of my life. There's not a morning that I wake up, and I don't remember the look in your mother's eyes when I told her I was marrying someone else. She wasn't angry, Jake. She pitied me."

"She'd been married a long time. She knew a bit about what it takes to make a marriage work. I can tell you her attitude has since changed. You won't find much pity in her heart these days."

I look away. This is where the rubber meets the road. This is where I get to prove that my commitment to God is a strong one, and I need his forgiveness. "I'm truly sorry, Jake. And if there's a way—any way at all—I can prove that what I did was about my weakness, not yours, just tell me."

"I know you're sorry. I never questioned that. I was sorry, too, believe it or not."

"Stop being so nice. Tell me the truth. Tell me what it feels like to hear my hollow apology. Now!"

He hints at a grin, his dark, blue-green eyes dancing, as though they possessed a secret. "It feels good. I've waited a long time for those words. I thought I'd take more pleasure in them. I thought they might change something."

"Change something? You sound disappointed."

"I'm getting married in a month. I suppose for years, I wanted to hear you grovel." He slaps his palms to his knees and stands. "Didn't work. Doesn't change a thing."

"You're getting married?" I finally register his words. "To a woman—"

"I haven't become gay in the last decade, so yes, I'm marrying a woman."

"I didn't mean that. Naturally you're getting married. I'm surprised you're still single now."

"Work's been keeping me busy. I had to make it a point to settle down. I want children, and I'm not getting any younger. Work isn't letting up. It's got to be a decision."

I hide behind a mask of indifference, but my jaw tightens. "I'm sure you'll be very happy. Is there something you came here for? Besides to hear me grovel, I mean, and really, I'm sorry that didn't bring you more pleasure. You deserved that much."

"There is a reason I'm here." He produces an envelope from his back pocket. Seeing a legal-sized envelope anymore strikes the fear of God in me. "I came to give you this. This is my apology, my way of clearing the air."

I rip it open. It's a check for $12,532.

"What's this?"

"It's the money you sent. I've added interest."

"Money I sent?" I feign innocence.

"I thought it was my mother for years. It came at the perfect time. I'd just finished Ron's and your house and was starting my own contracting business. Oddly enough, it was the exact amount I needed, so I assumed my mother had donated to my cause, but I later found out otherwise. And I figured you'd absconded with it from an account Ron didn't check carefully."

"I worked for every cent of that money, selling suits at Nordstrom's. Do you know how many dirty, old men I had to flirt with to scrape that together?"

Jake grins. "Well, thank you. I appreciated it. But I'm not a man who believes in debt, anonymous or otherwise. I kept it for a long time, because I thought it was the least Ron could do for me." He walks to the door. "Now that I know it really was your money, I should have let this battle go a long time ago."

"That's it? That's all you came for?"

"No. Lindsay. I came to kiss you good-bye."

I step in front of him, closing my eyes. He presses hard, sterile lips to my forehead. I open my eyes, and what I lost in Jake makes me aware of how easily I could trash what matters in life. It's hard to feel any kindness toward yourself when such a reality lands on your doorstep.

"You're still a beautiful woman, Lindsay. I hope you'll be very happy."

I nod dully. "I hope the same for you, Jake."

"Thank you for the money," he says softly. "My business has done well. You could've had it all, if you had been patient. Granted, not this kind of lifestyle, but I would have taken care of you. I would have protected you with my very life."

I step closer to him where I can feel the warmth of his chest. He still smells the same, an earthy mixture of sandalwood and musk. I could reel him in right now. I know I could. With one kiss, I'd have him questioning his fiancée's very name, but I have changed. The very idea now makes me ill and for that, I am thankful.

"I'm not a saint, Lindsay. Don't play with fire."

"I might have had it all, Jake. Patience is a virtue, and I'm afraid God isn't finished with me yet. I pray you'll be very happy." I squeeze his hand and let him go.

My neighbors' drapes are wide with shock-and-awe, Lindsay-style. Closure is a good thing, both in unrequited love and the neighbors' curtains.

Chapter 8

Jane

He'll be taxed on everything exceeding that. My best guess is two and a half million."

Two and a half million, he had said. And that's the last I heard of him. Mr. Hamilton Lowe, a lawyer too important for his own good. It's been excuse after legal excuse, and three more full weeks in this overcrowded, smog-ridden desert they call Los Angeles. Living here, I find reasons that the Mayans were so very violent. A human sacrifice here and there is starting to sound reasonable when there are so many humans abounding. This is a sign I've been here too long.

I could be in my courtyard, painting and laughing with friends. I could be on a backpacking trip on the ridge of Copper Canyon, but I am wasting my life in the city . . . waiting for money, which I couldn't care less about. I want to be sitting in the local Internet café, chatting with tourists from all over the world. I despise waiting for life to start.

I draw in a lung-expanding breath. *This is about my son, and he is worth it.* I've made his entire life difficult, and if I have the opportunity to make his future easier, I have no choice but to be here and fight for what's his. I'm the only advocate he has.

Probate. It's just a lawyer's excuse to keep squeezing blood from a client. The man has been dead a year, who do they think is coming to file a claim against the estate? The Mayan, "Fire is Born" is rising to stake a claim? "Ron, you and your financial games." I stare up at the ceiling and laugh, knowing he's probably listening as well as he did when he was alive. I might as well have spoken to the ceiling then, too.

I zip my suitcase and Kuku, recognizing the familiar sound enters into his cat carrier, excited for the next adventure. I bend down and rub behind his ears, "You can't stand being locked up either, baby? We're gypsies. We can't be held by these mere mortals, can we?" He sways his head for closer contact with his chin.

He meows long and laboriously, stretching his paws out of the container, and then retreats into the box in anticipation. I look at my watch, wondering when the princess might show her flawless face on this fine morning.

I sit on Lindsay's sofa with my suitcase and cat carrier at my feet. She'll appear soon, after her strange workout, whatever it might consist of. When I first heard her clunking around in her bedroom, hitting walls and odd, breathless noises coming from the room, I thought we'd had an earthquake. I thought to myself, *I leave Mexico for two weeks, and I have to be in L.A. when the big one comes.* This is my luck!

It turned out, the only shaking involved some form of praise and worship aerobics—these religious sorts have to get everything involved. They eat with prayer, talk in weird code, and even dance to music about God. I'll tell you, it's enough to drive normal people crazy. The first time Lindsay emerged from her bedroom with iPod plugs in her ears, singing God tunes, wearing shorts that really didn't have enough material to officially qualify as shorts, I thought to myself, *She questions* my *art?*

At nine-thirty, Lindsay finally appears at the top of the stairs, in taut Lycra shorts to her knees. The shorts are as tight as her muscles. She carries a bottle of 365 Water and her face is misted with sweat. It's a curse to look like Lindsay. Think of the maintenance! If there's a God above, He knew I wasn't ready for that commitment and graciously allowed me to be average. He definitely graced me with a complete lack of ability to care.

Her eyes rest on my suitcase. "What's with the bags? Are you going somewhere?"

"I'm leaving for a while. I've been here too long, and I'm getting restless."

"I thought Hamilton said—"

"Just to Ensenada for a few days. I'll be back before someone can mail something certified."

"Is that safe?"

"Lindsay, I live in Mexico. What do you mean, is it safe?"

"But you live on the other side of Mexico. That's like me saying I live in the U.S. and assuming it's the same in New York."

"I don't live my life in fear. I like to explore, and most of our fears are usually unsubstantiated. It's something completely unforeseen that will get you in the end. I have my breathable, khaki shorts on with hiking boots, my suitcase, and Kuku—what more do I need? I rented a SUV, and I'm going to drive."

"To Mexico? In an SUV? Are you nuts?"

"Lindsay, is that your way of saying you care?" I grin at her.

"You can at least take me out to breakfast before you go. I'm craving pancakes."

"It's all that exercise in the morning. You don't have enough fat cells to support that intensity of workout."

She rolls her eyes. "Is that a yes?"

"Fine. Breakfast is the least I can do before I go."

Lindsay wiggles into pants over her shorts and throws on a T-shirt. "I'm ready."

"You're going out like that?"

"This is L.A. I'm practically dressed for a funeral." She does a full twist for me, and if there's a trouble spot to be had on her, it doesn't show anywhere. Ronnie was right when he touted her beauty, and begrudgingly, I have to admit she's been sweet and most welcoming. I really had wished her to be the evil, little temptress I always imagined. I have no doubt she is an evil, little temptress—just one without guile or knowledge of her superpowers.

We get into her luxury sedan, which is showroom clean, like the condo. It's an odd statement that Lindsay goes out with her hair flowing every which way but doesn't allow a speck of dust on her dashboard.

"How's the wedding shower coming along?"

She starts up the car and it purrs to life. "Everything is done, with the exception of the location, so I can't send out the invitations. I was thinking I might ask Ronnie if he'd let me use the Pacific Palisades house one more time?"

I scratch the back of my head, wondering if she isn't plotting to end up with the house and my son in the process. For the life of me, I cannot imagine why she didn't ask for the house in the first place. "Why don't you buy the house from Ronnie? He's going to need to sell it, and you clearly have use for the home. It would make things easier on all of us."

"Never mind, Jane. I'll just rent out a restaurant."

"I didn't mean that. I'll ask him for you, of course. I can't imagine he'd mind. He probably won't even see the house before it's sold."

"He should see it. There's a lot of Ron in that house. I think he'd like to visit before it sells."

"Why would he want to do that?" I gaze across the black leather interior, wondering if she's messing with my mind. She realizes that Ronnie isn't Ron's son, doesn't she? Or is she questioning that fact, hoping to catch me in my tangled web of deceit?

She pulls to a stop sign and turns her head. Her blue eyes blink rapidly and the corner of her lip turns up. "Um, because he inherited a four million–dollar house from the man? Chances are, he'd be curious."

"Right." I watch Lindsay's easy smile. My hope is that she's happy for Ronnie. He did, after all, get what he deserved, for being raised without a father. Probably a good deal more than he deserved, but I do hope one day he'll know the truth and forgive me for what I tried to do for him.

We pull up to a restaurant that has plants hanging from hippie-themed pots along its storefront. Although it's nearly March, the day is bright and shiny, as usual, and a bevy of gym beauties fill the tables along the sidewalk.

"What time are you leaving for Mexico? Do you need to get back at any particular time?"

"I don't have a schedule. I was just anxious to get out of your hair. I don't know. I have this fear that as soon as I get out of here, something will go wrong with the will. Maybe I should just stick this out. It's not worth the chance of my being stuck here longer."

"Don't be silly, Jane. I have plenty of room, and you're not bothering me. I like the company, and you're better than a cat. At least you take care of the cat you came with." She giggles.

We enter the restaurant and someone even thinner than Lindsay (if that's possible?) seats us at a table near the window and all the other diamond-clad trophy wives in gym gear. "Doesn't anyone work around here?"

"For a lot of these women, going to the gym is work. They are either actresses or trophy wives, both of which require a certain physique."

"You say that matter-of-factly. Don't you find it sad?"

She shrugs. "Of course I do, but that doesn't make it any less true. Haley could never please her ex-husband, and there isn't anyone who tried harder. That's one thing I loved about Ron. We were both very flawed individuals, and we could respect that in each other. I loved him though he was older and drank too much. He loved me though I was flighty, can't cook for beans, and had to work hard to understand what he did for clients so that I could be of some help to him."

"You tried, Lindsay. That's more than I did, so I applaud you for that." And I do. The more I get to know Lindsay, the more facets I can see in her that are genuine and intelligent. But beautiful people are often charming and put one off their guard. I try to remember this as she orders a breakfast fit for a lumberjack. "I'll have the gluten-free pancakes with fresh strawberries on top and a side of organic bacon. Oh, and Diet Coke to drink."

"Organic bacon and Diet Coke?"

"You want that, too?"

I peruse the menu, which has an abundance of adjectives that mean nothing to me. Organic, gluten-free, farm-raised, non-hydrogenated, no GMOs. "I want two eggs, over-easy, with a side of toast," I say.

"Whole wheat bread all right?"

"Absolutely. Orange juice to drink and a coffee."

"Fresh-squeezed or flash-frozen?"

"Fresh-squeezed." I hand her the menu and peer at Lindsay, who is putting her hair into a large, tortoise-shell barrette. "I have to ask: are there chicken sausages which aren't raised on a farm?"

She giggles. "Look, I save my chemicals for Diet Coke. I want my chickens clean. Better living through chemicals, but not diseases from imported, dirty birds, you know what I'm saying?"

"I haven't a clue, actually. So what happens when you come to visit me in Mexico and someone in the neighborhood skins their chicken for your dinner? Is that street-raised?" The waitress fills my cup with something dark and cinnamon-scented. "This is coffee?"

"Our special blend," she says with a smile.

"Yum!" I take one sip and have to fight to swallow the bitter liquid.

Lindsay continues, "I'd be thrilled to have Mexican chicken from the streets of Campeche. Are you inviting me?"

"You're afraid to go to Ensenada. You're telling me you're going to take a Mexican airliner all the way to Campeche?"

"No, I'm afraid you'll go to Ensenada and won't come back soon, and the probate will drag on ever longer."

"Ah, so it's a selfish reason you want me to stay here." Secretly, I think it's because she doesn't want to be alone again, and nightmare that I may be for her, I'm still preferable to being alone for Lindsay.

"Maybe. Mostly, I don't like being alone. I like having you there."

"Aha!" It's as though she read my thoughts.

"Even if you don't like me very much."

"I like you, Lindsay."

"You like me, except when it comes to your son. You're just like Jake's mother. She never liked me, either—said I would break his heart."

"And from what I can tell, you did."

"True, but there were extenuating circumstances. And although you may not want to see it, your son is not interested in me. He's interested in the man he thinks is his father. I just happened to be attached to his history."

How I wish that were true. My son has the opportunity to do everything right in his life, and I want him to start fresh. Without the baggage I attached to him at birth. "So you wanted to bring me here for breakfast to tell me I should tell my son the truth. Lindsay, I know I should tell my son the truth."

"So what's stopping you?"

"I will tell him, of course. I'm waiting for the right time."

"After he inherits Ron's house? Is that what you are waiting for? Because the house will not eliminate the problems. He'll have to get it sold, have an accountant figure out what he owes for taxes on the sale. He'll have to find a place to invest that kind of money. Nothing comes without a cost of some sort." Lindsay has the face of an angel and the tongue of a viper.

"That money belongs to Ronnie. You may not understand it, but—"

She clutches the sides of the table until her knuckles are white. "I'm not stupid. Explain it to me, Jane. Explain to me why you can't tell Ronnie the truth. I'm all ears. I'm rooting for Ronnie. He seems like a man who will spend the money well, but I was married to Ron for ten years. We kept nothing from each other, but now I'm finding out about family I didn't know existed. It doesn't add up. You can't blame me for being curious, can you? I mean, your own son is curious."

"It was complicated, and obviously Ron thought it best to keep things the way they were: quiet. If he didn't tell you on his death bed, what makes you think I should share the truth?"

"If you were me, would you really want to remain in the dark, Jane?"

Yes, I would! I want to shout, but I know I wouldn't have been able to. I would have forced it and made my life all the worse because of my pushing. "That's not a fair question, since I know the truth and in knowing the truth, I can say it's a good place to be. The dark, that is."

She whistles like a teakettle, clearly frustrated she is not going to get Ron's secret out of me. He couldn't have trusted her with everything, or he might have told her. Instead, he probably drank away any guilt he'd stored up for decades and protected his princess from the ugly truth.

"I don't care if you think I'm stupid, Jane. Most people do. Most people think I'm a money-grubbing blonde like all the rest, but I learned early on that while money makes things nice, it doesn't take away your problems. So if you think making your son a millionaire is going to take away his desire to know the truth about his past, you're only setting the both of you up for disappointment." Her pancakes arrive and she pours a healthy portion of, no doubt, some natural version of what non-Californians call syrup.

My eyes feel as watery as the two eggs set before me. I have placed so much in the belief that I could make things better for Ronnie if I only waited the situation out. But darn that girl, she's given me the speck of doubt that keeps the fear alive in my belly.

"What reason do I have to lie to you, Jane?" She asks as she slathers organic butter over the syrup. "I'm a washed-up trophy wife whose husband is dead. I don't exactly have a well-laid-out future. What threat do I represent, exactly?"

"I've left my previous life behind too when I moved to Mexico. That's what happens when life changes, you move on. Considering

Jake's appearance, I would think you could understand the desire to do that."

"I understand it. I'm only saying it won't happen and neither will anything with Jake. That chapter is closed. But this thing with your son will haunt you until you come clean."

"I'll take my chances," I tell her as I stab at my eggs with my fork. "Why do you suddenly care about my sordid past?"

"I didn't, until I met Ron Jr. It just seems wrong to lie to him. Doesn't that get to you?"

"He's my son. What do you think?"

She shrugs as she shoves more food into her mouth and talks around the pancakes. "My mother lied to me. I guess the whole scenario hits too close to home."

"Moms do strange things for their children, and it may not make sense to you at the time, but later . . . when you're grown and gone."

"It still makes no sense to me."

I find myself getting tired of being questioned. "You got what you married for. What do you care what happens to the rest of the money? You didn't love him, and it's not a bad take for ten years of labor, is it?"

This isn't like me, and I hate the barrage of words coming out of my mouth. "I'm sorry, Lindsay."

She throws her water bottle back like a tequila shot and wags her finger at me. "No, that's all right, but for the record, I never said that."

"Said what?"

"I said I didn't *marry* for love. That doesn't mean I didn't come to love and appreciate whom I did marry. Ron and I had a great relationship in the end. Give me a little credit. I made the best of my situation. Some people who marry for love can't even say that."

"Who was Jake, then? Maybe you'll feel better spilling *your* secrets. Maybe it's not me you're concerned about at all. You don't expect me to believe you forsook Jake for Ron and stayed true." I laugh, but Lindsay doesn't and maybe it isn't obvious with so many men who want to be actors around here. But Ron is George Costanza next to Jake's Brad Pitt. "He looked like a movie star and seemed to know a great deal about you. So now what? You'll go to church and confess your sins and be free and clear and set for life after just a decade with Ron Brindle? Not a terribly steep price to pay for having it all."

Lindsay turns crimson and her expression puckers into an unflattering, bloated manner. "Is that what you think, Jane? That I'm happy Ron is gone? Chances are you didn't marry for love, either, or Ron Jr. would be named after his real father, whoever that is."

Below the belt. "I'll stay in a hotel when I return."

"I shouldn't have said that, Jane."

"No, I attacked first. That was fair." I take a bite of dry toast, and it scrapes my throat as I swallow.

Lindsay looks down at her plate and swishes the pancakes around in the syrup. She taps the fork, drops it and looks at me. "Money doesn't solve anything, you know. That was the thing I never understood until I had it. Sure, it makes some things easier, and it helps you to numb pain or hide your fears behind the stuff, but you never stop craving what you really want."

"More coffee?"

The waitress interrupts our conversation, and I stare over at Lindsay's beautiful face, wan from her troubles and pain. I wonder what anyone could have done to that girl to make her marry a man twenty years older. It's not like Ron looked young for his age. I shake my head to the waitress.

"What is it you really want, Lindsay?"

"I want to be a good person, not the bad kid my mother thought I was. I want to be good. I mean, I know I'm saved and all that, but I want my mother to see the goodness, and I don't think she ever will. She hasn't spoken to me since I married Ron."

Personally, I thought all religious sorts saw themselves as good. The reality may have been different, but that never seemed to change their views. I'm shocked to hear Lindsay admit such a thing, and against my better judgment, I find myself feeling for the girl again.

"Sometimes, people—even mothers—are critical because they don't know any other way to be."

"You're telling me I should have some mercy on my mother?"

"I have no idea, but my guess is that she only wanted the best for you, even if she went about it the wrong way. You seem to judge how I chose things for Ronnie pretty harshly." I drop my fork and lean in toward Lindsay. "I'm only saying, it's easy to think one thing without knowing all the facts. Maybe you should find out the facts."

"My mother doesn't like me. Those are the facts."

I shrug. "Maybe she doesn't. Having a baby doesn't make everyone a good mother, but wouldn't you rather know before she's dead and gone? Wouldn't you rather believe the best of her?"

"She hasn't spoken to me in ten years!"

"That only tells me she's headstrong, and I could have told you that by looking at her daughter."

A man walks by and practically hurts himself staring at Lindsay. Honestly, there are at least ten women in here who are nearly identical to Lindsay, but there's a warmth in her that charms in a way I find terribly disconcerting with a son her age. What's most upsetting is that it's not her looks, it's the invisible aspect that seems to mesmerize people, mostly men. There is no way to describe that, much less protect one's son from it.

"What's that like?" I ask her.

"What's what like?"

"Being stared at all the time."

"I'm not stared at all the time."

"Lindsay, you are. There's one man in this restaurant and at least twenty-five blondes, and he tripped over that chair right there to stare at you!"

"You're imagining things, Jane." She shoves another bite of pancakes into her mouth so that it looks like she has a giant gumball in her left cheek. She swallows. "Did you love Ron?"

"Lindsay, it's such a convoluted tale, you wouldn't believe you if I told you. I loved Ron like a brother. He tried to do the right thing, but I was too young and too vindictive to appreciate any of it. It's a terrible thing, how when you finally understand life, you look like this." I open my arms and look down.

"Will you ever tell Ronnie who his real father is?"

That's a very good question, and I suppose the answer is, not if I don't have to. "I'm not sure. Will you tell that young man who was over the other night you're not over him? I saw the way you looked when he left."

"I am over him!" she protests. "Honestly, I am." The way she says it, with all the conviction in the world, I have no choice but to believe her, which makes my heart pound because the last thing my son needs is Lindsay's heart being available. I'm sure I'm just being paranoid, but I've never seen that look in my son's eye. It's bad enough he chose to live here in Los Angeles, but if he and Lindsay do any research whatsoever, my secret is out. And with it will go all the respect my son ever had for me.

"I guess you are over him at that."

Lindsay pushes her plate away. "I don't think you should go to Mexico."

"So you've said. Why on earth would you care if I stayed?" I see her meekness when I ask—the shy little waif who answered the door when I appeared uninvited.

"I simply do. You should stay. You're free to go, of course. I have no hold over you, but I want you to stay. It's a feeling. I get them sometimes."

"A premonition?"

"I don't know, maybe . . . no, that sounds too important. Just a feeling. I think we might have something to teach each other."

"Did you have a feeling when you married Ron?"

She looks down at the table and then back up to me. "Yes," she says adamantly. "And I ignored it because it was too inconvenient, but I don't regret my marriage. Marriage taught me a lot about myself, most of it negative."

"That's your religion talking. All the guilt and shame. That's why I never cared for religion."

"Religion and guilt is what I'm trying to lose. Relationship with Jesus is what I'm trying to attain. I want to be more like Him. I want my mother to be proud of me, and I want to take what Ron gave me and do something in the world."

For some odd reason, I feel the skin on my arms prickle at her words. "All right. For once, I'm going to try sitting still, and I'll stay until probate ends," I tell her. "If only to seize a new experience."

A peace descends upon me. If I'd fought the current of life less, perhaps my journey down the river would have been easier.

Chapter 9

Lindsay

I'm glad my nosey neighbors don't speak. What happens here, stays here. Unless the cats start talking—then we're all in trouble. The Trophy Wives Club meets tonight. I'm in dire need of companionship, and if I have to force my way in, I will do so.

I hardly feel like explaining my odd group to Jane. She thinks I'm shallow enough as it is. I tell her the name of my Bible study, and I can hear her laughter now. We take our name from the Bible verse in Philippians. "I press toward the goal to win the prize for which God has called me heavenward in Christ Jesus." We are wives of Jesus, our eyes on the greatest Trophy of them all—a life well lived for the Lord. I race my BMW to the church, as though I'm making some sort of getaway like Bonnie and Clyde. Without the Clyde.

We used to meet on Tuesday nights, but all of the groups did, and since we're the redheaded stepchild of the church, we made an executive decision to meet on a quieter evening. When we could come and go, like the sinners we are. (Yes, it's true that everyone else should be right there with us, but they're not aware of that fact, apparently.) Besides, it's always easier to look at someone else's sin as bigger than your own, and we simply got tired of being the other side of the scale. Let them all compare themselves to the middle school group from here on out.

No one is in the room when I arrive. Too eager, once again. Eager to run from the live ghost who now haunts my halls, eager to see Bette, my mentor, and have her remind me to leave the past in the past. *Leave well enough alone*, she'll say. *We're on a forward journey. What good is it to dwell on the past?* Although I can repeat everything she'll probably tell me, I crave reassurance—hearing the words in her whispery, honeyed voice. I suppose I need to purge myself of the guilt, once and for all.

I keep replaying Jake's common nod toward me in the coffee shop, then his coming to my house with a check and a good-bye peck on the forehead. It's closure and I wanted closure, but I won't feel free of it until I admit the whole sordid tale to someone. Bette will listen and remind me the redemption I crave is already mine. She's the Miss Manners of First Community's Trophy Wives Club. Still not quite sure that there's an etiquette reference to dumping true love for money, but one never knows. I can't believe how easily those old feelings are stirred, like the mud at the bottom of a once-clear river.

You only think the past goes away, but it takes nothing at all to surface again. "Lindsay?" Bette comes in and turns on the light. "Why are you sitting in the dark?"

"Was I? The sun must have gone down some more since I sat down."

She looks at her watch. "The sun has been down for a good hour, at least."

"I'm going to start a ministry with the after-school program Ron used to support," I say, out of the blue. "I'm going to help the mothers with some of the financial decisions they make and see if their lives can't be slightly easier. I've been sitting here thinking about it."

"That's a very noble cause, Lindsay. It's good to hear you thinking of your future. What brought this on?"

"I've been thinking about what's next for a while, but I had an old boyfriend visit, and I suppose that's what made me start taking action. You have to accept when life has changed, don't you?"

"An old boyfriend? Is this something that has a future associated with it?"

"What? Oh no, nothing like that. Believe me, Ron was by far the best choice. Then and even now, looking back on my life with him."

"That's good, because there was a young man in here on Sunday looking for you. His name was Tim. Do you know him?"

Chinless Bond. "I met him at the singles' group."

"See! I told you that it was time to move on."

I shake my head. "No, it's nothing like that. Bette, do you think if you did something really bad in your past, it's possible to truly get over the incident? If it hurt someone else more than you?"

Her eyes crinkle with a knowing smile. "Well, I suppose that depends. Is it something that is still having consequences?"

"I'm not certain. Do you think I've wasted my life, Bette? I mean, Haley has become this agent assistant her boss can't live without. Lily practically runs the world. Penny is raising up those darling boys. Helena could tell you what Cleopatra wore at her death. But

I've decorated a condo and married a rich man. It's not much to show for a life, is it?"

"I think you're being hard on yourself. I agree that it's time to do something different. You're far too talented, and Ron loved to see you doing what you do best. You have a heart for women, and why shouldn't other people benefit from your gifts? Where would Haley be, if it weren't for you helping her get her life back on track, let alone the help you're providing for her wedding?"

"Oh, that's easy. She'd be asking Christina Aguilera for sequin advice. And I haven't done that much. Not really."

Bette laughs. "That girl sure knows how to enjoy life. We've all learned a great deal from her, don't you think?"

"I don't know where I'd be without Haley. But anyway, I'm sure you've heard my news by now. Ron's ex-wife is at the house. She's an artist. She's probably sixty, and it made me think I have a long way to go until I'm sixty."

"Heavens!" Bette gasps. "That old? It's amazing she manages to get out of bed each morning." She gives me just a hint of a smile.

"Bette, you know I don't mean anything by that."

"Of course I do. That can't be easy to see Ron's first wife at such a difficult time. We're almost upon a year now, aren't we?"

I nod. "Just past it, actually." My phone starts to buzz, and I look down to see a text message coming through.

MISSED U @ SINGLES. DINNER?—TIM

"Bette, did you give Tim my cell phone number?" I turn off my cell.

"Heavens, did I?" Her eyebrows arch. "Aren't you going to answer that?" she points to my handbag where I've plopped my cell.

"Bette, you have lived your entire widowhood alone. Why on earth do you think romance is the answer for me?"

"Don't accuse just me. We all think romance is the answer for you. So what's this big, dark secret? Spill it, so we can start setting up blind dates for you." I look into her eyes. Eyes that only shine brighter, now that her skin tone has faded with the years. She's one of those women who will always have the beauty of her youth, because it comes from within.

I trust these women with my life, no question. But with blind dates? Only a disaster can ensue. "Six months. Just give me six more months, and I'll start dating, all right? And please, don't encourage Tim. Our babies wouldn't have a chin."

"Oh, babies!" she claps her hands together. "Any plastic surgeon can insert a chin." She laughs at my apprehension. "I'm kidding, Lindsay. That's fine; I will call Tim off. When does Ron's first wife leave?"

"I'm not sure. It could be awhile." I glance at Bette. "She's got a son my age, and I think she's worried about him around me, so it may be sooner than probate is up."

"You're a beautiful, sweet woman. What would she worry about? If my son chose a beauty like you, I'd be looking forward to my beautiful grandchildren."

"You always know what to say to make me feel better, but seriously, those are probably not Jane's first thoughts of me. So, I made a mistake that I can't really make amends for, and I thought I'd ask your advice. I almost told Haley, but she's so joyful right now, I didn't want to bring her down. So I came to you. I hope you don't mind."

"Haley would never think you were trying to rob her joy. Friends are there for one another. You're so black-and-white, Lindsay, you just choose to throw the baby out with the bathwater. We've all made mistakes—"

I shake my head. "This isn't like that. I don't think I'm overemphasizing the fact that I can't make up for this one. Bette, have you ever committed a sin that had repercussions on others? But really, you couldn't see that it harmed you in ways other than your own guilt? Have you ever ridden off into the sunset and left someone else behind to deal with the fire you started?"

"You act as though living with guilt is a small price to pay. Sometimes, it's the biggest price to pay. Guilt is not from God, conviction is."

"I'm not sure if I have guilt or conviction. It seems that I got off easy."

"The others will be here soon, perhaps you can stay late and tell me more."

Bette unloads her canvas bag of study materials and pens while she speaks, and I have to admit, I'm feeling slightly ignored. *Um, I was talking here! I mean, breakdowns don't exactly come up when it's convenient, do they? Where's all this friend talk now? Hmmm?*

"Bette, I need to say this and hear your opinion. It's important."

"I'm sure it is, but Lindsay, I want to ask you to take over leadership of the Trophy Wives Club. Not forever, just for the first year while I adjust to being a wife again."

"Me? Weren't you just trying to get rid of me—to pawn me off to the singles' group?"

"Of course not. We're trying to get you to think about your future. We're not going to abandon you, Lindsay."

"Okay, now you've done it. Now I have to spill the truth. My conscience is getting the better of me."

"Lindsay, you're a natural leader and you love the Lord. You were a good wife to Ron, and you have so much to offer the younger women. I've watched you overcome an enormous amount of bitterness, and now you're starting life again. It's the perfect time to consider how your life can mentor others."

The Jezebel School of Mentoring. I shake my head. "This is not false modesty. Bette, you have no idea."

"Lindsay, you're shaking."

"Let me get this out before you offer me this job. This is important. It might change your mind. I ran into an old acquaintance." I rethink my words and pray for strength. "That's a lie of omission. I ran into my old fiancé. First at a coffee shop with Haley, and then he came by my house to give me something that I lent him."

"You were engaged? Before Ron?"

"Uh-huh. To my high school sweetheart. We were inseparable from the time I was fifteen years old." Doesn't that sound so sweet and innocent? And yet, I'm going in for the kill.

"Young love is so powerful." She sighs, shaking her head from side to side. "We think they'll never be another for us. We're so naïve, but that time is so special when—"

"No, Bette, I was anything but naïve. This isn't that kind of story." How my life could have been different if I had been! "The first time I saw Jake, I was a freshman in high school, and he was a junior. I thought I'd found my destiny. I know I was young, but that didn't stop me from thinking like an overeager Jane Austen fan. I think they fed me too much Shakespeare in freshman English. Anyway, I staked out his locker and conveniently got mine relocated next to his. Our first date, we went to see *Ferris Bueller's Day Off.*"

"He must have been quite a young man."

"His family helped show me what a healthy family—well, perhaps healthier than mine is a better statement—was like. My mother was an angry person in general, resentful for being saddled with a kid when she was young and beautiful. All the men wanted her, she told me. Until they found out she had a child."

"You know that's not true."

"Well, now I do, of course, but when you're sixteen, it can lead you to some rather stupid decisions. I realize she was just a hurting woman and I've forgiven my mother many times over. I still want her to be proud of me, but I think the problems may be hers and not mine there. She did the best she could, but she told me that I'd never amount to anything because I couldn't seem to do anything right. I made it my goal to prove her wrong. You know how obstinate I can be."

"Yes." Bette laughs. "I've seen a touch of that."

"Jake's family took me in as their own. They paid for my graduation gown and my prom dress so that we could go, but it was too late. I was already scheming subconsciously how to prove my mother wrong. After college, when everyone expected us to get married, I got nervous. Jake didn't have a college education and I did, paid for by the government. He was working in construction, and suddenly, I thought I could do better. I got nervous that if I married poorly, like she did, then she would be right about me. Then, I met Ron."

"And you fell in love!" She clasps her hands together.

"Wouldn't that be great? No, I didn't fall in love. I was in love with Jake. Ron was his boss."

"I see." She looks down at her Bible, clearly averse to hearing more. "Let me understand, Lindsay. Are you saying that you purposely dropped Jake for Ron"—she pauses for a moment to clear her throat—"because he had more money?"

My first inclination is to protect myself. "Jake was working on a job building Ron's Pacific Palisades home. Jake took me there after-hours one evening to show me a special bookcase he'd built with storage behind them in one of the dormers." The reality of the memory spurs the truth. "He was so proud, and I barely glanced at the bookshelves. I'd never seen such luxury. The kitchen in that home was bigger than my entire house. When I saw the chandelier,

I don't know, something in me shifted. I saw a way to prove my mother wrong because the person who lived under the light of that chandelier could never be viewed as a nothing."

"Oh," Bette murmurs.

It gets worse, but this part I keep to myself. I dressed in black slacks and stiletto heels went to the house looking for Jake . . . on a day I knew he wasn't there. I pulled my tiny, chip diamond ring off my finger and shoved into my slacks' pocket. I rang the doorbell and posed. The rest is history. Ron was easy pickings. He was mourning his wife, who had long-since taken off to a foreign country. For Bette's genteel ears, I pick up the story after the stiletto part, no sense giving her heart failure before the wedding.

"Ron had just moved from Texas to open another branch of his business—and he was lonely, a new Christian, and convinced that God had sent me to fulfill His plan. I never told him the truth about Jake, not even when we separated for a short time two years ago. We got back together, and I just went back to the facade. No harm, no foul."

She's stiff as a statue, her mouth slightly open. I thought getting this off my chest would be freeing, but actually, I feel worse having Bette look at me the same way Jake did. The same way his mother did. The same way my own mother did.

"Say something," I implore. "Call me a name. Something!"

"God did see that you got saved through your experience. What if you'd married Jake and never thought about your salvation?" She tries to add that upward lilt to the end of her sentence, but it's clear that it's forced. As if to say, *Oh yeah, that's a bad one.*

"Jake's family were all Christians. That's why they took me in when my own mother disappeared for a while."

"Lindsay, all I can say is that you either believe Jesus died for your sins, or you don't."

"I keep thinking about how I never apologized or explained. In their eyes, I'm the same person I was when I did that. I tried to be the best wife I could be to Ron, hoping to redeem myself, and I know God took it all away, but Jake's family . . . I'd used them like a trampoline and never looked back. Jake's forgiven me, but his family . . . I doubt they have."

Bette's voice takes a cold edge. "Then apologize, Lindsay. Apologize to his family and move forward."

The rest of the women come in, chattering and laughing. I plaster a smile on my face, but I can't look at Bette.

Lily Tseng is a tall, Asian woman, smart as a whip, tough-as-nails and knows Scripture like the back of her French-manicured hand. If I had to guess, I'd say Lily's spiritual gift was leadership. She thinks two years out and organizes people like an army, ever-marching toward the goal. I wonder why Bette wouldn't have chosen her as predecessor. General Lily seems far more the obvious choice.

"Did you get Haley's dress?" Lily asks me.

I nod. "It's gorgeous, and it was well within her budget."

Lily laughs, knowing exactly what I mean. "You should have seen her when I made her buy a real suit for work. I thought she'd have a conniption, right there in the shop! 'They want how much for this jacket? Are they going to come put it on me each morning?'"

"Girls," Bette says. "Let's not be mean-spirited." I feel Bette's glare upon me, and if it doesn't take me back to my youth immediately, I don't know what ever did. I'm not quite sure how it's mean-spirited to point out the obvious—that Haley is cheap as a two-dollar shoe—but I'm not in a place to be shooting my mouth off at the moment. I wilt back into the chair.

"Is Haley's dress sparkly?" Helena asks. Helena is our resident brainiac and usually makes it her job to state the evident without emotion. If Spock had a sister, she would be Helena.

"Just enough. It's beautiful. It really is," I explain.

Penny comes in late and frantic as usual. Today, her socks match, and this is a step in the right direction. She's our yoga mom who keeps everything in check by focusing obsessively on what she puts into her body. Her latest thing is "raw" eating— which makes me worry she's going to start munching on the trees one of these days and offer us all a leaf. Her sons (twins, nearly four) are now gluten free, trans fat free, and sugar free. If by accident someone ever feeds them McDonald's, they will go into immediate shock and learn to pray to the porcelain god. The family menu, however, is the one area of Penny's life that she can control, and naturally, she goes overboard.

"So when are you planning the bridal shower?" she asks me.

"The bridal shower." Everyone looks at me expectantly. "It's coming along. I'm getting the location firmed up." If Jane will ever let me talk to her son for permission to use the house.

All these years, I've allowed myself to exhibit a reputation that I can handle everything. I came here for support, and it's quite clear, no one thinks I need a thing and that I'll have everything under control. If they only had a clue. Bette watches me, her brows low, but of course, I'm probably imagining the judgment. Bette never thinks badly of people, but with my reality rearing its ugly head, there's always the chance to start. Maybe I'll get lucky and get lost in wedding shower plans without noticing.

Chapter 10

Jane

The concrete walls of L.A. are closing in on me. It's the only reasonable excuse I can find for "crossing over to the other side." This afternoon, I will be joining the Trophy Wives Club at a pedicure party. Someone touching my feet, religious women yapping on and on about how their men are rulers over them. I should just stay home and pull my toenails off for more fun, but here I am in a cab, riding the bumper of a BMW as we make our way downtown.

In Mexico, everyone's Catholic and I'm used to living around Catholics. I like them. They eat, drink, and they're merry. Everything's a familial celebration, and you don't eat meat on Friday. Those rules, I understand. Clam chowder is soup of the day on Fridays—that I understand. I suppose I don't understand how a clam isn't meat, but that's nitpicking.

The Catholics are reverent when it's called for: Hail Marys at funerals; black mourning clothes. They're joyful when necessary: *Las Posadas; Dia de los Muertos*—which means day of the dead, but it's really a celebration of life.

In contrast, Lindsay's brand of religion is all-encompassing. She works out to music about Jesus, talks about everything being a blessing, and seems unable to name her misery. Catholics admit when life is miserable and trust me—it takes a lot more to call something misery in Mexico than it does here. If the 405 is closed for an accident, they call that misery. Not because someone's hurt, but because they're stuck in their BMW thirty minutes longer. Their cars are far more luxurious than the nicest homes in the Campeche state.

Lindsay is the needy sort who feeds off others. See, that's where religion crosses the line for me. It has to be practical. That guilt of hers and wanting to make an offering for everything! No different than the Mayans, really, and she's made her view of them clear.

I throw the cabbie an extra dollar, and he grunts. Maybe that was exceptionally cheap, I think as he squeals off, but I never have understood why I want to tip someone who puts my life in danger.

My Mexican-made leather sandals squeak as I enter the salon, causing everyone to turn around and stare. People here are so shiny, is it any wonder they think making their feet glisten is a necessity? It's incredible to me how everyone in this town works to look exactly like one another, yet claims it's about their individuality.

"Jane!" Lindsay gets up and greets me at the door, pulling me in by the hand. "Girls, this is Jane, Ron's first wife." She says it with such enthusiasm, you would think J. Lo herself had just walked in.

Everyone stands and surrounds me. I suddenly feel very old. There's a woman about my age, but she's as shiny as the rest of them. "Hello, Jane. I'm Bette," she says and cups my hand in her own. It's the first time I've felt welcome since I've been in the country. I smile and then focus on the gorgeous, young redhead beside her.

"You're the one studying the Mayans?" she asks.

"Yes," I say, pleased someone knows.

"I've heard you named your cat Kulkucan, the plumed serpent. Directly related to the feathered Aztec god, Quetzalcoatl, but of course, Mayan."

"Yes."

"An odd name for a cat," she replies. "Cats have no feathers."

"No, that's true," I say, looking to Lindsay to rescue me.

"This is Helena Brickman. She likes facts," Lindsay explains.

"I see." I nod and look to the next trophy wife, wondering why on earth they don't have enough respect for themselves to come up with a decent name. The Trophy Wives? Ugh. Honestly, they seem smarter than that, and I wasn't expecting it from the name. "And this is?" She's a long-haired, brunette beauty.

"Lily Tseng."

"Pleasure to meet you."

"She works with Haley at the agency. And Penny is our young mother. She'll arrive harried in a few minutes with her twin boys in tow, and Haley will come and disappear with them. They have a mutual love affair going on. Haley would rather push them to the park, and play mommy than get a pedicure. I don't understand it."

"That's because you never had a little boy look at you that way, Lindsay. It's intoxicating." I wink at her. "Nothing will melt your heart faster than a little boy looking up at you with those big eyes and that tousled hair that needs a good washing. It makes life worth living."

"Only her little boy is now my age," she tells the group.

"But to me, he's still that little boy. Only now, he looks down at me instead of up."

Bette nods. "Mine are grown and gone, too, Jane."

"You have enough children to take care of with all of us," Lindsay says brightly.

There's a crash at the door, and we turn around to see a small display of nail polish knocked over, and splatters of pinks, reds and blues on the floor. Above them is the harried mother Lindsay described and two small boys. One reaches down to finger paint with the color when his mother grabs his arm and screeches. The Trophy Wives scatter to help clean up, and at the activity, one of the small boys says, "Uh-oh."

A waft of pungent nail lacquer hits us squarely. "I'm sorry," Penny says.

"Our fault. Our fault," one of the workers says. "We knew you were coming today." She bends over with some toxic substance and wipes the stains clear away while the Trophy Wife puts what's left of the nail polish tree back to rights.

"That's Penny," Lindsay says, as if there needed to be an introduction. Penny is still too involved in cleanup to notice me, but one of her boys comes up to me. Once a boy mother, always a boy mother. They sense it.

"Hi."

"Well, hello. Who are you?" I bend over and meet his gorgeous eyes. Children have eyes that melt any mother's heart. In them, you know that all is not lost in the world. When I start to feel that way, I could always find a child on the street with huge, brown eyes that made me forget all my troubles for a time.

"I'm Micah. That my brother, Jonah."

"You boys are very handsome."

"Haley will be here in a few minutes to take you to the park. In the meantime, you two sit on those chairs and don't touch anything!"

"They're darling," I tell Penny.

"They're their own weather pattern," she pants. "I wonder what it's like to go out into the world and not fear every second of it."

"But you know, these are the best days. Right now, you can hug them, and they're not the least bit embarrassed. Snuggle into that dirt smell and enjoy, because when they're gone, you'll cry for these moments."

"Somehow, I doubt that."

I laugh. "That's exactly what I would have said. I'm Jane Dawson, and my boy is now thirty-six and stands about five inches taller than me, but he'll always be this size in my heart." I pat one of the twins on the head.

"Penny McKenna, and you met Micah, and that's Jonah," she looks toward her son, and notices he's got red running down his leg. "Oh, Jonah!" She goes toward him and sees it's just collateral damage from the earlier polish crash, not a bloody gash. The same woman who cleaned up the floor comes and kneels before the small boy.

I know it isn't funny to Penny, but the whole scenario is perfect boy. Bringing them into a nail salon is merely asking for trouble, but I hide my mirth for fear of offending her or making her feel any worse than I'm sure she does. I had many a moment in the grocery store I wish I could take back.

Haley walks into the salon and looks straight at the boys. "Already? I'm only five minutes late."

Both of them scamper to their feet, Jonah avoiding contact with the cloth that's washing his leg, and the boys start to jump around Haley's feet. "Ice cream today!"

Haley looks at their mother and then back at them. "No more ice cream. Your mother says it makes you hyper."

It must be something else, I think to myself. *Like the fact that they're boys.*

The scene leaves me melancholy. How I miss the days when Ronnie would scamper in with some innocent, scaly critter and hold it up to my face proudly, causing me to squeal. Or when he'd play *futbol* and pass the ball into the goal victoriously and look straight to me for assurance. Jonah and Micah's dad has evidently played with their innocence by having an affair—that's what Lindsay said, so as I didn't think Penny was the only happily married one. I could have been like Penny—shut my mouth and given Ronnie the secure home that Ron offered us—but my pride was far too strong for that. Maybe it wasn't the life I wanted, but it was the one offered to me. Sometimes, looking a gift horse in the mouth turns into a sorrowful circumstance.

Haley and the twins retreat to a corner table with coloring books, and Penny gives a huge sigh as she settles into the giant massage chair. I am not at all frightened to hike the Copper Canyon alone at dusk, but having my first pedicure at fifty-three with a bevy of experienced fashionistas is enough to strike terror into my heart.

"I just get up here?" I ask, looking at the chair like it's a rocky crevice—and me without my hiking boots.

"You seem older than Ron was," Helena says, as I climb up gingerly. I have to laugh at everyone's gasps. Helena is exactly like the old women in my neighborhood. They wouldn't think twice of telling me how it is.

"It's all right, ladies. I'm used to people who speak their mind. I'm fifty-three, Helena."

"So he went much younger with Lindsay. Interesting."

"Seventeen years my senior—I'll save you the math," Lindsay says.

"A wide spread. If one were to take the median—well, the average alone would be 8.75 years in either direction for his choice of women."

"Would it? Fascinating," Lindsay says drily. She looks over at me as if to apologize. But personally? I like Helena. What's not to appreciate about someone asking the questions everyone wants to ask? People wouldn't lean in for the answer if they didn't care to listen, but they all lean in tightly, which says something about polite society. They may not purchase the *People* magazine for themselves, but they all pick it up when given the opportunity.

"I've always liked younger men. They're the only ones who can keep up with me," I tell Helena. "You can't imagine how many men my age are anxious to get married again, if they've been left or widowed. If you've never felt like the most popular girl in school? Just wait until you're fifty-five or better. We're all tens about then, because men can't stand the thought of dying alone."

Helena looks at me blinking. "I don't think anyone likes the idea of dying alone."

"Well, that's probably true. I just meant that I think it's a great and sad truth that men are so desperate to get married as they get older, while they battle it with all their might as young men." I let out a cautious laugh and finally I get a smile from her.

"You're talking to the wrong group," Lily pipes up. "We've had no trouble getting married. For us, the problem was staying married."

"Well, that's everyone's problem, isn't it? Marriage is never easy," I tell her.

"It's easier if you marry for love," Lindsay says dreamily.

"But that's the problem, isn't it? At eighteen, who knows the difference between love and lust?"

"She's got a point," Haley adds from across the room, and here I thought she was so into her coloring book.

"It's too pessimistic, Jane. I think marriage is a commitment to the institution."

I shiver. "You're probably right, Lindsay, and maybe that's my issue. I never did see the institution as being safe for a woman."

Everyone looks at me, and I want to slink down into my vibrating chair and take it back. The difference between these women and me? They still have hope. They still believe Prince Charming will be riding in at any moment. I know better.

Haley tries to break up the tension. "Jane, if anyone should feel that way, it would be me. But Hamilton changed that for me. He's never been married before, and I didn't think I'd ever marry again, but look at me! I'm marrying a man who writes prenuptial agreements for his vocation. Love obviously gave way to his ideals."

Yes, I think. *Let's do look at you. You're a size-two, gorgeous blonde with a willowy figure, and an enormous rack. Is there a man on earth that would pass up the opportunity to show you attention?*

"My son hasn't been married before, and I'm certain if he spent his young life single—which could happen, he's very committed to teaching"—I say to the other women—"I still think he'd want to be married when he was old and gray."

"Her son will be married in no time," Lindsay says. "He's young, gorgeous, normal, and Christian." Then she looks at me. "They go quickly."

The way she speaks of my son both puts me at ease about her interest and frightens me. "He's met a nice woman. Her name is Kipling," I tell them with more enthusiasm than I've shown my son, but it dawns on me that I'm with the queens of the broken hearts club, and they're not exactly concerned with my innocent son's reputation.

"Her son Ronnie is dating a wonderful woman, and you know how men are when they get close to commitment, they always want to make certain she's the one. So Jane's just making sure he doesn't have any questions, but they always have questions. Isn't that right?"

The women all murmur their approval and I loosen my grip on the armrests.

I open my eyes. "No one is perfect. Lindsay's made her mistakes; I've made mine. That's what you've been trying to tell me, right?" I look to Lindsay, but Helena answers.

"True enough, but Lindsay's given hers over to the Lord."

"Has she?" I look to Lindsay, and she doesn't seem any less burdened than myself. She still pines for her mother's approval and freedom from her guilt, while I run the risk of my own son not speaking to me once he knows the truth. I'd say Lindsay and I are about even on the redemption scale.

Helena goes onto ramble some more religious ideals at me, but I'm lost in my thoughts—that and the foot massage. Lindsay made better choices than I did. Whether I want to admit it or not, sticking with Ron made her a better person. Running from him made me no stronger. I was never really free from his pull because of Ronnie. It's with an extreme sadness that I realize I never faced up to anything. I thought I'd been the strong one, but all I've really done is run from the issues. I never faced them head-on, like Lindsay did.

"I'm done running," I say to Lindsay.

"That won't be easy for you," she says to me. "When the going gets tough, you seem to take off for long stretches of time."

"So I'll find out what happens when I sit still." But the very thought sends my heart racing.

"I hope you will," she says warmly. "And maybe I can find out what happens when I move on."

We stare at each other, trusting a little more, yet not fully. I think the real reason I hated Ronnie seeing something in Lindsay was because I couldn't stand to think of him seeing something good in me. Not when I'd lied to him for his entire life and robbed him of a father figure. I suppose Lindsay and I have more guilt in common than I'd like to admit. Ronnie deserves better than the likes of us.

"I'm going to tell Ronnie the truth. And you're going to go see your mother," I tell her.

"I am?"

"You are, because the fear can't be worse than avoiding the truth, can it?"

"What if she still hates me?"

"Then it's her loss, as it has been for the last decade. Any mother that wants to be right more than she wants her daughter in her life—well, the problem lies with her. Do you understand me?" I feel motherly for the first time in many, many years.

Lindsay nods.

"If she turns you away, you know the truth. If my son turns me away, I—"

I don't even want to think about what could happen. I just know Ronnie will find out the truth someday when I'm gone, and his memories will be tarnished anyway. The thought brings a lump to my throat, but it's time to tell the truth. To take all power away from his real father.

Chapter 11

Lindsay

My future years stretch out before me, long and empty. If I continue my path along the highway of scary, old women and cats, my life will continue to be a farce—playacting a role. I have to make peace with my mother. The Bible says not to bring your offering until you've made peace with your brother. I imagine He meant mother, too, and perhaps that's what has bothered me all along. Jane, a woman who's spent her life running and lying to those she loves, is the only one who seems to get me, which naturally strikes the fear of God into me. I may be simple, but I can see that my life does not line up with what I supposedly believe.

Other than finishing up plans for Haley's shower, I have no life goal, no actual destination now. And you don't have to tell me that Haley's shower doesn't qualify as a life goal, at least for my life.

It's been two weeks since I've seen the Trophy Wives, and our pedicure did anything but restore me. Jane and I had made a pact of sorts, but I haven't contacted my mother, and she has yet to tell Ronnie anything. So while our pact may have been made with the best of intentions, nothing has come of it. After several text messages from Tim, the Chinless Bond, I couldn't bear to step foot in the church. It only reminded me of the joke I probably am to the congregation. The joke I probably always have been.

"But of course, you have to go back," Jane says to me this fine morning.

"Why would I want to go back? I have to make peace before I make an offering. The Bible says that."

"Is it just me, or is there a simple fix for that? Those women love you, Lindsay, and I'm here to tell you, friends like that don't come along every day. I know you feel judged by Bette, but that's in your own head. For some reason, we women have a terrible time forgiving ourselves, but I saw nothing in her that day that implied she thought your trouble was any worse than the next girl's. Even if you think they did judge, you can't write them off for one mistake. Any more than they can write you off for a mistake. That's what friends do for each other. Do you want to spend your life running, like I have? Go make amends with your mother."

"We're both obstinate, aren't we?"

Jane laughs. "Not exactly a good trait. So who will make the first move?"

"I suppose that I have no choice. It's going to have to be me because of Haley's wedding." It's the Trophy Wives Club's final fitting for our bridemaids' gowns, followed by a ladies' luncheon, and I've dressed in my jeans and high-heeled flip-flops for the occasion. That's the biggest decision on my agenda—a salad or wrap for lunch. It's pathetic even to me. I can't imagine what Jane might say about joining me, but what do I have to lose? We both seem to be on the same page with our ineptitude.

"You'll come this afternoon for the luncheon?" I ask Jane as she sketches out a painting on the back patio. This one actually looks like something. I didn't know contemporary artists could actually make real art, and I want to say something kind, but I don't think my artistry opinion means much to her anyway.

"I don't know." She puts the paintbrush down and looks up at me with her fine, blue eyes. "I think I may have worn out my welcome last time, don't you think? Besides, the gallery owner sold my painting. I want to keep working while I'm here and build up a bit of a nest egg. I knew I should have brought more canvases, but they're so hard to travel with. I'll have to borrow your car and get to the art store at some point."

"Ron built the nest egg for you, Jane. He built one for all of us. Come have lunch with me."

"You're not fooling anyone, Lindsay. You just don't want to answer what you're up to. And you're wrong about the nest egg. I won't take Ron's money, Lindsay. What sort of woman do you think I am?" She drops the brush into a cup of liquid that smells like the devil. "I've made my own way. I don't need his money. I don't want his money."

There is accusation in her words, but I try not to take them personally. Jane did take his money—she just gave it to Ronnie.

Best to turn back to the luncheon—a safer subject to be sure. "Scaly feet belong on things that slither in the desert, not a free-spirited artist from Campeche, Mexico. Come to lunch, and we'll get a pedicure after." I say the country like Meh-hee-co, so she knows I'm being respectful.

Jane laughs at my paltry attempt in Spanish. "If I make a habit of this, you'll expect me to start buying shoes next. I can find them at a much better discount at the street market. Hiking boots even at the surplus store."

If Jane died tomorrow, her obituary would be full of accomplishments: renowned artist, doting mother, outdoorswoman and adventurer, but there would be no one to write it up for her, save for her son. If I died tomorrow, the Trophy Wives would be standing in line to write up my memorial, but what real accomplishment could they list? *She once got a pair of Jimmy Choos for less than $100 at Neiman's. She is survived by . . . not even a cat. Well, she's survived by her dysfunctional Bible Study group, and we loved her for her excellent decisions in nail lacquer and the party favors she chose for her best friend's shower.*

"So you won't come?" I stand with the door ajar. Jane is once again mesmerized by her canvas, and she simply nods her head. I leave the condominium and stand on the small porch for a moment and wonder if I shouldn't go back in and try again. Someone needs to light a fire under the two of us.

"Why won't that boy knock on your door?"

"Huh?" I look up to see my neighbor on the porch across from mine. Her name is Cherry, though she's got the palest pallor and honestly, she's more like a molded raisin than a cherry. Her cheeks are a roadmap collection of lines covered by overtly pink blush, but her brow is taut and lifted, like she's in a state of constant surprise. "Are you talking to me, Cherry?" She's one of the quiet ones, but when she does speak, her voice booms like a clap of thunder in the clear, blue sky.

"Do you see anyone else out here?" she snaps. "You blondes are all the same. You don't know how to reel your men in. When I was your age, I didn't waste my time with this teasing business. I had men eating out of the palm of my hands. Men like Tyrone Power and Dean Martin, and you can't even get that simple boy to ring your doorbell. It's dismal. You girls run around half-naked today and still can't get your man."

"I don't run around half-naked! This is Chanel!" I inform her on my blouse choice. "What boy?" Naturally, I know Cherry sees everything that goes on in this complex, but she's also claimed affairs with every A-lister in Hollywood. She was either the biggest tramp in Hollywood history or has trouble with her memory. For her sake, I'm hoping it's the latter.

"That boy. The one with the work boots and the sexy buns in the jeans." She puts her arthritic hands out and pretends to squeeze. *I think I'm going to be sick.*

"Jake?" I say hopefully.

"Well, I don't know his name. I'm not psychotic."

Yes, you are, but I believe you mean psychic.

"He's been here four times in the last week, but he always chickens out before he rings the bell. Sticks his hand out, pulls it back again, like an amusement park ride. Back and forth, back and forth. Come here, girl." She motions with her bony forefinger. I step closer to her. "Sex!" she yells. "Sex is how you reel them in!" She mocks a fishing action. "Get yourself some lingerie and a fur coat and you—"

"Thank you!" My ears hurt, and my hands automatically cover them for protection. "Thank you, Cherry. I'm a Christian woman, so that's not the answer." And I desperately need a bath now. Maybe with some Brillo pad loofahs to remove the grime.

"Maybe that's why the boy is chicken. Too much religion dogging him. Never did understand that guilt world you people live in."

Right now, that makes two of us.

"It's nothing like that. I'm not even sure who you're speaking of. He was probably here to check the PG&E meter."

"No, our meter reader is a fat, Cambodian man! This man is young and virile."

"My husband just died."

"That can't be your excuse. Your husband died eons ago. You should have yourself a new husband by now. You're not a Lebanese, are you?"

"I have to run, Cherry. If you see the man again, encourage him to ring the bell." Something tells me, I shouldn't have said that.

"Have to do everything for you kids. What happened to this generation?" She goes into her place, mumbling as she does so, and slams her door.

I walk out to my car, but glance back into the entryway. Did Jake come looking for me? My heart starts to pound at the very thought, but reality strikes at my soul. Jake is off-limits. I owe Ron that much. It's like saying I never truly loved my husband. And I did, but the thought that anyone is looking for me fills me with a hope that I know it shouldn't. If I spend the rest of my life alone, I want to be content. Hope for me is a dangerous avenue. Once taken, you can't go back. The route without expectations is easier.

The voice of God has grown silent in my ear, no doubt helped along by Cherry, who has a way of drowning out any godly thoughts whatsoever. I love my neighbor, but her advice is something like you'd find in an all-male barbershop of my father's day.

I feel exceptionally alone as I drive to the bridal shop, trying to muster up excitement for Haley. She has come so far, and she's going to make the most beautiful bride. I have to put on my party face because Haley seems to have some sort of guilt about having a big wedding. If I don't relay excitement, I worry she'll continue to go through the motions, just wanting to be married and not enjoying the process. Everyone should enjoy the process.

The salesgirl inside the boutique opens the door for me. The shop is closed with a sign saying, Closed for Private Fitting. It's so non-Haley to have anything resembling favored treatment, I think I have the wrong place.

"Haley Cutler?" I say through the crack in the door.

"You must be Lindsay, matron of honor." The gal gets a little snippy. "You're the last to arrive. Fitting Room A, down the hall. You're wearing heels. Make certain they're the same height you'll be wearing the day of the wedding. Or find the right size in the fitting room. It's most important that your gown be the right length."

Naturally, I want to snap at her that I could pull this entire wedding fitting off without her, but I'm still reeling from my Cherry conversation, so I think it's best to just shut up. I wander down the hall and step into a room. On a pink-carpeted pedestal, there's a beautiful bride with long, dark hair wearing a tasteful white gown. Her ample chest fills out the beaded bodice, and her tiny hips disappear in a full skirt. An exaggerated, draping train tells of her youthful zeal, and I realize I'm in the wrong room.

I pause in the doorway, gazing at the vision of a formal wedding. What my life might have been if I hadn't taken so many shortcuts? To have been the princess for a day, the bride whom strangers cheered for—the loss seems overwhelming now that Ron is gone. We should have done things slowly, appropriately. Instead, we eloped, rather than face people's concerns. I was a wimp, even when I thought I stood tall in the face of adversity.

"Lindsay? Is that you?"

In a chair beside the bride sits . . . Jake's mother. My stomach tightens, as I realize this tiny, virginal-looking bride has to be Jake's. She is a vision in her gown. And honestly? I'm thrilled that Jake will get the chance to do things correctly. "Mrs. Evans?"

With a flash of the eyes, I see the bride comprehend who I am, and I wish I had the ability to fade into the wall or disappear instantly, like the cats in my complex.

"What are you doing here? Surely, not getting married again?" Mrs. Evans says with reproach in her voice.

"No. My best friend is getting married. I'm here for the bridesmaid dress. My fitting. That gown is absolutely divine on you."

The bride smiles. "Do you really think so?" She pulls at the full skirt and twirls slightly on the platform.

"Hold still!" the seamstress snaps, and she puts her demure fingers to her lips and laughs.

"Absolutely. You look straight off the cover of *Bride*."

"You haven't changed a bit." Something in Mrs. Evans's tone tells me she doesn't consider this is a positive. I feel as old and questionable as Cherry herself against the dark-eyed bride.

"Excuse me." I back out of the doorway, unable to find the proper way to address Mrs. Evans.

"Lindsay," I hear Mrs. Evans say, and I halt in my tracks. I turn to face the music like I should have done years ago.

"How is your husband, Lindsay?"

"Dead, I'm afraid."

"I'm so sorry to hear it. Was he good to you?"

"He was." I feel like there are ants crawling all over me, I have an incredible urge to run. "Is that Jake's fiancée? The bride?"

"It is. Isn't she a beauty?"

I nod. "Exquisite."

"Such a sweet girl, too. She loves my son so much. That's all I ever wanted. For my son to be loved and appreciated for the wonderful boy he is."

"What mother wouldn't want that?" I sputter.

"No kids then?" she asks me.

"No."

"Well, God certainly spoke about what He thought of your choice, now didn't He? Barren as the Sahara, no doubt."

"Perhaps, but I don't proclaim to speak for God."

"You're too old now, I suppose. For children, I mean. It's a pity. Being a mother is the most fulfilling job in the world."

"I'm sure it is. Hopefully, you'll get to be a grandmother soon and double your pleasure. I should go. Haley will be waiting."

"Lindsay, I've waited a long time to speak my piece. Give me my moment, won't you?"

"Of course." I steel myself, clutching my hands into fists. Mrs. Evans always scared me. Even when she took me into her home and taught me to braise my first cut of beef, she did it implementing a critical eye, ever-watchful of errors.

And just like that, hearing her frightening tone again, it's like I've been transported back in time. I suddenly know why I married Ron and why I wouldn't have married her son. Ron loved me unconditionally. I was worth something to him. I wasn't a project that he could mold into something else. He was simply happy to have me alongside him. He loved to watch my face light up when we discovered new restaurants, or the delight in my eyes when we'd get a rare electrical storm over our canyon view. When I saw myself reflected in Ron's eyes, I was charming and good. In Ron, I saw just a glimpse of what I would look like to my Heavenly Father. *I didn't repeat the unhealthy patterns of my childhood. That was the lesson!* If I'd married Jake, I would have been repeating the pattern of my own mother! A smile spreads across my face as I recount that maybe I wasn't so naïve as a young woman, after all. I wanted to be loved. Not for who I might become, but who I was all along.

"Mrs. Evans, thank you so much! It was wonderful to see you. I wish you all the best!" I turn toward Fitting Room A when I hear Mrs. Evans's voice again after me.

"Incidentally, I didn't marry Ron only for money. I married him for acceptance!" I grin as wide as I can as I see Haley and the girls in the fitting room.

"Lindsay, you're here!" Haley says as I enter the doorway. "What was that?"

"I didn't marry Ron for money. My whole life has been this puzzle, and I feel like I put it together. Ron thought the best of me."

"I think the best of you, but all right." Haley kisses my cheek. "Now get your dress on."

"Oh, Haley! You make Heidi Klum look positively plain in that gown!"

"Do you like the dresses?" Haley asks, pointing to where mine hangs on a rack.

"I do! I think they're beautiful. You did a fine job all by yourself, Haley."

"Does this mean the mourning is over?" she looks me straight in the eye. "Is my best friend back? I know that Ron would be happy to hear it, if so."

"I am back!"

"Good, then I can start whining. I still feel completely stupid having a white wedding again. Oh, and if you're not bringing anyone to the wedding, Hamilton has someone you might like to meet."

"Hamilton! Haley, no offense, but no one wants to be set up by a lawyer who writes up prenups all day, all right? It's not exactly romantic."

"Hey! Hamilton is very romantic. I wish you'd spend more time with us. I used to spend time with you and Ron all the time."

"You lived in my condo. It's not like we could avoid you."

"Not every landlord is so hands-on, if you know what I mean."

"Not every tenant cooks like you. Ron got the best of all worlds— I helped organize the accounting business and you took care of cooking. We were like his very own young, gorgeous, blond harem. Now you're ready for me to transfer my affections to Hamilton, is that what you're saying?"

She grins. "No, but I feel like I never see you. For the last two weeks, you've been like a ghost."

"I've just been busy with Jane at the house. Would you stop worrying about me? You're a blushing bride. Where's your mother?"

"I sent her to the florist. She was driving me crazy." Haley looks at her bridesmaids, each of them donning their gowns. They're all the same color (fuchsia) but designed differently. One can't really put an older Bette in the same dress as the yoga-bodied Penny.

"I hope everyone is okay with this," she whispers. "My mother has been telling everyone to lose a little weight. I thought Bette might clock her before I sent her to the florist."

"Haley, it's all right to enjoy this. In fact, you *should* be enjoying this, for Hamilton's sake. Otherwise, you're just back in guilt mode, and you might as well still be with Jay."

It's so easy for me to dole out advice. Me, who has been living alone for a year and doesn't have anything to show for the time.

Haley sits with her tiara-capped veil on her head, moving it with her fingertips. "I was born to be a princess."

"You were born to be a Fabergé egg. Sparkly, gem-encrusted, and invaluable."

We laugh when a seamstress reminiscent of the Cold War comes in and barks orders. "Bride, stand over there! Bridemaids, in order of appearance, over here!" I scamper to get my dress on and back into place before I get sent to the rock quarry for punishment.

Haley salutes and stands on her pedestal, and she speaks directly to me. "If it's all right for me, then it's all right for you to go on living. Ron wouldn't have wanted this for you. Live your life, Lindsay. What do you want to do with it? Bette mentioned that you were thinking of a women's ministry. Go home and make a list to get it started. Do something! It's my turn to live vicariously through you. I'll be the boring housewife." She giggles.

"As if that were possible—for you to be boring. There are too many rhinestones in the world for that to happen." I look around the room and all of the Trophy Wives are nodding. It seems there comes a day when friends run out of grief for you and mine was about up. It is time. I'm ready.

The room suddenly gets quiet, and for the Trophy Wives, that's an amazing feat. I turn around and see Jake's bride has entered the room. Slowly, I walk across the room, and soon the chatter starts up behind me.

"I wanted to thank you," she says.

"Me?" I turn around to explain her presence, but the women have all given me the luxury of a little privacy. The young bride and I walk into the hallway, away from listening ears. Even if they're talking, I know them well enough to know they can do two things at once if the conversation interests them.

"Yes, you, Lindsay. I feel as though I know you. Mrs. Evans is always going on about how surprised she was when you up and married another man. Forgive me for being forward, but we're both practical girls, Lindsay. If you hadn't broken Jake's heart all those years ago, I might never have met the man of my dreams. So I wanted to thank you. I happen to believe everything happens for a reason."

"You're welcome." It's such a warm moment that I don't confess what I really want to tell her—Jake's mother scares the daylights out of me, and I have been thanking my lucky stars since being reminded of her oh-so-charming personality that I did not marry into that family and repeat my childhood of constant critique. But my mother, and life in L.A., taught me manners and not to speak such thoughts aloud.

"It's all right," she says, lowering her voice to a whisper. "I know you married for money. I understand completely. It was a practical choice, and I for one, commend you for it."

"Actually, I think my reasons ran slightly deeper than that. As I was watching Jake's mother, I realized—"

"So, do you have any tips for me?"

"Pardon?" I feel a pit at the bottom of my stomach as the motive of her conversation comes to light. Is she telling me she's marrying Jake for his money?

"Tips?" I ask her.

"You know, so that the younger version of me doesn't come along and snatch him from my arms. How did you keep your husband's interest?"

She is the most elegant, young woman with a perfectly regal profile and the same, captivating eyes that Jake himself possesses. She means no harm. I can tell her words run no deeper than their surface meaning, but I can only pray she learns the errors of her ways as I learned mine.

"Love him well, despite the money. The love of money is the root of all evil," I tell her. "In the end, it's not worth a plugged nickel."

She laughs. "How could I help but do anything else but love him? I am so glad I got to meet you. Jake's just ready to have kids now and look how old you are! That would have never worked. You see how things are?"

I force a smile. "I do. Good luck to you."

"You too! You're not too old to remarry, you know. Good for

you." She trounces off to her dressing room, and I roll my eyes.

"You only think you know your destiny," I say under my breath to her back. "Then reality bites you in the—"

"Lindsay!"

Gazing at Haley, I watch her try on a giant rhinestone necklace. As if she reads my mind, she looks back toward me, and I shake my head.

"Killjoy!"

If I died tomorrow, maybe I'd be sorry I didn't wear more sequins. Who knows? If I controlled less, I wonder if I wouldn't have enjoyed more. I can't help but envy the Future Mrs. Jake. Innocence protects one from harsh realities for a long, long time. I'll bet she had a nice mother who filled her with wonderful Cinderella dreams. Too bad Mrs. Evans comes in the deal. And too bad, the future Mrs. Jake will eventually have to learn the truth.

Chapter 12

Lindsay

"G reat, I'll see you then." I hang up the phone and look to Jane, who is absorbed in her current painting, which is nearly done and turning out beautifully. "Guess who that was?" I ask her.

"Nordstrom's. They're offering you a job. You're going to be measuring people's feet again soon."

"I sold suits," I tell her with a laugh. "And they're not interested in me. I'm too tall. I make the men feel short."

She doesn't look away from her painting. "You really need to find a new excuse, like the fact that you haven't worked for ten years. No one buys the tall thing."

"Is it my delivery?" I ask.

"It's the message." She faces me. "No one is going to feel sorry for a six-foot blonde who weighs less than the average Labrador. It's not in the cards for you to win sympathy, I'm afraid."

"It was your son on the phone."

She drops her paintbrush and faces me. "Ronnie?"

"Do you have more than him? And is he inheriting a house, too?"

"Very funny. What did he want?"

"You're not going to yell at me for talking to him?"

"Not yet. Did you call your mother yet?"

"Did you tell Ronnie his history yet?"

"Touché. What did my son want?"

"He's going to allow me to have Haley's shower at the Pacific Palisades house before it goes on the market. Thank you for asking him." *Though, if you let me speak to him, I could have asked for myself.* "But in return, I'm going to help him stage it for sale, so he'll get the most for it. I'd like to sell it furnished and so would he. What's he going to do with all that? He plans to donate the proceeds to the school he works with in Mexico during the summers. He's like the male Mother Teresa, I must say. We're a beautiful team, don't you think?" I see her flinch at the word team, but to her credit, she says nothing.

"You've got quite a commodities exchange going on between the two of you. When did all this come about?" She tries to keep the pinched tone from being noticeable, but I know full well what she thinks about me talking to Ronnie, and honestly, I wish I could tell her that Ronnie is too practical of a boy to be tempted by the likes of me.

"It was his idea. So I'm innocent. He just called here and asked if I'd help with the sale. He says he knows Hamilton will do it, but he doesn't trust him to get the right amount for it, hence the staging. I've got a great realtor too, so he'll be in great hands. He's hoping to build a brand new school with the money."

"My son is planning to give away this money? All of it?"

"Am I not speaking out loud? When he called, I thought he was looking for you, but he said no, he was calling me."

"Really. And you said yes, you'd help him with the sale?"

"You're welcome to chaperone me if you don't trust us together. Naturally, I said sure, I'd help him, but then I thought about all the women Haley wants to invite, and I thought he could help me as well. A restaurant is so formal and the clubhouse condo, with all the neighbors who scare Haley, not to mention the cats . . . " I look down at Kuku. "No offense. I thought we could throw one last party at the Pacific Palisades house. I brought up the idea to Ronnie and he agreed we could help each other."

"What does Ronnie's girlfriend think about this arrangement?"

"I would think she'd want him to get the most for his house. If they get married, it will give them a nice start in life."

Jane lifts her eyebrows. "Not if he's planning to give it all away. Are you kidding me?" She shakes her head. "For your sake, Lindsay, I hope you never have to taste reality."

"Oh, I didn't mean it that way. Quit checking my words. You're an artist; you're not supposed to be so literal. He's on his way over here after work, and we're going to do a walk-through together. Feel free to join us if you worry I might pounce."

"A walk-through of what?" She sounds testy.

"Of what furniture he should keep for the showing and what he might want to add."

"You're going to help him? You, who designed this mermaid house?"

"Is something the matter, Jane? I thought you liked my place."

"Nothing's the matter." She slams her paint box shut and wipes her hands on her apron. "Yes, something's the matter. You told me you'd stay away from Ronnie."

"And you told me that you were going to tell him the truth. I haven't told him anything about Ron, and he's asked, so I think you can trust me."

She picks up her paintbrush.

"Would it be so terrible if Ronnie did see me in a romantic light?" I mean, I couldn't care less about Ronnie, but must she keep bringing up how thoroughly unworthy I am for her precious son? I'm letting her stay in my place, and she's just rude!

"So you are planning something! You can't help but use those supermodel looks, can you? It's what you fall back on!"

"You know, I'm getting tired of all the quips about my looks. I'm thirty-five, Jane! And even you have to notice that I'm not a twenty-year-old bimbo any longer—not that I was a bimbo, mind you. But I'm getting tired of you talking down to me as though my blond hair gives you the right to disrespect me. I thought you were a feminist. And why change from day to day? Two weeks ago, you were supporting me in front of my Bible study. But wherever Ronnie's involved, you're like a pit bull. I never know when you'll turn on me. It's your own guilt, you know. Tell him the truth!"

"I'm not turning on you!" she shouts before she's had any time at all to figure out if she's turning on me or not. The ground seems unstable when Jane is near me, and I find myself questioning my own thoughts and deeds. "But I've worked hard to protect Ronnie from the truth, and I won't have you blabbing it now. I'll tell him when the time is right."

"Blabbing? Why would I want to hurt your son? Did you notice how you managed to bring this back around to you again? I'm helping Ronnie, and it's about you. Give the man some thought, will you? Why would you be upset that I'm helping him? Don't you want him to get the most for the house?"

She shakes her head. "I know you are not that naïve. Ronnie's going to own everything Ron left him—everything that doesn't belong to you, that is. That's going to make him quite the catch, isn't it?"

"Jane, you can't think—" But looking into her eyes, I see she does, indeed, believe it, and our friendship has been nothing more than a farce built on the shaky ground of mistrust.

"It's not like you haven't done this before."

I am stunned silent. I thought she trusted me. I thought she wanted me to go home and make it up to my mother, to see if reconciliation was possible. Now I see it was all a ruse to simply keep me away from her precious son.

"You're a blond bombshell, who claims she can't get a job because she's too tall, she's not skilled enough, she's planning to help homeless women, blah, blah, blah. You haven't lifted a finger to find some sort of path for your future, and now, you've conveniently planned to meet up with the new owner of Ron's mansion. If Ron fell for you, Ron Jr. should be like taking candy from a baby."

I feel as though I've been punched in the stomach. "It's *my* mansion, too, Jane. Don't you think if I'd wanted it, it would have been left to me?"

"You're saying it was *your* choice that Ron left that house to Ron Jr.? That's convenient. I suppose that will be one of the first things you tell him."

"Well, of course not. I didn't know there was a Ron Jr., until two months ago! But go ahead, and look up the deed of trust. It was in both our names at one time. We had an agreement."

"If that were true, Hamilton couldn't sell this house without your approval, and I went through all the paperwork. That house was clearly in Ron's will to give as he pleased."

"All my rights for the house were transferred back during our last separation. Look it up. Better yet, ask Hamilton." I slam my hand on the counter. "Forget it, I don't care if you believe me or not. I'm done trying to prove myself to your level of perfection. If you think

so ill of me, I'd appreciate it if you'd leave my house and take that
furry mongrel with you!"

"Is this part of your plan? To get me out of here so you can see
Ronnie alone?"

"You are paranoid! You think I'm a money-grubber, so keep your
son away from me. You did a good enough job keeping him away
from Ron. I'll get a hotel conference room for the shower, because
I'm glad to be done with the both of you. I was only being polite
for Ron's sake, anyhow." I clench my teeth and hear the grinding
sound in my head. It shouldn't matter what Jane thinks of me.
She's entitled to her opinion, after all. But I hardly see how she
pictures herself much differently than me. She didn't stay married
to Ron. At least I stuck by my promise. Say what you will about
me, I was loyal to the man. And this is how he repays me. By bringing his ex-wife back to town so she can accuse me of every atrocity
in the book.

"I don't care what you do anymore, Jane. But I don't want your
precious son. A nasty mother-in-law is one reason I didn't want
Jake, either! And I *loved* him!"

I clamber up the stairs, slam my bedroom door and then breathe
deeply. Guilt exudes from every pore in my being. "I tried, Lord!"
But I know I failed. Even if I'd wanted to stand up for myself, I
didn't have to be so hateful.

The phone rings, and though it's probably for Jane, I answer it
anyway. As I imagined, Jane picks up the phone before me and says
hello, and a man's voice greets her. "Jane—"

"Davis! How did you get this number?"

"Ron gave it to me. The gallery is low on art. I've brought in a
few of your favorite locals for display, but at some point, I'd like to
know if you're returning. I miss you."

"Ronnie gave you this number?" she asks, by way of an accusation, and I realize this is none of my business. I put the phone toward the cradle when Davis responds, and my curiosity wins.

"I would have gone with you," he says. "Why didn't you tell me you needed to go?"

"I didn't know how long I would be gone."

"Jane, this is getting ridiculous. I have put up with this crap for ten years. One day you're here. One day you're not."

"So leave. No one's holding a gun to your head."

"Then, you could claim I left, just like you knew I would."

"Spare me the dramatics, Davis. If you want to leave, leave. If you want to stay, stay. Our relationship is based on trust."

"In that I can trust you to run when the going gets difficult, you mean? You never answered my question. I see you left the ring here. Is that my answer?"

"I told you a piece of paper means nothing."

"It means something to me. It means something to Ronnie. Why don't you ask your son about it? Not that you seem to give him a choice in anything."

She slams the phone down on him, and I rub my ear, where my drum just received significant damage. "I know!" I say to the ceiling, "I shouldn't have been eavesdropping!"

I drop to my bed and hear a pronounced meow. I pick Kuku up and place him on the floor gently and collapse back onto the mattress. The more I know about Jane, the less I understand. She has littered portions of herself here and there, and tiny clues unfold about different aspects of her life, but naturally I wonder if there's anyone on earth—including her—who sees the full picture. This man, Davis, sounded heartbroken, and she met his long-lost voice only with brisk curtness. He gave her a ring! And she abandoned it, along with him.

She hurts. It's the only fact I truly know about her. Now my guilt mounts higher than ever. I march downstairs with resolve, to put my humanity aside and try to avoid the thought that she thinks I'm a complete manipulator. She's avoided answering some tough questions.

She's packing up her art equipment when I get downstairs.

"A man asked you to marry him, and you didn't have the decency to answer him before coming to the States?"

"You're wrong that you don't fit in here at this complex, Lindsay. You seem to do quite well minding other people's business."

"He loves you. That's obvious."

She rolls her eyes. "You sure have a lot of time to get into my business. Why aren't you interested in any of the other women in your life? That Helena has a lot to fix, if you're into fixing people, and Haley certainly needs help planning the wedding of the century."

"I don't want to do any of those things."

She sighs in exasperation. "You never want to do anything to change your life!"

"And you never want to do anything to keep things in yours! I can't believe you've had a man in your life for ten years, and you never thought to mention it. Was that him who called from the California Department of Corrections? Is he a guard?"

"What? No, he's in Mexico. Listen, Davis and I, we have an arrangement. I don't have a man in my life!" she claims.

"So you haven't had him in your life for ten years? Is that what you're saying?"

"Did you listen to the entire conversation? What is wrong with you?"

"It's my phone, and I'm worried about you. You're like ET living here, getting whiter and paler! Go back to Mexico if you need to. For crying out loud, Jane."

The doorbell rings and as I open the door, Cherry is standing there on my porch holding Jake by the ear. "Cherry, what on earth?"

"He was going to leave again! I caught him! I'm faster than I look, ain't I, boy?"

"Cherry, let him go." I pull him into the house protectively.

Cherry slaps her hands together as though her mission has been accomplished. "Don't forget what I told you, either, Miss Lindsay. Your husband's been dead a long time now. Your religion ain't doing you much good, is it?" She points her crooked finger at me, wagging it a few times before she turns and, with her lurching walk, heads back toward her door.

Jake shuts the door behind him. "Nice. Friend of yours?"

"I like her. I may *be* her one day."

He looks to Jane and nods. "You don't believe this for a second, do you?"

"She's nosey enough to be one of them. Don't underestimate her. I'm going to pack." Jane picks up Kuku and heads to her room, slamming the door.

"Bad timing?"

"I suppose you heard I met your bride. Is that why you're here?"

"I did hear," he says. "My mother thought that you may have planned it."

"Yes, running into your mother is just the kind of thing I would plan. She was thrilled to see me."

"She was?" He laughs. "That was a joke, I suppose."

"Does your bride know you're here? A week before your marriage? Or were you trying to get a bounty on my head?"

"She doesn't know I'm here. Does that make me a cad?"

"It doesn't make you ready to commit, that's for certain."

"You're not going to tell me, then?"

"'Tell you what?"

"That she's marrying me for my money."

"Even if she told me that, I wouldn't believe her. There are plenty of reasons to marry you besides your money. Those blue eyes on one's child are quite enough. The money's just an added bonus."

"But she did tell you that, and you weren't going to tell me."

"No, in fact, she didn't, and I don't believe she is marrying you for money. Marriage is hard, Jake. It's hard enough without questioning everyone's motives in everything. Assume the best. That's what Ron always did for me. You've waited a long time to get married—embrace it. She thanked me for giving you up. That doesn't sound like a woman intent on marrying for money."

He exhales deeply and peers down at me. His gaze darting down the hallway to check if we're alone. "What if I want out?"

"Most men want out a week before their wedding. It means nothing."

"I don't want to marry her."

"Well, it's a little late for that!" I exclaim. "And aren't you telling the wrong person? I'm not marrying you!"

"Isn't it better now than after the wedding?" he asks, and I look behind me and then back to him.

"Are you practicing on me? Because really, Jake, I don't understand. She's not here."

"I haven't seen you in ten years, Lindsay. All of a sudden, you're in the coffee shop, I pay you back the money I owe you, you meet my fiancée at the dress store. I'm worried it's not a coincidence. What if it's divine intervention?"

I swallow over the lump in my throat, unwilling to look him in the eye. The young Lindsay within me could run off with Jake and never look back, leaving that poor princess standing all alone at the altar, but the mature Lindsay—the one I've become because of Haley and Bette and the rest of them . . . heck, even Jane—that Lindsay can't bear to be thought of as the immoral woman ever again. Besides, how would I know if he's supposed to marry her? If you look at the shambles my life is currently in, my life choices haven't been anything to imitate.

He shakes his head. "It's not cold feet."

"Maybe it's not cold feet, but the fact that you're here doesn't speak well of that. Jake, you have no idea who I am today. You're thinking we can go back to being sixteen and carefree, but marriage isn't like that, I'm afraid. It's not just sugarplums and gumdrops. Make the choice to be there, and you'll be there."

"It was time to get married. I'm getting to that point where you're either gay or eternally questionable as a partner. I didn't think it mattered."

"You didn't think it mattered who you spent the rest of your life with?"

"I know. That's sick, huh?"

"Jake, why are you here? What do you think I can help you with?"

He rakes his fingers through his hair, which now has a touch of gray at the temples. I think about the years I've missed in his life and wonder if he ever would have had the guts to stand up to his mother. It was one of the first things that attracted me to Ron. He answered to no one. Certainly not an overbearing mother. My experience with mothers had made me more than skittish to ever become one. Would I have been under Mrs. Evans's rule all these years later? With a baby on my hip?

"Cherry says you've been coming here to see me. Is this why?" When I look into Jake's eyes, it's impossible not to feel the butterflies in my stomach that I felt as a young girl. It's impossible not to feel the soaring emotion of my first love, but to imagine that's something worthy of stopping someone's wedding is ridiculous.

"I haven't been able to sleep well since I saw you at the coffee shop. I came over here with good intentions to put an end to the questions in my mind, but it didn't work. I thought giving the money back would ease my anxiety, but I'm here now because I have feelings for the wrong person, and I want to know that you're not coming back. I need to hear it from your mouth that there isn't a chance in hell of you coming back to me before I commit to Tristin."

I want to slap him. I mean, seriously take my hand and thrust it across his face until he's red from the sting of my palm. "Jake, you don't even know who I am anymore." But as I look in his eyes, I know he does see a good portion of it. He knows what I'm capable of, and still, he's standing here. "I am a flawed person, and I don't want to take the chance to break your heart again. You have a bird in the hand—my advice is to fly away with her. She's a beautiful girl. Don't question this Jake. It will only haunt you."

"Let's fly to Italy tomorrow."

"Jake!" I back away from him. Really, I should send him down the hall to Jane. She likes to flee commitment, too.

"I know it's the one place you've always wanted to see, and I want to be the one to take you."

"You're getting married next week. You have always done the right thing. Well, except for maybe right now. How would you feel if you broke this girl's heart, and left all your friends and family stranded? I *had* to live with the guilt, Jake. It's not fun to get what you want at the expense of others. There's an enormous price to pay."

"I'd feel terrible, naturally."

I don't feel flattered, as I should. I feel branded, and I know as sure as I stand here that I would take the fall again. I would be the Other Woman, while he got to keep his reputation as the nice guy. I won't be the *her* again. I'm not strong enough to take it. I'm a Trophy Wife, and we have standards. Biblical standards.

"Jake, get married. Sometimes the price of what you want is too high. This is one of those times. Do the right thing, and God won't let you down."

"That's what I'm trying to do. The right thing."

"Then break up with Tristin. You're not in love with her if you can show up on my doorstep a week before your wedding. Either that or you're a complete commitment-phobe and at this point, I don't have a clue which is true."

"You're not promising me anything if I break it off with Tristin."

"No, I'm not."

His dark blue-green eyes still have power over me. Their soulful plead begs me to don a red dress and take my place as the man-stealer. After all, after one betrayal, what's one more? It's better than spending my life alone in this cramped condominium with a dozen cats. But I think about Bette's sorrow-filled eyes when she heard my confession. And Haley's upcoming wedding to a man who thinks she invented beauty. *This is not love I feel. This is about winning and loneliness. I'm in the race for the long haul, for the crown above.*

"If you love her, marry her. If you don't, let her go before it's too late, but do me a favor and keep me out of it. I've had enough drama for one lifetime."

Jake steps forward, and I look down at his work boots, not briskly new, but not hard-worn like when I knew him and they'd have to last until he could afford a new pair. He is a different man. I am a different woman. He surrounds my cheeks with his fingers and lifts my eyes to his.

He kisses my forehead, and I'll admit, I fight the urge to lift my lips to his and dwell in the flesh. Being a Christian never really gets easier, does it? As I watch him, I don't feel sure of anything. Cherry is perched behind her curtain, but she opens it so I can see her shaking her head. I know just how she feels. Failure is my middle name.

Chapter 13

Jane

Even Kuku is looking at me with scorn, pacing around my feet.
"I know. I shouldn't have said anything. Even if she is after
Ronnie for his money. I raised him smarter than that, didn't I?"

Kuku meows.

"You're turning on me, too? Listen, just because she's pretty and
doesn't throw you off her bed, don't get any ideas. What am I talking to you for? You're male, and you all react the same way to a
gorgeous blonde."

I fold my cotton pants. They're the wrinkled style that travels
well, and I get frustrated with folding so I twist them into a ball
and drop them in the suitcase, throwing a wadded-up Guatemalan
T-shirt on top of them. Everything else, I yank off hangers and out
of drawers and pile into the bag. I did my best. I made it nearly

two months and considering the circumstances, that's about seven weeks longer than I thought I'd last.

Inside the bathroom, I scrape everything off the counter in one fell-swoop, my arm like an elephant's trunk swathing a new path in the jungle. Only in this case, it reveals a fresh, clutter-free countertop. Just as pristine as the day I found it, with only the brightly-colored, fish-shaped soaps and tropical blue hand towels, in a clam-shaped dish. I straighten the coordinating bath towels and stand back to admire my work.

Every trace of me is gone, except I put the Retin A back where Lindsay so graciously left it for me. *Yes, I'm old.* I know this without her subtle hint of medical products left on the bathroom vanity. Unlike Lindsay, I have more important things to worry about. I leave the prescription tube on the counter, convinced she'll need it more than me, regardless. Her looks are still a commodity; mine are long-gone, and they never did me any favors, anyway.

"Why do I say things I don't mean?" I ask the mirror, as I think about what I told Davis. "I feel terrible afterward, and then I can't even apologize."

It's a terrible character flaw, probably right up there with talking to oneself. One of these days, Davis isn't going to be waiting when I get home. My lower lip trembles when I think of an empty house, and I still it with my finger. I flatten my palms against my cheeks, pulling back the extra skin. I'm in there somewhere, my fresh, girlish self, whose eyes are bright and full of life. I came here, angry at Ron, sure, but Ron was only a symptom of when I didn't have control over my life. Now I have so much control that no one but Davis seems to want to be around me—and I think he's just been a glutton for punishment. I thought I could show Lindsay the right path. Now that she's on her own, and I've completely bungled it.

She just thinks I'm a crazy, old lady who belongs with the rest of her neighbors.

Most of my life is over now. Though math has never been my subject, it doesn't take a genius to know that at fifty-three, the best years have come and gone. I wish I could just call Davis, and blurt how much I miss him, that I wish he was here with me, and the thought of going home to a house without him tears me up inside. But there's something different about me—there always was. I'm missing some deep, functional part of womanhood. An inner portion of my heart is dead. It doesn't operate the way other women's seem to, offering up nurturing words and a warm meal. It didn't used to be that way. I was the mother all the kids loved. Now, I'll leave the house and avoid the guilt of what I can't provide. Something prevents me from saying how I feel, if it will make someone else feel good and reduce me to a lower plane. In fact, often it makes me do exactly the opposite of what I desire.

I'm tired of living this way. But it's too late now, I suppose. "I yam who I yam," as Popeye would say.

My son is the only one who breaks through that barrier—the sole person from whom I do not fear rejection, though even that's a lie, since he doesn't know anything but my version of his youth. He is the last vestige of my best years. The only thing I ever did right, and someone could easily make the argument I didn't even do that well. At the very least, I didn't do it honestly.

A letter slides under my door, and I greet the blue stationery with astonishment. In Ron's handwriting, it reads RON JR. As I clutch the letter, I see that the seal has been broken. I open the door. "You read this?"

Lindsay's sneaking up the stairs, and she turns toward me when I call out. "I didn't know there was a Ron Jr. when I read it. I thought

Ron might have thought I was pregnant. I didn't know. Either way, I didn't give it to the charity in the desk. I had it all along, but I didn't know how to tell you."

"You let me call all over town looking for the desk?"

"I knew there was nothing important in it."

"So why didn't you tell me?"

"This may surprise you, Jane, but you don't exactly invite warm and friendly information. Everything you do feels like judgment. Maybe you don't mean it that way, but I'm afraid of you. I imagine a lot of people are afraid of you. And I think you like it that way."

"What does this letter say?"

"It says nothing, but I thought you'd want to read it before Ronnie got it, so I'm giving it to you. Do whatever you'd like with it. Give it to him, don't give it to him—it's none of my business. Considering Ron left him the mansion, it's probably the least you can do for his memory."

She continues up the stairs, and I rip what's left of the envelope and find his old-fashioned script in a letter to my son.

Dear Ron Jr.,

You won't remember me. We haven't been intimately acquainted for a long time, but I loved you. If God deems it in heaven, I will love you from above. Children are often the recipients and thus, innocent victims, of adults' poor choices. I should have done more for my health. I should have done more for your mother. I have prayed for you, and I know His will is perfect. Someday, I have no doubt, we will meet in the clouds and my intentions will come to fruition. Your mother is a good woman, regardless of what she says about *herself at times. Love her well, and I will see you when your race is finished. Put your hope in Jesus and He will not leave or forsake you.*

In His Love, my son,
Your Father, Ron Brindle

I wasn't just afraid of Ronnie's father. I was afraid of Ron, too. The two of them blamed me. "That's why I left." I breathe deeply trying to calm my racing heart. I see Ron's rage-filled face when I told him I could never love him, the spilled milk of Mitch's fateful choice that night . . . and I see Mitch all over again, young and full of zeal. Before my life was split into fragments. No house in Pacific Palisades will ever make up for it. I rip the letter into tiny shreds and the pieces float around me in whirling, floating circles . . .

"Mom? Mom?"

I look up and see my son standing over me. "I didn't deserve you."

"What? Mom, wake up!"

I notice that Lindsay is standing next to him and she has the phone in her hand. "They'll be here any minute. Can you get her on the bed?"

I sit up, but the world is still spinning, so I lay back down. "Who will be here? What's going on?"

"Mom, we heard you fall." I look around me frantically for the letter, only to see Lindsay is slyly putting the pieces away in her back pocket.

"I called 911. They'll be here any minute now," she says.

I stand up without help. "What are you talking about? I'm fine." But as I stand, I feel dizzier than ever, and more than slightly hung-over, sort of like that time Davis and I had the homemade tequila margaritas.

"Just sit down until they get here." My son checks my pulse and the worry in his eyes brings tears to my own.

"Ronnie, I'm fine. Don't worry about me." I pat his arm. "You're such a good boy. Always wanting to take care of me, when it's my job to take care of you."

"When you're found collapsed on someone's bedroom carpet, it's generally understood that you are not fine. Stop fighting me."

I roll my eyes. "Fine, I'll wait for the cavalry."

Ronnie starts whispering something to Lindsay, and the thought incenses me. "What are you two whispering about? I'm right here! Say something out loud if you want to say it."

Lindsay darts out of the bedroom, and my son is watching me as if I'm on fire. "Ronnie, I just fainted. It's not a big deal. I just had a busy day and forgot to eat."

"When Ron fainted, he never got back up, so I'm not going to take your word for it."

"Ron had a stroke. I didn't have a stroke." If I could find the words, I'd tell him the truth right now. God forbid I die and leave Lindsay to break the news to him.

"How many fingers am I holding up?"

"Three."

"How about now?"

"Four. Are we going to do this all evening? Maybe we should get a pad of paper and play Pictionary. You always loved that game. When he was little, he could draw absolutely anything." I look around. "Where did Lindsay go?"

"Is Davis at home?"

"It's late there, you're not calling Davis. Besides, I don't know if he's home."

"It's a Monday in March, where would he go?"

"We had a fight."

"You had a fight. Davis never says anything back to you, though Lord knows, he should."

I smile at Ronnie's sad assessment of his mother. "You know me too well."

Soon Lindsay is back, and she's carrying a glass with orange juice. "Here, drink some of this."

I take a drink, realizing I am really thirsty. I gulp the entire glass down and hand it, empty, back to her. "Thanks, Lindsay." I feel fine and stand again. "I just need to eat, that's all." They're both looking at each other again. "I'm diabetic, my blood sugar got low. There is no sense in alarm. This is what happens."

"You're diabetic?" Ron says. "Since when?"

"I don't know, a year or two officially. I always have been slightly. That's why I can't hold my liquor."

Ronnie crosses his arms across his brawny chest. "Mom, it's all right to tell people pertinent information. What if I have a kid with diabetes, and I tell the pediatrician there is no history of it in my family?"

"You don't have any children, and I thought you said it wasn't serious with Kipling." I watch Lindsay's eyes as I state this, but she makes no move toward Ron. At least she has the wherewithal to do her dance without me watching.

The doorbell rings, and Lindsay disappears out of the room again and returns with two brawny EMT guys, who are probably out-of-work actors struggling to get by. I can imagine them saying, "I'm not an EMT, but I play one on *ER*."

"My son overreacted," I tell them. "I'm diabetic, and I didn't tell him. I just got low on my blood sugar, that's all." One of the men takes my pulse, while the other gets out a blood glucose monitor and pricks my finger. "Ouch! Why don't you warn a person?"

"They only scream louder when I warn them. Besides, you should

be doing this every day. I get seven year olds who don't even react.
I've taken to a surprise entry." He has gorgeous blue eyes, and if I
were a younger woman . . . "Forty-nine," he says with raised eyebrows. "You need to get yourself a glucose meter and keep track of
this daily."

"Do you need anything from us?" Lindsay asks, and my strapping
young EMT notices her for the first time and, naturally, looks again.
I'm glad I'm not dying here.

"No. Thank you, miss. We have everything we need. You drank
some juice?" He asks me, still looking at Lindsay.

I take his chin and turn his head toward me. "I did."

"Are you on any medications?"

"No, sir."

"Any feeling of pins and needles in the fingertips?" He takes his
fingers, and they meet mine.

"No." Well, save for the fact that I do feel slightly tingly at the
touch of a thirty-year-old hunk . . . never mind.

The other EMT has a stethoscope to my back. "Inhale deeply."
He holds his cold piece to my back. "And exhale. Any history of
heart disease?"

"None," I state proudly. "I'm a hiker. Bet I could out-hike you two."

"I bet you could." He pulls the stethoscope away. "I'd like to get
you an EKG tonight, just to be certain there are no underlying pressure problems that led to your fainting."

"I'll make an appointment with my doctor in the morning."

"Mom, you don't have a doctor here."

"I'll find one. This is L.A. I assume you have doctors besides plastic surgeons here. They have to have someone to work on, right?
That means doctors' wives."

"Mom!" Ron says, in that "you're so embarrassing" tone. I look
back at the EMT with the blue eyes, because if I'm going to look at

one of them, it might as well be the one dreams are made of. "I'm not going to the hospital, so you can pack up all your equipment and start writing your report."

He takes the blood pressure cuff off me. "You might as well take her to dinner. She'll probably benefit from that more." He says to Lindsay. "Speaking of dinner—" He raises his brows at Lindsay.

"I'm calling Bette," she says to me, ignoring the gorgeous man making a pass at her. *What is wrong with that girl?*

"Bette? The older woman from your pedicure group?"

"Yes. You don't listen to me, and you don't listen to your son, and I know that Bette won't give you a choice. She demands respect. Therefore, I'm calling Bette. She'll take you to dinner, slap some sense into you, and we'll all come back tonight for a rousing game of Pictionary." She smiles at me. "I heard you from the stairs. How does that sound, Ronnie?" She turns to my son and flashes her giant baby blues.

"Positively brilliant. Though at the moment, I'm up for slapping some sense into her myself."

I narrow my eyes. "Ronnie—"

He kisses my cheek. "You scared the life out of me, you know? Diabetes?" He shakes his head.

I start to stand, and one of the burly EMT guys holds me down. "We're almost through here. Would you mind waiting downstairs? We have some more tests we want to run and get a full history."

"I told you what was wrong with me."

"I'd like a full history, too!" Ronnie says to me.

"This is California. People sue here, so forgive us if we can't listen when you refuse service. Too many lawyers. Something happens to you, and I don't have these stats? My job is gone. Just a few more numbers to get for the forms."

"Your California law is the reason I'm stuck here in the first place!"

"Calm down. Henry, check her blood pressure again." I sit and wait while he cuffs me again, and it doesn't take a test to tell me my blood pressure is, indeed, through the roof. "You sent my son down there with that woman!" I squeal. "Sure I have high blood pressure!"

"Your son's a lucky man. Can I trade places with him?" The blue-eyed wonder asks.

Henry whistles long and high. "She's a beauty."

"Ah, beauty." I open my arms. "You see what happens? It happens to the best of us. Better make sure you find more than a pretty face, know what I'm saying?"

"You're a beautiful woman," the handsome one says. "You have that flirtatious look. You flirt a lot when you were younger?"

"Was I supposed to stop when I got older? Someone forgot to tell me the rules."

The men finish their work, and I reach for the telephone. I dial the number at home to tell Davis that I want him there when I return, but a strange woman's voice answers. "Hola."

"Who is this? ¿Quién es este?" I demand.

She hangs up the phone, so I dial again. There's no answer. My world is crashing in around me, and I'm stuck watching my son make eyes at my ex-husband's trophy wife. *If You're up there, God, this is definitely not the way I want to go!*

Chapter 14

Lindsay

S he likes you, you know," Ronnie says as we get into my BMW. My car is old by L.A. standards—a 2006—but it doesn't show its age, and I'm attached to it. I get like that. Too attached to objects that represent times in my life, coupled with an extreme inability to let go. I could barely stand to watch Haley leave the condo. I can't bring myself to sell the condo, and now, there's Jane. Even though she doesn't like me, she likes me as much as she's able, and the last thing I want is for her to leave before this will is finished or she's feeling better. Though everything about her appearance and demeanor may deny it, she is not a spring chicken.

Ron goes on. "If she didn't like you, you'd know it. She's very obvious about such things."

I smile back at him. I know it's true. The fact that he's in my car right now tells me his mother likes me as much as she's able to.

Either that, or she's met Kipling and isn't overly fond of her. The idea of my husband's stepson is even less palatable to me than her, so I don't know what she's worried about.

When Jane kicked us out to go to the mansion—together—I held my shoulders back, feeling confident she'd accepted the fact that I was not after her son. It was a sign of acceptance, weak-willed as it may have been. Though it could have been the drugs the EMTs gave her or Bette's soothing words. Either way, it feels good to escape the condo and drive into the crisp, clear evening of an early, cold spring.

"Sometimes I think your mother endures me, and I'm good with that."

"My mother does not *endure* anything she does not like. Trust me on this. She picks on those she likes. She doesn't bother with people she doesn't like." I look over at Ron, realizing for the first time his charming, boyish good looks—the misty, green eyes under a crop of light brown hair, highlighted with natural streaks of blond. He has that California surfer look—everything about his body is in perfect order, topped by a head of hair in complete disarray.

"You must have really stood out in Mexico. How come you didn't stay?"

"It's hard. I want to fix everything, give the kids everything I have. Here, I can do that without being ineffective. I tend to be a sucker. Have it written on my forehead."

"I can relate."

"People sense the suckers. Have you noticed? There can be four hundred people on the street, and a kid in holey clothes and bare feet will find me to ask for money. He just knows. I have a beacon."

"Well, you look like a hero. There's something about a six-foot-four guy with muscles. Your presence makes people want to believe you can do anything. Like Superman." *I did* not *just say that.*

"Is that so?"

"Your mother told me how tall you were. I didn't measure or anything." I wish I could find my way back to the moment before we started this conversation. I now feel very schoolgirlish and ridiculous.

He holds up his hand. "You don't have to explain. It's not the gringo looks, though. It's the same way here in California. I am a sucker. People sense it."

"That's why your mother is so protective of you, I'll bet."

"Meaning?"

"Well, she's worried about the girl you're dating." She's more worried about me, but I don't make mention of that. "You're going to be inheriting a lot of money. All the same things Ron's friends probably warned him about with me." I shrug.

"Anyone who would marry me for money wouldn't get much. "

"Why not? This house is worth a fortune. Even if you give a significant amount away, you'll be left with money," I tell him. "Wait until you see its location and how beautiful it is."

"It's a house. You feel attached to it. To me, it's just a house that will help attain my goal. Once that's done, I'll be poor again. Rich by Mexican standards, but poor by California standards, any way you look at it."

"I don't understand."

"I work with kids on the south side. I send extra money back to Mexico for my friends running the schools there. I don't need much to survive. Any woman I'm with will have to accept that. Doesn't make me much of a catch, does it? At least not in L.A., where people spend more dressing their dogs than caring for the poor. This house is going to purchase a new wing for that schoolhouse."

"It could build several schoolhouses," I tell him.

"I know," Ronnie admits. "But that overwhelms me, so I have to start small and build from there."

"Hamilton will help you with any of this, you know. Managing this kind of money can be a full-time job. It's not as much fun spending it as you might think."

He looks over at me questioningly.

"Ron never relaxed very well. He was a wonderful husband but having that kind of fiscal responsibility makes it hard to just pack up and go. Not to mention all the other accounts he managed."

"That is not the life for me at all. So if that makes me a catch, any girl will be sorely disappointed when she realized I gave it away to be rid of the responsibility."

I laugh. "It will make you the right catch for the right woman," I offer. "Do you think this woman you're seeing needs much to survive? Mowgli?"

"Kipling!" He corrects. "Did my mother tell you to say that?"

"No, we just have the same sick sense of humor, I suppose. Mowgli gives me such an image, and she doesn't suit you at all." I'm smiling as I drive through a green light. I can see his eyes upon me, and I'm embarrassed to admit, there is a distinct chemistry between us. So I do my very best to ignore any connection.

"Kipling spends a lot of money on purses."

"All women spend money on handbags." I look over at him. "Unless there's something physically wrong with them, I believe it's genetic. Even my friend Haley spends money on handbags, and she's as cheap as a indie producer."

"All right. I won't hold that against her."

"Shoes don't count either."

"Anything else?"

"Getting her hair done. No one wants bad hair. That comes at a price."

"Purses, shoes, hair. I'm beginning to think I would be better off with a dog." He laughs.

"You can't leave a dog to run off to Mexico. You'd have to spend money to leave the dog in the kennel."

"All right. I give up. Is that what you want from me? I am too low maintenance for human consumption."

I laugh out loud at his comment. "Would she move to Mexico with you, if you went back?"

He looks at me and smiles. "I'm not going back. Not permanently. Unlike my mother, I can't shut my heart down like it's a machine."

"I told you, you're preaching to the choir. I'm a sucker, too!" For some reason, I bond to this admission, and it makes me see him in an entirely different light.

"Did you love my father?"

It's such a pointed question, and I admire him for asking. He's much more like Jane than I thought. "I did love Ron. There was a lot about him to love." We come to a red light, and I take a good gander. Ronnie has a Matthew McConaughey charm without knowing he possesses such charisma. He really does have a lot of Ron's characteristics, but he's entirely individual to himself, and that's what I can't help but find attractive. This admission, even to myself, sends a surge of guilt through me. "Ron was a very lovable man. He accepted people for who they were. Warts and all. Those people are hard to find here in the plastic surgery capital of the world."

"Says the five-ten blonde."

His comment stuns me, and I stare at him. "That was rude. You don't strike me as the rude sort." The light has turned green, and there's a BMW honking hard behind me, but I'm waiting for my apology.

"Was it rude? I hadn't meant it that way. It was supposed to be a compliment, but Cary Grant I'm not."

"He had his words written for him, so I suppose that's all right." I grin toward him, and I feel the power in his smile back at me. It warms me inside.

"But seriously, Lindsay, you are so striking. It's hard for a guy to see past that. I didn't know Ron like you did. In a way, that ticks me off, so maybe some of that is coming out in inappropriate comments. I mean, I think you have a great heart, but it is wrapped in a pretty nice package and I am male. Moaning about things that aren't meant to be is a solid waste of time."

"You're right, but pain in life shapes you. It molds you in ways you don't want to be molded."

"Only if you let it. We give others too much power over our thoughts, don't you think?" I should take my own advice, but it's so much easier to see your problems in others, it just warrants a sermon—but then, you feel completely hopeless after giving it, because it would be so simple, if only I heard myself. "I hope your mother is going to be okay with Bette tonight. Maybe we should have stayed home. I'm feeling guilty." See? I can't even get past the thought of a sermon, without a healthy portion of guilt.

"She wouldn't have let us do anything. Trust me, the faster this place is gone, the faster she can go home. That's what she wants. To be back in her world where she can escape at random."

"Did she do that when you were growing up?"

"Believe it or not, she was the consummate stay-at-home mom when I was growing up. She baked cookies, she let the neighborhood kids in, she fed half of them dinner since she knew they wouldn't get it when they went home. Surprise you?"

"Not really. I saw a lot of that in her when she first came, but the longer she was caged up here, the more I saw the other side of her. Bette will straighten her out."

Ron laughs.

"No, really. She will. She has this presence of the Holy Spirit in her that one can feel emanate from her. She can seriously smack you upside the head so softly, you never know you've been hit. I've only heard her say one mean thing in my life, and I probably deserved it."

"I doubt that. She sounds like the perfect woman to be there. So let's not worry about her. If there's one thing I know about my mother, she's tough enough to withstand the whirlwind that is L.A."

The house is as beautiful as ever, and when I drive up to the courtyard driveway, I can't believe I ever lived here. It's still magical. Undeniably the most beautiful house near the Palisades Village, with some of the best canyon views in the area. "I'm so excited for you to see the house."

"Why?"

"Because there's so much of Ron in it. So much of me here. I'm anxious to show you all I did, I guess. I'm proud of it." Naturally, I think of his mother making fun of my "mermaid" house, but this place is different. It's understated, traditional, and beautifully furnished. "It's everything you'd expect of a good, trophy wife."

He glances at me to see if there's a joke involved, but I don't offer the hint of a smile. "I still don't understand why you didn't stay here if you love it so much."

"When Ron went back to drinking, I was devastated. When he returned to me, I wanted him to know it wasn't the house that brought me back. We spent the last year in my little condo after Haley moved out. I would have lived in a shack with him. You'll find out when you have everything stripped from you and all you have left is each other—you either sink or swim. Money can really do more to tear apart a relationship than bring it closer. I suppose I learned that the hard way."

"He was so much older than you. How did you two find anything to talk about?"

"We just did. I was raised around my mother's friends, so I was probably much older than my years." As we pull up to the house, I watch him scan the vines growing up alongside the three-car garage, and his eyes widen. "I didn't start out with the best of intentions with Ron."

"I've heard."

"But I fell in love with him. He was such a light and so warm, it was impossible not to. The age, I never noticed. I'm like that. You know how people will say, 'Oh, you've lost weight' to someone? I never, ever notice things like that because I see the inside of the person. Okay, with the one exception being my best friend Haley. She thinks it's her life duty to sparkle."

"I don't follow you."

"She likes to wear rhinestones and sequins, animal prints—you know what I'm saying. It's hard for me to see past that. I have this innate need to tone her down."

He looks at me like I am a rambling idiot. "I can't believe this house is just sitting here unoccupied."

"I know, it's a shame. The schools are excellent here. This will be a fabulous house for some lucky family."

"Do you want children, Lindsay?"

"I have myself to worry about now. I made a mess of things, why pass it on? Ron didn't want children and I didn't, either. I never thought I'd make a great mother, I guess."

"Everyone makes a mess of things, but that doesn't stop them from becoming parents."

"I suppose I should have told you."

"Told me?"

"I have perfectionist tendencies."

"There's no perfect parent, trust me. I see them all in the schools."

"Your mother would do anything for you. My mother sort of blamed me for everything."

"My mother spends too much time pondering life and not enough with people."

"I thought her house was a fiesta house!"

"Oh, it is. But having a party and sharing yourself can be two different things."

I push the gate code, and we arrive into the private Mediterranean courtyard. I watch Ronnie as he spies the canyon view for the first time. "Wow, this place is—"

"I know, huh?"

We climb out of the car, and the gate closes behind us. I can see a thousand reasons to spend the rest of my life in this house. Its walled-off perfection from the bustle below and its European charm makes me feel as though I've been transported to a private, Spanish island. There's just something about being here that makes me feel alive. I close my eyes and let the remaining sunlight fall onto my face.

We walk behind the iron gate to the tiled courtyard, which is centered around a lovely fountain. I flip a switch and the water bubbles serenely into the pool at its base. "All of that along the staircase is hand-painted Italian tile. I picked it out online when I felt something was missing here." I pull him over to the studio at the end of the patio, overlooking the canyon. "Can you just picture your mother out here painting?"

"She'd hate it here." He chuckles. "It's too clean for one thing."

"Probably, she would. Come inside. This front door is hand-hewn alder from the Sierras." I rub my hand along it. "This wrought iron design was made especially for the door by a craftsman in Montana."

"I thought you weren't around when Ron built the place."

"I've made a few changes since it was built. Just added a woman's touch here and there. Ron had great taste for the most part, but colors don't seem to be in a man's repertoire."

"That's a bit sexist," he says.

"I'm in a Bible study called the Trophy Wives Club; you think I care about PC, sexist garbage?"

He grins. "I suppose not."

"The house beams were created to look like they were a hundred years old. This mantel is actually from a castle in Italy. It's solid marble, and I worried that it didn't fit in just right, but I got over it when the fireplace looked naked without it."

"So what would you change in here for the sale?"

I scan the room. "It needs to be cleaned up." I look at the Italian vases on the bookshelves. "That's a distinct style. You don't want to have in a staged house."

"All right." He walks around looking at the walls. "Where are all the pictures?"

"They're in scrapbooks. Ron didn't appreciate clutter, and I learned to like the clean look, as well."

"That's odd. I mean, you don't have any on your mantel. Makes it feel like it's already staged. There are pictures all over your condominium."

I ignore his assessment. "We'll need to take out the extra furniture or rearrange to make the best possible flow. We could put a seating area over here." I point to the corner. "And then keep this furniture to surround the fireplace as a focal point. We'd need to pull all these books off the shelves and add some pottery or stoneware that would go with the decor but isn't too distinct, like what's in there now. With these clean, off-white walls, we want to keep the beachy lightness."

"The beachy lightness? Right." He fights a laugh. "I don't have the stomach for this."

"You're making fun."

"I'm not, but I would never buy a mansion and I know why. Even if I had the money, I couldn't make it through the sales pitch." He stares at the fireplace. "This place is incredibly romantic. What woman wouldn't fall in love with a guy in this house? It's impossible not to feel like James Bond here."

I nod. "It has an air about it, it's as though God kissed it with His grace. Ron's drinking made being here hard sometimes, and I moved out of it to find some peace when alcohol took over. Still, nothing deters me from the serenity that this house brings. It's like the red dirt of Tara for me. I feel home."

"The what?"

"You know how Scarlett O'Hara wants to go home to the red dirt of Tara in *Gone with the Wind*?"

"I saw it in Spanish; it's translated differently."

We laugh, and I sink into my cream-linen sofa, tucking my feet beneath me. I stare at the fireplace. "I can hardly believe I possessed that fireplace at one time. Can you imagine the lives lived in front of it?" I pick up the remote control and start the fire. I sigh. "The sunsets are magnificent here. I think we should stay so I can word the marketing brochures correctly."

"I'm sure the realtors will handle that."

"The realtors don't love this home. I do, and I'm convinced I can write the copy better than they can."

"I have a hard time believing you want to sell this house, Lindsay. Why'd you move?"

"I'm wondering the same thing right now. I guess, unlike you, Ronnie, I do need a lot to survive. That's not a great thing to learn about yourself. Giving up this house was the first step to being a better person."

"No one needs this much." He sits down on the sofa beside me.

"It's true. It's mythology that the world can't touch you here. It feels like it, doesn't it? Like you're free of fear and turmoil, but it eventually gets in and undermines the idea of perfection. There's no such thing as perfection."

"An afternoon of *futbol*, my mother's tamales with good friends, and the neighbor's flan for dessert. That is as close to perfection as you're going to get here on earth."

As the sun begins to set, I jump up from the sofa. "Oh I forgot the best part. You have to see the bathtub. It's the perfect time." I pull him into the master bedroom, and sigh at the sight of my beloved. "It's my favorite place to be. This tub at sunset. Do you have any idea how difficult it is to get a bath at sunset? Husbands want dinner, guests arrive for cocktails, business associates have meetings—it's wholly inconvenient to bathe at sunset, which is why it's the most coveted time."

"It seems like you were born to live in this house." He says it as though he feels sorry for me.

"That's how I felt the first time I came here. I was engaged to another man. The contractor, actually. One of them."

"So then you fell in love with my father? Or this house?"

"It was a bit of both. When your mother doesn't grocery shop or come home at night, a house like this makes you feel like this is a person who would never let you go hungry. I'd say my affections were pretty tied up in my fears."

Ronnie nods as he lets his eyes take in my image. I wonder if he hears my tale as just a lie to win his sympathy. Lord knows I wasn't above using them in the past.

"So the bathtub." I point to my pièce de résistance. "The Italian tile on the wall is like having my very own Sistine Chapel. Oh, we'll have to take the chandelier down. They're illegal over tubs—did you know that? At least that's what the builder told me. We had to wait until the inspection was over to put it in."

"If the builder was your former fiancé, I'd say you were lucky he put it up solidly." Ron stares at the light. He's got about a week's growth on his face, and the rugged appearance against the soft green of his eyes is mesmerizing, especially under the fading sun. It's been a long time since I noticed a man, but I quickly remind myself just how off-limits this one is.

"I suppose you're right. I never thought of that." He catches me staring at him. "So, I am thinking of having the shower in the evening, out on the patio, and coming into the family room for gifts. Then, I'll take care of getting the house staged, and you should be set."

"Oh." Ronnie shakes his head. "The wedding shower. My mind was on the bathtub, so I thought we were still discussing cleanliness and you had an outdoor shower on the patio."

We avoid looking at each other when he says this and I find my jokes at Jane's expense about the chaperone to be slightly less funny than I found them earlier.

He changes the subject and I'm grateful. "I have a lot of questions about Ron. My mother won't answer them."

"I won't either, Ronnie. It's not my place. He left you this house, I think that shows you how he felt about you. Why didn't you call when he was alive?"

"I didn't want to hurt my mother."

I nod. "What do you think your girlfriend will say about the house?"

"She broke up with me. I called her my girlfriend earlier, didn't I?"

"I'm sorry." I stammer for the right words, but instead I blurt, "Why?"

"How would I know?" He brushes his arm. "I mean, I sure can't see it. I'm a fabulous catch." He holds his arms out and smiles.

"Well, what did she say?"

"You're not going to let this go. You want the gory details on how I got dumped."

"At least there's enough of a social life to get dumped. I'm getting text messages from the only man in my church singles' group, and he doesn't have a chin."

"You would dump a man simply because he didn't have a chin? That's cold."

"You forgot shallow. It's shallow, too," I remind him.

"Kipling said my family being broken apart, and my late age without marriage was a warning sign to her father and he didn't approve of me as a proper choice. He said my family history didn't speak well for my commitment ability."

"Thirty-six isn't that old in California. It's the new eighteen. Isn't that what they say?"

"They should say that. They're an old-fashioned family. She was home-schooled through college, and her father's probably right. It's not many fathers who want to see their daughter married off to a California schoolteacher who sends half his paychecks to Mexico. I don't exactly have 'Trump' written in my future. It wasn't serious." He shrugs.

Ronnie doesn't seem like a man who gives his heart easily, and he certainly doesn't seem like the type who can't commit. He's committed to making no money while he does what he's passionate about. "Just tell her father he needs a higher dowry, that's all. Is she a one-cow wife or a ten-cow?"

He laughs. "She's a ten-cow wife. Just not my ten-cow wife."

"I wonder if this house would have made a difference. This has to be worth a thousand cows easily, don't you think?"

"If it would have, then she definitely wasn't right for me. I need the thousand-cow wife who can live on the one-goat salary."

"True. I wonder what her father would say about me? I made my own mistakes; I can't blame them on genetics. You either buy into the grace thing, or you don't. So, I have deemed her completely unworthy of you and her father a very bad judge of character."

"What about your parents? Are they still alive?"

"They are, but I'm dead to them, unfortunately. I don't know my father. We have that much in common, and when I married Ron, that was the end of my mother and me. She married several times before I left. She's probably found herself eight more husbands since then. I'm not sure I can even find her. Every time I plan to go back and try one more time, something always seems to come up and another Christmas passes. I have to be willing to accept whatever happens when I see her, and I'm not there yet."

"I see the children in my classes and I couldn't stand to abandon them. How can parents do this?"

"I guess that's why we both found God, huh? He'll never leave or forsake us. Though I have to remind myself of that more often than I'd like."

We walk back out to the family room, where a gas-induced fire roars under the antique mantel. The sun is starting to set in the canyon and the pink dusk light illuminates the room.

"He'll leave the ninety-nine to go after the one. That's my favorite."

"We have this hope as an anchor for the soul, firm and secure."

"He raises the poor from the dust—"

I smell the sweetness of Ronnie's soul, the purity with which he speaks, and my heart is moved to places it has not dared to visit since Ron had gone. We look directly into each other's eyes and both of us recognize what we see there. A connection that simply cannot be. A reading of each other's heart all in the split second of our eyes meeting.

Ronnie's warm voice and the promises of God remind me, *I'm alive. I'm still here, and I'm good enough.* We sit across from the fire, not looking at each other for our own protection, but without feeling the action, I snuggle into Ronnie's shoulder. Sitting silently, we're each in our own thoughts, and notably thankful that we can get away from the troubles of the outside world, if only for a moment. Both of us know, the minute we move, our time is up. Reality sets in and deals us yet another blow. But for now, we are silent in the warmth and peace that surrounds us.

Chapter 15

Jane

Bette Taylor is about my age, but she's much younger in appearance. She's kept up with the facials, and the creams and all the goodies that keep a woman in high style. Her teeth, though not neon as many people's are, boast a brightness that cannot be natural. At times I wonder, if I'd married easily to a more common man, if my life would have turned out like hers, with some of the shine still left on me.

"I have the perfect restaurant for dinner," she says. "Not one of these loud places the kids always want to go to. Nothing makes me feel my age quicker than going into a loud restaurant. Doesn't anyone appreciate the fine art of conversation anymore? Where you're not screaming over a guitar solo?" She looks at me briefly. "I'm feeling my age again, Jane. This generation does everything quickly and loudly. I'm at the mall the other day and there's a 'brow bar.' To get your eyebrows shaped inside the makeup department. Right by the door where everyone is coming and going, can you imagine? There is no feminine mystique left. Remember how we were taught not to have our Mary Janes so polished a boy could see up our dresses?"

I nod.

"Now they wear their underwear instead of clothes. No need for boys to peek any longer."

She's impossible to dislike. Sweet-natured with beautiful, warm eyes that interact with you when she speaks and an enthusiastic, contagious smile. Like a magnet, she draws people to her affectionate nature. There are not enough people like her any longer. Even I find myself drawn to her. I like her, despite my instincts to *not* do so. It's not in my nature to endure the Bible-thumping sorts patiently. Imagine me . . . with a Bible study leader for an evening out on the town. Wouldn't Davis have a good time with this one?

"You have something that generation needs, and you love them and you know it. I've seen you with those women, remember?"

"Oh, well, those women—how could you not love them? They've all made mistakes, but they're repentant and trying to better their lives. That zeal is joyous to be around. Energizing, I would say."

"It's a two-sided sword. The young make you feel young, and they make you feel old."

"I feel old as dirt though, Jane. Glad to be here, but old nonetheless. Have you ever seen the show, *The Real World*?"

"I haven't, no."

"My niece had it on when she spent the summer. I about had a coronary. I turned it off, but after she was out of distance, I turned it back on just to see if I was hearing correctly. It's young men and women, thrust into a house together. Then they try to have sex, they talk about sex, they have one-night stands and discuss the sex afterward. It breaks my heart. It really does."

I try to change the subject to lighter fare. "Remember when Lucy and Ricky couldn't say 'pregnant' on television?" I laugh, but Bette shakes her head some more. It's clear she's really upset, and I don't know—there were loose girls when we were young, too. I may even have been one of them, by Bette's standards.

"But you know, it's in God's hands. I can only do what I can do. I have my Trophy Wives, and they keep me going. I've asked Lindsay to take over leadership when I get married. Did she tell you?"

"No, she didn't tell me. It's sometimes a bit strained with us. We're just so different." This wasn't really true, but it felt true. Lindsay and I, we were more alike than I care to admit, but we have to work so hard at relationship, it makes us feel worlds apart. Each of us reading something that isn't there from the other.

"Strained with Lindsay? I can't imagine. That girl is one surprise after another, but she's forthright, if she's anything. Even when her humiliation is plain to see, she is straightforward and the first to repent." She looks down at her lap briefly. "Well, usually."

"We were married to the same man. I imagine that makes things strained by their very nature, wouldn't you admit?" I am not in the mood to hear Lindsay's wonderful traits recounted to me. She does have this natural spark of energy, and I do not want to hear about it while she's with my son. Ron Jr. is so trusting, and he needs a woman who sees the world as innocently as he does. "It was so nice of you to come, but I would have been fine. As soon as I got some juice in me, I was okay." I tell her, humiliated by the entire scene. "I'm easily sidetracked, and I forget to eat. This has happened before. It's just a gentle reminder to take better care of myself."

"It's no work for me to be here, Jane. It's a gift, and I'm grateful for the time. With you, I doubt I have to be aware of what Justin Timberlake is up to. You're a fascinating personality. A real artist. I've never met one before." The way she says it, as though I'm Van Gogh himself . . . well, not that I liked to be fawned over, but who doesn't like to be fawned over? At least slightly?

"It's time to go home, that's all. Ron left my son the house in Pacific Palisades—"

"Yes, Lindsay told me. She was sorry he wouldn't be keeping it in the family though. She does love that house. We had many a nice Christmas tea there."

"Why didn't she keep it? Do you know?" I ask, wondering if I might finally have the answer. "You're not the first person to mention how much she loved the house."

"It's not really my place to say, but I know she's happy with the decision."

That's another thing I don't get about Lindsay's religion. Everyone's above idle gossip—and I find that hard to believe. Maybe it's just Bette, and she's learned it's wise to keep her trap shut. In my town, we know what's going on in everyone's house. I feel eased out here.

"Ron Jr. will appreciate the money. He keeps a few schools running back home in Mexico. Buys them books and supplies each year, so I know they'll be thrilled to have more. He can probably buy decades of education now, as well as a house for himself. He says this year, every child will get a backpack and a new pair of shoes."

"Yes, Lindsay has spoken very highly of your son. It seems as though you've raised a gem."

"Lindsay's being kind. She hasn't spent that much time with my son, so she wouldn't really know." I hope to ward off any encouragement anyone might give to Lindsay about my son. "Yes, he is a gem, but I got lucky. I can't really take credit. He was gentle-spirited from the start. Nothing like his mother."

"I wouldn't say that." She pats my hand. "I'm so glad you're here. Every once in a while, it's important to be around women our own age, so we know that we're not completely out to pasture yet."

"I agree. I'd love to return this favor when you're married. Perhaps you and your husband could come visit Davis and me in Campeche." Davis's name rolls off my tongue before I remember he may not be there when I return. The woman who answered my phone may be packing his navy blue suitcase as I speak.

"Davis?"

I'm not up for the explanation of living in sin. I'm fifty-three years old, and don't believe in such rules. I've earned the right to do as I please. "You'll have to visit *me* in Campeche when you're married. You'll see that the same things are not valued in my country as yours. L.A. would depress anyone about the natural state of aging."

"The same things aren't valued five miles out of the thirty-mile-zone. That's the zone they say holds Hollywood and has the most impact on the world. Frightening, isn't it? Considering what goes on in that area."

"Horrifying." I try to avoid thinking about the woman who answered my phone. If Davis were leaving, I have a hard time with the fact he'd bring another woman into my house. *Just leave already.* Don't taunt me, and employ my house as your own personal bachelor pad. I feel rage welling up within me, and I know it will consume me if I allow it, so I focus on the lovely people walking along the street. "What city is this?" I ask Bette, as there are a million little cities in L.A., all chained together like a tightly strung strand of pearls.

"Santa Monica. It's still a posh neighborhood, but there's a crepe place you'll love. Do you like crepes?"

"They're fattening and taste divine—what's not to like?" But I do hope she won't be offended when I have something without pastry in it. My diabetes has taken a licking since I've been here. Davis used to ensure that I ate several times a day. The thought makes me smile that, at my age and experience, I would still require such ridiculous coddling in such a basic area.

"See, right there. That's something you don't get with the younger folks. They're counting their calories all the time so they can drink with dinner. If I'm going to pack on the calories, I want some substance and chocolate in mine."

"Chocolate. There's something I miss since being diagnosed. I always wondered why I could get fat saying the word."

Bette pulls the car to the side of the road, amid a few honks as cars swerve around us. If they weren't right on our rear, there would have been no trouble. "I completely forgot about diabetic eating. Here I am, taking you to carb central for dinner. Well, I'm turning around the car, and we're going somewhere else." She presses the gas pedal to the metal and the next thing I know, we're streaming along PCH with the Pacific to our left. "Oh, I have an idea." She takes a turn, and we zoom toward the hills. I will never get used to L.A. driving. Soon, we're climbing the hill with the dark, vast ocean behind us. "This is where Ron Jr.'s house is. The one he inherited."

"We're not going in, are we?" I panic. Lindsay will think I'm stalking her.

"Heavens, no. It's behind a great gate, but I thought you'd want to know where it was. I'm sure he'll take you before it gets sold. It's quite a beautiful home."

"Of course, he'll take me. They're planning Lindsay's friend's wedding shower and how to move the furniture to sell it. In Mexico, we usually just buy the furniture that's already there. No one cares enough to move things." I laugh at the concept.

We drive until we're nearly at the top of the hill, and she points to a great, iron gate. "That's it." She pulls to the side of the road and a car goes whizzing past us, as though waiting for the opportunity.

Naturally, I can't see a thing but the gate, and I'm disappointed. "I can't see the house."

"It's beautiful. A lovely Mediterranean with Spanish and Italian details. It doesn't have an ocean view, but the grounds are beautiful and there is a view of the vast canyon behind it. It's like being in Tuscany, right here in Pacific Palisades."

"I wouldn't think that type of thing would impress you, Bette."

"Oh, a show of money doesn't impress me. It's the warmth in the house. It's not like these cookie-cutter mansions that everyone builds to impress others. It's someone's home. Even without the Pacific view, I'll bet it will go really quickly." She touches her chin. "Well, perhaps not. People like to impress others here, so maybe the warmth won't make a difference. It does to me, but I'm not purchasing multimillion dollar homes. Not anymore."

"Your husband was wealthy when he was alive?"

She nods. "In the worldly sense. I did what Lindsay did all those years ago. Only I had two kids to manage, and I didn't enjoy throwing soirées as Lindsay does. That girl can order up a catered affair in two seconds flat. She's got everyone who matters on speed dial. Me? I'd serve anyone meatloaf. An executive's wife is expected to have better taste. I learned eventually, but the heart got him before he had a chance to appreciate it."

"I thought I'd be a good wife like that. I dated the boy in high school who everyone wanted to date. Captain of the football team, member of Future Business Leaders, he drove a '57 T-bird when the rest of the kids had jalopies."

We drive into a small, expensive-looking village of quaint boutiques and restaurants. Bette waits forever while a car backs out and the traffic collects behind us. Although there is a great deal of honking, she is completely at peace, not missing a bit of the conversation.

We enter the restaurant, which is little more than a casual café with diner-style tables and French coffee prints in grand frames along the walls.

"So is Mr. T-bird Ronnie's father, then?"

"Oh, you know about that."

"I'm afraid I do. It was troubling to Lindsay, you understand, that Ron may have had a son she didn't know about. I consoled her when she found out, then she said it wasn't his son, just his name, but that it was a secret. Secrets make life so complicated." Bette says, as though she might have one of her own. But judging from her demeanor, I would doubt it.

"Well, she covered it all then, didn't she?" I feel my jaw get tight as I think about them speaking of my private business. There are just too many people who know the truth for Ronnie not to, and with each reminder of that, I am tense beyond belief. I have to get this done. Lindsay and I promised each other. I would tell Ronnie, and she would call her mother. And now, we both may feel guilty when we face each other, but neither one of us has made a move toward real action.

"She's a lovely girl. Lindsay respects other people's life truths, even if she might not agree with them."

Judging by that comment, I can only assume that Bette doesn't agree with my life truths. "Would you like Lindsay for a daughter-in-law?" I ask Bette to see if she'd put her money where her mouth is. I mean, Lindsay may be a lovely girl, but that doesn't mean she didn't marry for money and make some horrific choices you'd hope the mother of your grandchild hadn't made.

"She is precious and so open to what God has for her."

"That doesn't answer my question." As if I haven't tried that kind of answer myself.

"Lindsay doesn't seem ready to date to me. Although Ron's been dead for over a year, she doesn't seem to have found her way without him yet. She's not ready to embark on something new, in my opinion, but I have tried to set her up on a few dates here and there. There's nothing wrong with her getting back into the game for fellowship's sake. She keeps flailing over this ministry idea of hers, and it's taken her forever to plan something as simple as a wedding shower. Lindsay used to do that kind of thing in her sleep. But I'm babbling. Do tell me about Ronnie's father. Did you love him very much?"

"I did." I smile thinking back to when romance was fresh and new. "He used to charm all the girls, and I felt so lucky that he only had eyes for me. I'd sit in the passenger seat of that T-bird like I was queen of the Rose Parade."

"So what happened? Did you marry him?"

I clear my throat. "No, I never married him. We had planned to marry when something horrible happened, and all of our dreams were shattered in one night. When you're young, you don't think about consequences."

"That's devastating. Is he . . ." She pauses for a moment. "Is he dead?"

"No, he's very much alive. He's here in California. A guest of the state, you might say." My cell phone trills and I look to see it's Davis on the line. "Davis?" My voice oozes desperation, but I don't care. I just want to hear his voice. "Davis?" I say again. There's no one on the line.

"It's hard to get a signal in here. Why don't you try going outside?"

I punch in a return call, but nothing happens. I walk a little farther until I see more bars on the phone and try the operator this time, and beg her to put the call through, telling her it's an emergency.

"But you don't have an international line, so that's why the call isn't going through. Give me the last four digits of your social security number."

I do, and soon, the blessed ring takes place. "Davis. Davis, I am so sorry. I'm coming home, Davis."

"*Hola?*" The same woman answers the phone.

"*¿Donde esta Señor Davis?*"

"*Si, no está aquí.*"

"Where is he?" I ask again in English.

"*Señor Davis no aquí.*"

"*¿Cuándo llegará él?* When will he be back?"

"*Yo no sé.*"

She doesn't know, my foot. Davis never goes out unannounced. "This is *Señora* Dawson. *¿Quién es este?* Who are you?"

She clicks the line. I walk slowly back in the restaurant, fear barking at my heels.

"I'm going to lose them both, Bette. Both Davis and Ronnie. I feel it in my bones. My teeth are chattering like they did thirty years ago."

"Your health isn't good, and it's cold outside. Things always seem worse when our health isn't up to par. What can I do for you?" I look down at the table, and she's ordered me a full meal, steaming and diabetic-friendly. "Eat something, Jane. You'll feel better."

I shake my head. "Ronnie is going to find out everything before I tell him. I need my son. I need Davis." Hearing myself say that I need people is a surprise to even me, and Bette is probably right— I'm only hungry, feeling weak. I've spent my whole life believing I could live without anyone but my son, and he may be the one I have to live without. "My son is probably head-over-heels for Lindsay by now."

She laughs aloud, a sweet tinkling laugh, but still one that lets me know how ludicrous she thinks my premonition is. "Nonsense. Lindsay has enough on her plate without falling for her deceased husband's son. Or whoever he is. You were telling me the story about his father. Sit down and eat. Lindsay has a good head on her shoulders, and she's grown to care about you, Jane. Nothing is going to happen."

"There's a strange woman answering my phone at home. Davis isn't there, but I just got a phone call from there. He *has* to be there."

"He probably just went to the grocery store."

"Then who is that woman?" My feelings are getting the best of me, and try as I might to suck in a deep breath and try to find some balance, I only feel like hyperventilating.

"Men don't know how to operate on their own when women are gone. The first thing they usually do if their wife dies is sniff out someone new to help them manage. It hasn't been for lack of offers that I haven't married again," she tells me. "It's just there's finally a man I want to care for the way he deserves. I'm sure Davis simply found a local woman to cook his meals or clean up after him. You should be thankful. Can you imagine what the house would look like when you got home if he didn't?"

"I've never taken care of a man that way," I admit, more for myself than Bette. I force a mouthful of chicken in, because evidently I have to get my strength back.

"Maybe it's time you started."

"Maybe," I answer, but I'm doubtful. One doesn't exactly start being June Cleaver at fifty-three.

"You seem to me a very intelligent woman, Jane."

"Thank you?" Somehow it doesn't quite seem like a compliment, but Bette isn't one to give me a backhanded word either.

She continues, "Sometimes, intelligent women are their own worst enemies. What would it cost you to put yourself on the line for this Davis person? He seems like a safe bet. He's hung around this long, hasn't he?"

"Davis doesn't need that. He's a very independent thinker."

She looks at me doubtfully. "I've found that sacrifice, when called for, is better for the one who gives of themselves. I'll bet there isn't a thing Davis wouldn't do for you if you came forward."

Now it's me who looks doubtful. What has a woman like Bette had to sacrifice in her life? Did she have to give up the life she knew to run to a foreign country? Did she have to lie to her son about his father? I did what I had to do, and I'll do it again before I let Ronnie give up the future Ron handed him. Clearly, we may have disagreed on how to raise Ron Jr., but I can't deny Ron did love the boy he came to call *son*. After all these years, he didn't forget him. He didn't forget his responsibility to family. Perhaps I've been too harsh on Ron Brindle.

Chapter 16

Lindsay

As I stare into the fire, my cheek resting on Ronnie's shoulder, it dawns on me that the ties that bind us one to another are difficult to rationalize. Most notably, the unspoken connection that creates intimacy with someone you've only recently met. No wonder I've always appeared irrational and impulsive. Once you've felt this way, it seems ridiculous and unappreciative to pretend the moment was simply imagination.

I've heard this phenomenon romantically referred to as "love at first sight," and pessimistically referred to as straightforward lust. By nature, I'm not given to lust. I don't want to set myself up for failure, but I have always carried the ability to focus on the inner person, regardless of the exterior. Which is why I could love a man who looked like Jake, straight out of action hero Hollywood, and Ron, straight off a Hair Club for Men ad.

It's why I was able to speak up harshly to Haley when I met her. I knew she needed some tough love, and our immediate intimacy has created the best friendship I've ever had—even within the confines of the Trophy Wives Club, where I had plenty of great friends already.

Haley was different. I draw in a deep breath. *Ronnie is different.*

Although Ronnie has a great exterior—lust-worthy by anyone's standards—it's his inner sensibilities that attract me. His ability to see the mansion as a means for his ministry shows his mind is not swayed by materialistic goals. As someone who is easily swayed by materialistic pursuits, I find that endearing and balancing. I am not blind, though, to all the reasons his goodness is for someone other than me. I will myself to sit up and pull away to the corner of the sofa. Without another word to each other, we get up, I lock the door, and we head to the car. Once inside, Ronnie suddenly speaks.

"Is something wrong, Lindsay?"

Yes! I want to shout. *Just once, I want it to be convenient to fall in love. Is that too much to ask? There has to be some nice widower at church who needs a woman who knows how to call a caterer, plan a party, and lay out his suits for him before work. I need that man. Definitely not you.*

My stomach flutters at the memory of being surrounded by Ronnie's arms, followed by another immediate and healthy portion of guilt. No more guilt. I want to live life without a steady diet of guilt. Am I so desperate for attention that I have to throw myself at the one man I can't have?

"We were caught up in the moment. The house was warm and inviting. We're both lonely," he says. "Nothing happened anyway."

"Right. That house brings up a lot of emotions for me. You're so right. That's it!"

"I was caught up myself. It's such a beautiful house. Yeah," he says looking out the window. "Just beautiful. A beautiful house."

"Don't forget," I say with a forced laugh, "you did just break up with your girlfriend, so what's a hug between friends? Plus, I'm feeling lonely and planning my best friend's wedding shower. It was a natural reaction to snuggle. Nothing more." Bringing it up again did not salve either one of us, and I tremble at my *faux pas*.

"Snuggle? You would call that a snuggle?"

"A hug. It was simply a hug."

"I hug people all the time," Ron states. "I hug my mother! Heck, I even hug my neighbor's dog."

"Well, if I still had a mother, I'd totally hug her too. See? Completely innocent."

"Completely."

I suck in a deep breath. "So why do I feel so blasted guilty? Nothing happened."

"We're not perfect."

"So you're saying it was a mistake. Well, I never claimed to be remotely close to perfect. My mistakes are laid bare for all who wish to account for them. At least I dropped my fiancé before YouTube came on the scene, that's all I can say. Public isn't nearly as bad as it could be. I'm blathering. I have nothing to be nervous about, so why am I blathering?"

"I don't care to account for them," he says. Then he turns his shoulders and faces me. "Your sins, I mean. Anymore than I wish to have mine reiterated to me if I've moved forward. Hopefully, we've learned and won't make the same mistake twice. Growth. It's all about growth. We're growing. Tell me about dumping your fiancé; you'll feel better about this."

"Absolutely, you're so right," I agree. "Okay, so I was dating my high school boyfriend and that was nice and all. He was handsome, and he opted not to go to college. He went straight to work for his father, a contractor. After I got out of college—"

"What college did you go to?"

"UCLA. I majored in Art History. It was a pretty useless major, but college was great."

"You didn't meet anyone at school?"

"I worked during school and was only there for classes, so there wasn't much chance of that. I saw my boyfriend on the weekends, and that was that. Maybe I lacked motivation, but it was enough for me. I didn't have the gumption to look for anything different, and you know, it was fine."

"So tell me then, how did you meet my father?"

"Jake, that was my fiancé. He was working for Ron building this house, remember? I saw that chandelier in the dining room and I thought to myself, 'Can you imagine what it's like to eat your meal every night under something that fabulous? That would make me a really important person.'" I look to Ronnie, and his face is crinkled. I shrug. "I was young and naïve. I don't think that now."

"No, of course not."

"So I dressed in what you might call provocative gear, for me anyway—nothing like what the girls wear nowadays—and I came to the front door one day when I knew Jake wouldn't be there, to meet the owner."

"You purposely came here to meet him because of the chandelier?"

"I see it differently now. I see that God was watching over me, and He gave me grace when I didn't deserve it. Ron had just found the Lord, and he was eager to share what he'd learned with me. Jake's family was all Christian, and I understood everything, but I didn't have a real faith. Not really. Part of my falling in love with him was falling in love with Jesus, and the Lord knew I needed him. When I read that story about Ruth laying at the feet of Boaz and taking the leftovers from the threshing floor, I thought to myself, 'That's me. That's all I want, just what's left.' It seemed like a sign from above." It seems to be working. My telling Ronnie about my old self is definitely separating him from the new self. Never underestimate the ability to repel people with truth.

"So you married him."

"I think that he liked that I wasn't going anywhere. Maybe he did know it was the house that kept me here at first, but that soon changed."

"So what now, Lindsay?"

"I don't know. I don't feel the passion for life I once did. I used to love to help people with their financial planning. Ron taught me to do that with such skill that I don't think I'd feel poor even if I made minimum wage. It's a mind-set." I point to my temple. "Though I must say, it's hard to keep it when surrounded by all this. I get tempted. Naturally. I suppose that's why Jesus asks us to flee from temptation."

"Where are we?" Ronnie asks as we look out over the crashing surf.

"I don't know. The car came here. It's part of the trip, to see the ocean. Besides, it's sunset at the beach now. We'll follow it. I couldn't resist the temptation. Ah, you see. I told you. I am easily tempted."

He leans in toward me, and I shut off the car. I know the ocean is before me, but I can't hear the thundering surf over my heartbeat. I stare at his chin and feel my eyelids slide shut. I drink in his warm scent and it sends my body emotions I know I can't handle. My eyes fly open.

"So!" I say with an obnoxious clap of the hands. "A walk, maybe?"

He's thinking what I am, that once this evening is over, we'll have lost these moments forever and there's a loneliness in my heart that can't bear to say good-bye to this stolen time sooner than I need to.

"No. No walk." He brings his cheek to mine, and I breathe in this deep peace that I know cannot last.

But my mouth betrays me. "So did we regret our snuggle? I mean, hug? Or didn't we?" I ask him as I pull back. "I just want to be clear."

"I believe we're still debating the issue."

"Let's debate outside. On a walk along the pier."

"It's cold out there."

"I won't feel it."

"Neither will I."

We both get out of the car, and Ronnie comes around to shut my door, but he doesn't get that far and I find myself in his arms. We lean against the car and my head falls into the crook of his neck. I can feel the sweetness of his breath upon my face and the strength of his devotion in his grip. Something about the way he holds me says he won't ever let go, and though I am at a loss to explain this, my trust is vast and deep like the Pacific.

"How long until the wedding shower? I imagine I won't see you much after that and the house is on the market."

"Two weeks." I force the whimper from my voice. It comes out strong and overly loud. "Then, you'll be able to sell the house and this whole difficult incident will be over."

"Is that what this is?" he croaks. "A difficult incident?"

"Ronnie." I put my palm on his chest and step back. "I promised your mother. I promised her this very thing wouldn't happen. She knew something." I pull away from him.

"My mother knows me and she knows I have never looked at another woman like I did the first day I was allowed into your home. It's not your beauty; it's the spark that lies within you. I couldn't begin to explain it, but I felt it being in the same room with you."

"What if she's right, Ron? Did you think of that? What if she does know you so well, and this is about your devotion to your father and not me?"

He grips my arms. "Is that what you think?"

"I don't know what I think. I know I want to be a good person. I want to prove my mother wrong and yet I keep ending up exactly where I shouldn't be. That doesn't make a good person, Ronnie!"

"Doesn't it? You're not seducing me, Lindsay. You're not taking anything from me. You're here for me, and I want to be here for you for as long as I'm able."

I shake my head. "No, this is all happening too suddenly."

He backs away. "I've got nothing but time, if that's what you're worried about."

"Your mother doesn't believe I'm a Christian, and why would she? I made one vow to her. One vow and I haven't kept it."

I feel Ronnie's soft kisses on my cheek. "Ronnie, don't."

His firm lips are soon on my own, and I am swept away in the moment, lost in his closeness and desire. Part of me acknowledges it can only feel so good because it's wrong. *It's sin*, I remind myself. *Sin!* I push him away and wrap my arms around myself as I run to the pier, away from the temptation. The wind is ripping across the pier, and it's sharp and brisk. But I'm thankful for its thunderous noise because warmth envelops me, and I want to get lost in my head and forget that this will all come to an end soon. Because I am Lindsay Brindle, and it is not my fortune to walk in such easy sentiment.

After I find my voice again, I walk back toward him. He meets me on the pier.

"Your mom says he did it on purpose, made probate for the house while everything else was in a trust. She said he did it on purpose to keep her here."

"Why would he do that?"

"Your mother thinks I'm after your money. Maybe she thinks Ron orchestrated all this so that I might be taken care of."

"That's ridiculous."

"Then why did he bring her back here, Ronnie? You know as well as I do that I could have handled this. Quickly and without the drama. He wanted you both here." I know it has something to do with Ronnie's real father, but does he?

"Maybe he was trying to keep me a secret. Did you ever think of that? He wanted to be your hero. Maybe he wanted to stay that way in your eyes and having a son you've known nothing about— well—"

The waves crash hard against the shore and slap up against the pier underneath us. Ronnie brings his arms around me and tightens them so that the roar of the wind is silent against the deep beating of his heart.

"Does any of it matter anyway? They lived their whole lives like this, with secrets and questions. Do you want to live the rest of your life like that? Because I don't."

"Oh no, I know what you're getting at, and we're not telling your mother this happened. Any of it. I'll have the shower in two weeks, and we'll put this all behind us."

"And we'll share a secret. Just like my parents did."

I pull my head back and look into his eyes.

"He thought my mother was running away by living in Mexico. But she loved it there. She's so much more at home there, I wish you could see her in her element. She's so tense here. I think Ron just thought he knew my mother, but maybe he never did."

I feel a tear fall knowing that it has something to do with Ronnie's real father and will he be able to handle the loss when it comes? What will he think of my betrayal in this madness?

After a long, silent drive in my car, Ronnie and I pull up to my condo, and the lights are all off. Only the orange streetlights illuminate the front walk leading into the darkened hallway.

"I guess my mother is still out with your friend," Ron says. "Diabetic. Can you believe she'd keep that from me? I was hoping to check on her before I trekked home."

"I'll take good care of her, Ronnie. Drive safely," I say, patting him on the shoulder like a Labrador.

He lets out a haggard sigh, and we both know what it means. Our night of romance is over. We're about to wake up from this fantasy we managed to create for ourselves tonight. This element of peace in our chaotic worlds.

As we get out of the car, Cherry's porch light goes on, and I notice there's a man in front of my stoop. Her curtains move as she sends my visitor a non-welcoming message.

"Who's that?" Ronnie asks, putting his arms around me.

"I'm not sure. It looks like . . ." It looks like Ron, but of course, I don't say that out loud.

"Stay here."

I grab the back of his jacket and stay close. "I'm coming with you."

I'm not hallucinating. He sees the resemblance, too—the man looks nearly identical to my dead husband. A car pulls up alongside the curb and parks and I hear a door slam. It's followed by flashing lights, and I look back to see a patrol car slide in behind Bette and Jane. There's a rash of slamming doors.

"Mitch!" we hear from behind us. "Ronnie. Lindsay. Come back here!" It's Jane's voice, but my eyes are fastened to the door and the mirage I'm seeing.

I jump as a cat creeps along my calf.

The feline blinks at me. His eyes are blank and without life behind them, and my shoulders drop. Ronnie stands alongside me, and holds me firmly. "Mitch." Jane scurries beside us, out of breath and wild-eyed. She tries to catch her breath. "Stop this—we need to talk. Ronnie," she barks back at the two of us. "Go inside with Lindsay."

"What's going on, Mom?"

"Go inside! Do as I tell you!"

"Mom?" The man says, focusing on Ronnie. "This is my son?"

"This is *Ron's* son," Jane says definitively, and she looks away from me as I express disappointment in her.

"Janey, please. It's time," he says.

We're all standing around in a half-circle. Bette, Jane, Ronnie, myself, and this policeman, waiting for answers from a mysterious stranger bearing a striking resemblance to Ron. I imagine even Cherry thought she'd gone to the next world when she laid eyes upon his portly shape.

"Is this a domestic dispute?" the officer asks.

"This is *my* son, Officer. I'm here to meet my son."

The officer looks to Jane, whose eyes are as wide as lagoons. She shakes her head. "A minute, please. Can we have a minute?" Jane pulls the man she called Mitch aside and even in the dim light, I can see her trembling.

I step back, certain now that this man isn't my long-lost husband, but uncertain of everything else. He looks remarkably like Ron, but where Ron had smiling eyes, creased in the corners with delight, this man has lowered eyebrows and that straight line above his nose that has become rutted with anger.

Ronnie looks to his mother, back at the stranger, and then steps forward, ignoring his mother's request. "Mom, do you know this man?"

Her shoulders slump. "This is Mitch. Ron's brother." She crosses her arms across her chest. "Can you just give us a moment, son?"

Jane and Mitch walk away again, but their emotions are high and their words float across the yard like Jesus giving a sermon on the lake.

"Mitch, this isn't right. You need to give me a chance."

"That's what I've been trying to do, Janey," Mitch says. "Trying to call you and tell you about my release, but you kept hanging up on me. I've done my time. I'm begging you, don't make me do anymore."

"Everything all right here?" The officer calls, his hand ominously on his revolver. "We've had a call about a strange man lurking about the property."

"That would be me, Officer. Mitch Brindle, I'm a free man." He walks toward the policeman, his eyes perusing Ronnie as he walks by. "Just came to claim my kin is all."

"Is that so?" Jane says. "Stay here for a minute, Officer. I have some questions for him, and I'd appreciate protection."

"Protection? Janey, you know I'd never lay a finger on you. What is this? Haven't you done enough to make Ronnie think ill of me?"

"You wanted Ron's money!" Jane accuses. "That's why you were calling, so please don't act like the long-lost family now! Don't think I don't understand what you're up to. I'll send you back to jail for extortion if you try anything with me."

"Extortion?" Mitch asks. "You're going to talk to me about extortion? If anyone ran off with what belonged to someone else, it was you. Exhibit A," he says, motioning to Ronnie.

She takes the familiar stranger and walks toward the street, her expression pleading. Ronnie looks as though he's been sucker-punched. "Let out? My father? I'm in another dimension." He takes two fingers and pinches me.

"Ouch!"

"I'm still here. That's good."

"Don't jump to conclusions, Ronnie." But of course, my own mind is rabid with conclusions. If Ron did indeed have a brother in jail, why on earth wouldn't he have told me? In Ronnie's eyes, I see betrayal flicker across his brow at he stares at his mom.

"She wouldn't lie to me about my father." He looks to me for support. "She wouldn't."

"If she did, it would have been for your protection, Ronnie. Your mother loves you more than life itself. She'd never do anything to harm you."

His questioning look of deception now focuses on me. "You knew about this."

"I didn't. I swear. I didn't know Ron had a brother."

"Is Ron my father? Answer me, Lindsay."

I swallow. "I don't know." And I don't. I only know what Jane has said, which isn't much of anything. But seeing Ronnie now, I want to protect him. If Jane did lie, seeing his face now, I know exactly why she did it.

He shakes his head back and forth. "I trusted you."

"I didn't have anything concrete to tell you! I didn't want to gossip and make it worse."

"Look at my mother's face. There's desperation in her eyes. She's despondent talking to that man, whoever he is, and I've never seen him before in my life. If my father isn't who she said he is, how could she have kept that from me?"

"I'm saying we don't know the whole story. We'll find out the whole story eventually, so there's no sense in filling in the blanks. Ronnie, please." I clutch at his hand, and he thrashes it away from me.

He stares at his mother, the pain in his eyes worse than anything I've endured with my own mother.

"If Ron is not my father, there's no inheritance. There's no money for the schools in Campeche. It's stolen. It's not mine to give away."

"Trust your mother to finish this, Ronnie. Think about the kids. Ron left the money to *you*. Not to Ron Jr., his son, but Ron Jr., the man. It's yours, free and clear. He had to know."

His eyes darken. "You did know about this!" His gaze is accusing and angry, and I feel my throat swell. I'm afraid for Ronnie to find out the truth, whatever it might be. Not here. Not like this. And the way he looks at me with disgust in his eyes, it's worse than I could have imagined. The problem with such a quick connection is that it's just as easily detached. The beach, only a half an hour before, feels light-years from my present.

"Ron considered himself your father, Ronnie. He wouldn't have left you the money if he hadn't. I know that much about my husband."

"You didn't even know he had a brother," he scowls. "You didn't even know I existed until Ron mentioned me in the will. You only knew what Ron told you, and clearly, it wasn't much."

My stomach roils at the painful truth. "I guess that's right." Is it any wonder I was such an enabler to Ron's drinking? Out of the shadows breaks another strapping figure into the orange glow of the porch light. My eyes narrow as I see Jake's smiling face come into view. *Not now!*

"What's going on out here?"

"Nothing's going on." I look at my feet. "Just some family business. Can I call you tomorrow Jake? This isn't the best time."

"Cool. Hey, Linds." Jake grabs my arms. "I did it."

"You did what?"

"I broke off my engagement. There's no wedding on Saturday. I'm free. I'm a free man!" He rakes his hand through his hair, oblivious to Ron's presence or his current crisis. "I feel invincible!"

"Jake, that's great. Would it be all right if I called you later?"

"Jake?" Ronnie comes and stands in front of him. "This is the fiancé? The one you dumped for Ron, the man who may or may not be my father?"

"Jake." I shake my head briskly. "Please just go."

He claps his hands and shouts to the air, "Ah! I'm a new man. A new man I tell you. No more doing what I'm supposed to. I'm going with the flow from here on out." He picks me up at the waist and twists me around. Truly, he's oblivious. "I owe it all to you, Angel!"

As he places me on the ground, I see Ronnie's expression turn. "You'll excuse me." He marches toward his mother and Mitch.

"Did I say something wrong?" Jake asks with false innocence.

"Jake, can I call you later? Please."

"Aren't you happy for me, Linds? If anyone would know how I hate to be boxed in, it's you sweetheart. Look, you married that pruned-up old man to get a commitment."

"I am happy for you if this is what you want. Of course. But that pruned-up old man was my husband and I loved him, so I'd appreciate it if you would show him some respect." I can barely think of the words to answer him. *Clueless*, I want to shout at him. *Go tell someone who cares!*

"I made the right choice. For me. For us." He motions between the two of us.

I blink a few times. "What did you say?"

"We're free and clear, Lindsay." He stands over me with his hands on the back of my neck. "Didn't you hear what I said?"

Free and clear. Free and clear. I search for meaning in his words when my brain finally dislodges from where it's stuck. "I have to go." I clamber for my keys.

I want to be good, God. I want to be good. Why can't I be good?

I enter my condo, collapsing against the wall. "What have I done?" I search my memory for if and how I led Jake on—and if I did, how is it I ended up in a cozy snuggle with Ronnie all night? My cell buzzes, and I scramble hopeful it's Ronnie, but there's another text message from Tim at the singles' group.

ONLY DNR CALL ME!

If Ron were here, he would clear this all up for me. Perhaps not, but if he were here, I wouldn't be in this mess. I'd be married and planning parties for his clients! Even Ron might not understand my situation this time. Mexico is sounding better by the minute. *Ay carumba.*

Chapter 17

Jane

I can't believe I'm standing here, mere feet from my worst nightmare coming to life. Bette is leaning against her car, the officer stands with his hand on his gun, and the neighbors' prying eyes are everywhere. But the worst of it all is Ronnie. He knows that I've lied to him, and nothing I ever do can make it up to him. The look of disgust in his eyes is palpable.

"You can't tell him right now, Mitch. Please. If I meant anything to you." I plead with him and clutch his forearm. The years have taken their toll, but certainly so have his choices. Gone is that innocent puppy look that I remember, the one that helped me believe anything he tried to sell me. The other girls would watch him as though I were the lucky one who got to be the victim of his charms. "It's been thirty-six years. What good can it do now to tell him?

You'll only hurt him. Look at him, Mitch. He's turned out so well. He's happy. Why can't you just leave well enough alone?"

He looks back toward the stoop. "He's my son, Jane. You're the one who hurt him in this, and you can't admit your lies led to this. A man has a right to know his father. Think of what this might mean to him—to learn his father isn't dead."

"You think it's going to be a great solace that you've been in jail for his entire life?"

"Don't you think I've paid enough for what I've done? Yet, you don't want to pay for what you've done. There are consequences to actions. No one knows that better than me. I've been paying them practically my whole life, and now that the law says it's over, you want to continue the sentence."

"You took another man's life."

Mitch doesn't defend himself, which surprises me. "And you took mine and handed it to my brother. Janey, wake up. Ron always wanted you, and he saw a way to make it happen. Do you think I'd give the woman I loved to another man? Even if he was my brother?"

"Why did you go that night, Mitch? You didn't have to go!"

"I did, Janey. I had to go. It was what I was taught to do my whole life. Take care of my little brother, and I did."

His words bring tears to my eyes. "What about me? What about taking care of me? I was pregnant, Mitch. You knew it, and you went anyway!"

He still won't apologize for the choice, and I want to throttle him. In the thirty-odd years since, he hasn't taken responsibility for his stupidity, and his family honor still blinds him.

"It could have been anyone to raise my son, but you had to pick him. I wanted Ronnie to have a good life, so I said nothing. Not until you came back here for the will, to reclaim my brother as my son's father. That was the last straw! Ron is dead now, but you want to act like I'm the one who's dead, like I never existed. Tell my son and give him the option of whether to kill me off in his mind."

I wonder how he knew about the will, how he knew I was back, but I don't ask. Mitch always did have a web of contacts and informants I will never understand. "Don't you want your son to have an inheritance? I thought I did the right thing by giving him your last name. Ron left him a great deal. Can't you just leave it be?"

Mitch turns his head to the side and spits on the grass. "I can't. Did you like being managed by my brother, Janey? Did you like him telling you how to act in all situations? The proper respectability for each occasion? But that's exactly what you want from me right now. To shut up and let you keep right on lying."

"Your brother tried to do what he thought was right. He gave your son a home and a name to be proud of."

"How can you say that to me? He gave him my name. The name he should have had. Don't act like Ron did us any favors by marrying you."

Looking at Mitch's worn eyes, I see the humanity in him and all the lost years. The part of him I've tried to erase from my mind. Making him a monster made what I did bearable, understandable, but he's not much different than me, and I hate acknowledging that. He fought for what he believed in. He paid the price. I didn't and I don't want to. I want to go on running and leave the past behind me. "Please, Mitch."

"What are you afraid to tell him? He knows, anyway, Janey; you're fooling yourself if you think otherwise. Besides, you know I didn't pull that trigger. His father isn't a murderer. If I was in any other state, I wouldn't have served a day. Tell him the truth and be done with it. Will it be so bad? Right now, he thinks he was abandoned by his father. Trust me, alive and a crook is something, anyway."

"So he should believe he was abandoned by two fathers? That's your suggestion? And what about the armed robbery that put you back there? Don't think I didn't hear you went back."

He smirks. "It's hard for a felon to get a job, Janey."

"Excuses. Always excuses. Do you need money? Is that what this is about? What do you want? I'll get you the money; just leave Ronnie out of it."

"My brother owed me. He stole you and my son, and he couldn't even do that right. How long did you stay with him? Two years? Three?" He shakes his head back and forth. "No, you're not going to do this to me again. We're not talking about me. I know what I did. We're talking about you. If you can't give me one good reason why I shouldn't tell that boy who I am right now, and why I didn't marry you, there's nothing to stop me. I gave you the chance to tell him. I'm not giving you anymore."

My eyes clasp shut. I have no idea who or what I might be praying to, but I am definitely desperate enough to look for help anyplace I can get it. "Mitch," I say calmly. "Will you give me a week to tell him? Let me tell him the whole story. Let him Google it, and see the truth before he meets you."

Mitch rubs his chin, eyeing me with curiosity. He has no reason to trust me, this much I know, but I can't lose my son. I can't even count the number of times I've thought about how I'd get through this if Mitch ever did reappear in our lives. I'd lie and say it was his brother's baby. Why Ron pulled me back into this forsaken state to make amends with his brother, I'll never understand. I suppose it was a trap to punish me in some way. To give Ronnie the money and point to me as the villain in all this.

Ronnie strides toward us, his long legs resolute in his conviction to spare his mother from some unknown person. I don't deserve his allegiance, but I'd wither without it.

"Mom, is there something you want to tell me?"

I nod.

Bette comes and stands beside me. I feel stronger with her at my side, but the truth doesn't come tumbling out of me like I hope it will. I babble for a minute, trying to form words.

"Jane has had a stressful night," Bette says. "She fainted earlier from a sugar low, and I do think she might be having trouble again."

I look at Mitch and Ronnie. Father and son. I wonder why on earth I ever started this facade. It made sense all those years ago, when I worried my son would think he inherited the genes of a criminal. It's true that Mitch wouldn't have gone to jail in another state. California had a felony murder rule. It essentially meant if you were present at the time of a murder, and you didn't run or try to help, you were guilty.

Mitch believed his little brother Tommy wouldn't pull the trigger. He was wrong. Ron, on the other hand, must have questioned Tommy's sanity. He ran.

One night. One mistake and so much pain. I had made my own prison that I had to deal with, so I never thought about Mitch. I thought about our child and my inability to raise a baby with no diploma, no way to work and watch him grow . . . and it was so easy to turn to Ron. He made it easy, and I was searching for a hero. I suddenly feel weak, and Bette grips me. With the help of the policeman, she brings me into the condominium. Kuku is there to greet me, and he meows at my feet.

"What am I going to do?" I ask the floor.

"The truth will set you free," Bette says, and I look at her.

"Not this time." I shake my head. "Not this time."

The thing is, even though I just left my son outside with his real father, I know Mitch won't tell his son the truth. His loyalty is that which keeps the mafia in play. It's what put him in jail for most of his life.

"It's time to tell him," I say.

Bette and Lindsay nod.

"Go get him Lindsay, will you?"

"Then we'll be upstairs if you need us," Bette says.

Undeserved loyalty. I received far too much of it in this lifetime, and the debt has come due. I wish Davis were by my side for this.

Chapter 18

Lindsay

So now probably isn't the time to tell Jane I snuggled with her son. Although we never really did determine if it was actual snuggling, did we? This much I know: when he's not standing here, I obsess on how ridiculous it is that I'm tempted by a man sharing the same name as my late husband. Utterly obscene, in fact. But then I see his boyish grin, his gorgeous face, his warm eyes, and soft-spoken manner, and reason flies out the window. It's as if something clicked between us that can't be turned off—but that's exactly why it should be. Ronnie's life is in turmoil at the moment. He doesn't know who his father really is, his mother has been lying to him his whole life, and I've been aiding and abetting the deceivers.

What's he going to think when he finds that out? Will his fantasy of me pop?

What's Jane going to think when she finds out I've been kissing her son?

What's Bette going to say about my Christian love for all involved?

And then there's Jake. This man I loved, once upon a time, back from the dead (to me) to stake a claim in a future he thinks I promised him if he broke off his engagement.

Oh yeah, I'm fried. Anyway you look at it.

I'm stunned at how different Jane is now from the calm artist who arrived on my doorstep with a cat. She's weak from her illness, stunned by the arrival of a dangerous stranger, and worst of all, the whole of it seems to have broken her spirit.

I've been there. I've paid the price for my past, and it's not fun. I can look at Jane and see she's aged about ten years in the last two months. That's the thing about life—you can run, but you can't hide. Eventually, our past catches up with us, and the wave is that much higher, the longer we've waited. It's stronger and more powerful, ready to pull us back into the depths.

Bette paces the room, and I turn the computer on, and type in my mother's many names. The last known husband's name shows something in San Dimas. I dial the number, and I hear Nick's familiar voice. I'm silent for a time as I take it in.

"Hello? Anybody there?"

"Nick?" I finally say. "Is that you?"

"Lindsay? Well, by golly, girl, where ya been?"

"I'm here in L.A. still. Are you by any chance . . . are you still married to my mother?" I bite my lower lip as I wait for his answer. The thought of my mother being close by brings an excitement in me that I can't explain. I feel like this could be it. This could be the time we finally see eye to eye.

"Baby girl, your mama's in the hospital. Some days she remembers me; some days, she don't."

I gasp and cling to the side of the desk. "No, Nick. No, don't play with me. Put her on the phone. Is she telling you to say that? Put her on the phone right now!"

"Lindsay, honey. Your mama's not here no more."

I knew this could have happened, but the reality of it makes me sick to my stomach. I can never make it up to her. I can never make her proud of me, or tell her I was grateful for what she did do. What she was capable of. "Do you think she'd recognize me if I went?"

"She might, Lindsay. She always remembered you as the best thing she ever did. So maybe it would be good for her to see you."

"What city is she in?"

"She's right here, in San Dimas."

"Is her health good, other than her memory?"

"Yes, she's strong as a horse. Just the mind is gone. You remember how your mama liked her cookies? Well, she went into a diabetic coma, and she wasn't right when she came out of it."

A diabetic coma. The irony of my mother forgetting me for the same reason Jane struggled earlier isn't lost on me. It's like a great cosmic joke that is in no way funny.

"She told me not to call you, Lindsay. When she's lucid, she said that you wouldn't come anyway."

"Nick, you know that's not true. You know it."

"Well, I knew it, but I was trying to go along with her. When she knows who I am, I want her happy."

"So she didn't try to find me."

He's quiet. He doesn't want to tell me what I already know. That she never gave a thought to me in her life, that telling me I was the best thing to ever happen to her was a lie.

"I've made a mess of things."

"Your mama was a stubborn woman, Lindsay. You come here and visit me when you're ready, and I'll take you to her. There's more chance she'll remember if you're with me. You got the address? I got some of her things for you. Some of the memories in picture books and her ear bobs and things. Stuff she's not going to be using there."

I nod. "I'm going to go now, Nick. I'm not up to talking."

"No, course you're not. You call here when you're ready, you hear?"

"I will, Nick. I promise." I hang up the phone and run into Bette's arms and just let her hold me while I sob it out. All the regrets, all the realities that come with ugly truths from the past. It never seems to end. "My mom, she's in a home now . . . I guess her memory's gone, Bette. Why did I wait so long? Now I can't tell her that I loved her. I forgive her. I always did, but I didn't know how to go to her."

"Oh, honey, you told her. You did tell her. She didn't want to hear it is all." Bette pats my back soothingly.

But nothing can soothe this ache. When will the regrets end?

Chapter 19

Jane

S it down, son." I can't bear to look him in the eye. I should have told him the minute I came to this forsaken city.

"I don't want to sit down, if you don't mind. I just want the truth, and no more partial truths or half-truths or anything else resembling a lie. I want the truth. You even told Ron's little trophy wife more of the truth than you told your own son." He shakes his head, the treasonous thoughts on the tip of his tongue. "Why didn't you tell me?"

"We were in Mexico, for one thing. I never married your father, and the Catholics didn't take kindly to that back in the day. You went to Catholic school. It was bad enough you were a gringo from a broken home."

"That explains why you didn't tell others. It doesn't explain why you didn't tell me."

"Ron sent us money while we got on our feet. He always wanted us to come back, but we weren't compatible, Ron and me. I had nothing but contempt for him, and every time I looked at him, I saw this pale shadow of your father. The man I did love. You shared Ron's name, and I didn't want to explain that you were his brother's child. What would you have thought of me?"

"Maybe I wouldn't have understood at eight, but at some point, I got old enough to understand the truth."

"And by then, I'd been telling the lie so long, I was far more comfortable with it than the truth. I knew Ron would remember you in his will, so as far as I was concerned, I did what was best for you."

"When did I ever care about money?"

"It was what I could do for you, Ronnie. I wanted to do what I could. I knew if I ever got into financial trouble, Ron would be there as long as the lie was there. But Ron lost heart in the end. He found God and wanted me to come clean about everything. He wanted me to bring you here to meet your father in jail. When you moved here, I thought certain he'd find you, but I guess his trophy wife kept him busy enough. That and the bouts with alcohol."

"I want to know it all. From the beginning." He's still pacing, his brawny arms clasped together behind his back.

"Ron had a brother. He had two brothers. The younger one was killed by a police officer that night."

"What night?"

"Let me finish. Ron and Mitch. They had a little brother. Tommy. He was always in some sort of trouble with the law. One night, he got high on something and took a gun. He said someone owed him money at the pawnshop, and he was going to get what was his. Well, a pawnshop is no place to take a gun, let me say that first. It wasn't like it is today, where you just get money on credit so easily. If you didn't have the money back then, it was all-encompassing; you didn't gas up your car and you didn't get to work."

"Spare me the trip down American nostalgia lane and stick with the facts."

His coldness hurts, but I want this over as quickly as possible. Like ripping off a band-aid. "The pawnshop owner didn't unlock the door, so Tommy never made it inside. The police showed up, and Mitch—that's Ron's brother and your father—stayed to talk some sense into Tommy. He never thought his little brother had bullets in the gun or that he'd shoot. But he did. He shot a policeman dead. The policeman's partner, in turn, shot Tommy dead. Mitch witnessed the whole thing." Jane looks to me. "Ron ran before any of the shooting occurred, convinced that Mitch could talk Tommy down, and it would end well. He'd always done it before."

"But he didn't."

"No, he didn't. Tommy was killed, and Mitch was there for the death of a police officer. He'd known why Tommy had gone down to the pawnshop, and that was all it took to convict."

"That doesn't explain why you married his brother, Mom. You were supposedly in love with this guy."

"Ron convinced me that we could raise you, and Mitch would be out soon when his conviction was overturned, and everything would be fine. Just without Tommy."

"How long did we live with Ron?"

"Do you remember him?"

"Not at all," he tells me.

"You were almost three when we left. I tried to stay for your sake, I really did, but the longer we were there, the more Ron seemed to forget that Mitch ever existed. The more he seemed to see you as his son and me as his wife. I'd already betrayed Mitch once. I couldn't do it every single day of my life. Believe it or not, we left because I couldn't pretend anymore."

"So why not tell me the truth at some point?"

"Mitch never returned my letters. He never commented on the pictures I sent. I assumed at some point, he couldn't forgive us, so we just went on with life. That's what you do, Ronnie, you just go on with life. Ron obviously wanted to make it up to us. His will was his way of doing that. Bringing me back here was in a sense giving me back to his brother."

He steels himself and crosses his arm. "Thanks for the truth. Goodnight, Mother."

"Ronnie, don't go just now!" I run behind him and grab his arm, but he shakes me off.

"I need some time." He pulls open the door, and outside, the police officer and Mitch are still talking, shooting the breeze as if my whole life hasn't unraveled in the last thirty minutes.

Mitch smiles and puts out his hand. "Ronnie."

Ronnie takes his hand and the two of them embrace. The moment is not lost on me—that and the irony that I should be the one left out of the beautiful reunion. I slowly let the door close and leave father to son.

"My life is in ruins," I tell Bette as she comes down the stairs.

"So is Lindsay's. Maybe the two of you could help each other. I'm going to get home. Lindsay's just found out her mother has lost her memory, and she's pretty upset. I think this is a time for the two of you to come together."

"You're leaving?" I ask incredulously. "Isn't this the sort of thing you do, Bette? Make people feel better when their lives fall apart?"

"I've found God puts us where He wants us. Sometimes that place is very uncomfortable, but until we change our behavior, we stay there. Sometimes, even after we change our behavior, there are consequences. You girls can work this out and be there for each other."

"You're saying this is some sort of divine grounding?"

"I'm saying that when we don't let our kids be who they are, we're the ones who suffer. I speak from experience. Your life isn't in ruins, as you might think. It's always darkest before the dawn."

I need a cliché right now? "I signed my life away to get my son that money."

"He never asked you to do that. I'll call you in the morning." Bette stops at the door when she sees Lindsay come out of the kitchen, her face red and puffy.

It's clear she's been crying, and I feel a pang of guilt at the sight of her. She has a pink suitcase in her hand. It's clearly expensive leather, and it's never been used. It's as pristine as the day she brought it home from the store. "What are you doing with that?"

"I'm going on vacation. I need a vacation."

"Lindsay, this is your house. You need a vacation from me, and I'm leaving."

"I've already booked a cruise. I'm leaving in the morning from the Long Beach pier, sleeping at a little hole-in-the-wall hotel so I don't have to get up too early. I need a little sunshine and buffet-style eating, and I'll be fine. It's what my mother might have done. I wish I'd given her the opportunity to come with me a few years back."

"A cruise?" Bette says. "Lindsay, by yourself?"

"Why not? I never do anything by myself; it will be good practice. What trouble can I get into on a boat?"

"What trouble, indeed?"

Lindsay purses her lips. "Well, if I do get in trouble, you'll never hear about it. Look at it that way. What happens on the boat, stays on the boat. I promise not to fall off. That's the only trouble you usually hear about."

"I'm sorry about your mother, Lindsay."

"Thank you."

Bette makes her way to the front door and holds her hand up in a wave good-bye.

"Tell Haley not to worry, Bette. I'll call her. I have everything for the wedding shower under control. Promise!" She pulls her bag behind her and walks out the door before Bette has had a chance to leave.

"Father in Heaven, I will be in deep prayer for Lindsay." Bette stands with her eyes closed.

"Why do you say that?"

"Trouble follows her. She's going to have more than that pink bag tailing her."

"Lindsay will be fine." She's a scrappy little thing, and the good news is she's out of my son's life for good now. I can only pray that I'm not.

Chapter 20

Lindsay

A cruise. Never thought of myself as the cruising sort, but as I walk down the gangplank and show my passport, I realize escaping into the bowels of a boat might be exactly what I need more of in life. Just like *The Love Boat*, I can guest-star for a week in a different role, and then go home to my life, no worse for the wear.

Why shouldn't I live a life of virgin daiquiris with paper umbrellas, listening to bad pickup lines at the poolside bar? It's as good a cause as any to find myself. Maybe. Clearly, it wasn't selling suits, or I wouldn't be this tall. It wasn't helping single mothers with their money, or one of my friends might have said it was a good idea. And it can't be planning wedding showers, because I don't have that many friends.

I'm stuck, so naturally, I turned on the television and saw *Titanic* playing. Granted, most people wouldn't think of going on a cruise when watching *Titanic*, but my luck on land hasn't been very good, so it can't be that bad on sea. There wasn't a lot of prayer involved other than the deep desire to get away.

As Penny often says about her twins, I create my own weather patterns. Where I go, storms seem to follow, and at some point, I have to say to myself, what did I do to create this Category 5?

What better place to work on all that than a cruise? There will be no one to mix me up, no one to tell me I'm doing it wrong, and most important, there will be no Jake and no Ronnie to make me believe Prince Charming can rescue me from my pathetic self. Ron, God love him, he was a good man, but he didn't fix my problems, my fears, or my abandonment issues. He only helped me avoid them with cold, hard cash and tasks to keep me busy.

I've brought my Bible and an excess of self-help books, and if a girl can't get fixed in a week's worth of solace, prayer, and self-help books, I don't know that there's hope for anyone.

"Tickets, please." A young steward takes my ticket and scans it. "Welcome to the *Exploration Princess*, Mrs. Brindle."

"Thank you. And it's Miss. Miss Brindle." I look down and see my wedding ring and I yank it from my finger and shove it into my pocket.

"The elevators will take you to the eighth floor, Miss Brindle. There's a buffet being served in the Starburst Room, and your dinner is at eight o' clock. Enjoy."

"I plan to."

I used to be a tough girl. I've turned into a whiny, soft person that I detest. I'm like Bette without the substance.

"So who is it going to be?" Cherry asked me as I left the condo last night. "The handsome one with the nice—ahem—backside, or the sweet, young son of your ex-husband. He probably has a little money now. And those eyes . . ." She sighs. "Can you imagine what it's like to wake up to those eyes?"

Hearing Cherry talk about men like that is always disturbing, and it never quite loses its shock value. "It's not going to be either. I'm off to have some fun."

"You go, girl! Woowoo!" she squealed as I left. I laugh just thinking about it.

"What's so funny?" a man in the elevator asks me.

"I was just thinking about my neighbor. She was excited I was going on a cruise."

He gives me one of those smiles and nods as though I'm crazy myself.

I think back to her advice. "Lindsay, don't waste your life on appearances. Look at my face—looks forty, doesn't it? My chest, maybe twenty-five, but honey, there ain't no denying I am an eighty-year-old woman. I feel it in my bones." She releases her grip and pats my arm. "You go sail around the ocean and come back, ready to commit to someone or something. You're not a loner like us. Hear that much. I may be just the crazy old lady who lives across the porch from you, but I learned a thing or two in these decades."

Maybe I should have gone to a spa—less contact with humanity there. Bette's expression told me exactly what she thought of the cruise, and the fact that Cherry approves doesn't say much for my choice. I have this knack for creating conflict, and only when I'm in it do I see the steps that I took to get there. I like to think myself a victim of circumstances, but really now . . . I've stopped a wedding from happening, I've kissed my dead husband's nephew and I've offended my houseguest by breaking the one promise she asked of me. I couldn't have stumbled into all of that, could I have?

As I step off the elevator, my cell phone rings, and I look at it to see that it's Haley. I plop the suitcase down and answer. No doubt she's calling because of Bette's panicked phone call to her. "Yes, Haley?"

"Girl, I don't know what you're up to, but you do remember me right? Your best friend? The girl you saved from a lifetime of chocolate frosting and nights of bad TV psychology? I feel like you're running from me, and I can't keep up. Where have you been?"

"I'm not up to anything." I'm not in the mood to be around a bride, full of hope for the future. Even if she is my best friend.

"I know, Bette says you're going on a cruise."

"Don't I deserve a vacation? I just wanted to have some time to myself. Mull things over a bit. I don't even know what to say about my mother. She wasn't all bad. Right? Maybe I'll like the woman she's become. Who knows?"

"Well, I suppose so. I wish I could take some of this from you."

"But you can't because you're the charmed one, remember?"

"It's when I stopped wearing rhinestones, my life suddenly got so rocky. I'm thinking a cruise is an excellent place for you to pick up a new wardrobe. A tacky, vacation wardrobe."

"I got the invitations out for the shower. Did you see them?"

"They're gorgeous. I can't wait to see everyone. My mother has forgiven everyone, now that I'm marrying a man my own age. She invited Gavin's wife to come down with her for the shower."

Gavin is the man Haley's mother hoped she would marry. "That has to mean Hamilton's in like flint now, huh?"

"And why wouldn't he be? How on earth did you book a cruise so fast?"

"They had the presidential suite still open for this week. They usually upgrade it if it's not sold, and it wasn't so I gave them my credit card number, and for the next four days, the suite is mine. The storm in the condo should have blown over by the time I get back. Jane will have found a new place to live, or better yet, be on her way back to the life she lives in Mexico. Jake will figure out what to do with his sorry, commitment-phobe life, and if I had to guess, it's to run into his bride's arms and beg forgiveness. Ronnie will have realized he made a mistake—" My voice trails off.

"Wait a minute. What was that?"

"Nothing. Look, we'll talk when I get back. It's four days; you'll survive without me."

"What did you do? You can't leave me hanging like that!"

"Uh-oh, you're breaking up. Better run!" I snap the phone shut and pause outside my double-doored suite.

I open the door and jump onto the bed, stretching out wide across the king-size mattress. I pull out a book. "Okay, Dr. Phil. This is the last time I take a bald man to bed with me."

Chapter 21

Jane

I'm packing my suitcase, ready to get back to a world that makes sense to me when the phone rings. I see Ronnie's name light up the caller ID screen, and I about burst.

"Hi, Sweetie!"

"Hey, Mom, how are you this morning?"

"Well, I'm getting things packed up, once again racing from the shambles I've managed to create in L.A. This city doesn't like me, and now it seems, neither do you."

"Mom, I need time is all. This will blow over. It has to because I know you would never do anything to hurt me, and you're my mom. I love you."

"I wouldn't, Ronnie. I've done some stupid things in my day, but never would I hurt you on purpose."

"So I have a favor to ask of you then."

"A favor? Anything son."

"Find Davis and marry him. Mom, he loves you, and you've given too much of your life away trying to protect us. You can't keep running. Sometimes, you have to stop and feel the pain. It's no fun. Trust me, it's no fun, but it's necessary."

"You're giving me advice on romance?"

"I would never feel qualified to do that." He laughs. "I'm giving you advice on keeping what's good around."

"You met Mitch then?"

"I did. I like him. He holds his pencil the same way I do."

"How would you know that?"

"We had breakfast. We're going to have breakfast every Sunday for a while. Get to know each other."

"I'm glad. Can I give you one piece of advice?"

"That depends."

"Don't rescue women. Your namesake always did that."

"I'm not rescuing anyone."

"I know what you like in women, son. I saw it in the sixth grade, when you went on and on about Julia Suarez. The poor girl had that lisp, and everyone made fun of her. You fell in love immediately."

"I'm afraid I wasn't that sympathetic, Mom. She hit puberty early, and I was twelve. That's when I was making my decisions hormonally. You take care of yourself."

"I'll take care of myself. The diabetes is in check. I promise."

"When are you leaving? I'll need you to leave the fax online so that anything that needs to be signed can be sent down there and returned quickly."

"Oh, that's right! I still haven't talked to Mitch about—"

"Mitch and I have the will all worked out. Don't you worry. He won't be making any claims."

His comment fills me with questions, but I don't want to lose my son over telling him how to run his life, so I clamp my mouth tightly.

"I'm leaving tomorrow. I think it's best if I'm gone when Lindsay returns. She's ready for her house back, and I'm sure Davis is ready for me to get back to my old life, if he still wants me in his old life. I haven't even spoken with him since he called about the gallery being low on stock, so I'm certain that—"

"Davis isn't there, Mom."

"What do you mean he isn't there?"

"Davis isn't at the house, and he isn't running the gallery. He hired a woman from Xalapa. He's gone. He wanted me to break it to you gently and asks that you respect his wishes."

"Ronnie, Davis has always said that—"

"No, this time, he's gone. He left the house and gallery in the care of this woman. She has a son that I'm going to enroll at the school. Davis left you a note. I'm so sorry, Mom."

I feel as though my heart might stop. "You talked to him? Didn't you just tell me to go back to him?"

"I did, but I didn't say it was going to be easy. Nothing worth having ever is. Davis called me because he thought if he talked to you, he might change his mind. He still loves you deeply. I wish you could tell him you feel the same, but it may be too late this time. But I have faith in you, Mom."

"You're telling me I'm going home to an empty house, and that he couldn't wait to tell me personally? But I should run after him and not be too proud to beg?"

"Precisely. Davis is gone. He said he couldn't playact as your husband any longer."

"Playact?" I force myself to catch my breath. Those are nearly the exact words I used to describe my own situation with Ron. I couldn't have done that to another human being. "We've been through so much together. Surely, he'd tell me this himself. Ronnie, you know that Davis and I—"

"He was worried he wouldn't follow through. I told you, Mom. You don't always make it easy for people to tell you their truth."

I'm crushed and in disbelief. "You can't trust anyone in this world."

"You can trust God."

"Oh, for crying out loud, Ronnie. Grow up! I'm talking about reality here."

He hangs up on me.

I believe in the law of attraction. Clearly, I'm attracting a swell of garbage, so I must be doing something to get such a violent reaction from the men I love.

The world is a very dark place to be sometimes.

Chapter 22

Lindsay

I have my whole life in front of me. That's what I think when I go to the front of the ship and hold my arms out like Leonardo and Kate in *Titanic*. Like every idiot on a cruise ship hasn't done this before me. Well, everyone under the age of sixteen, I suppose. Seeing someone my age is probably disconcerting for many.

"You're the queen of the world!"

I turn around to find a man behind me smiling at my antics. I step down from the bow. "Like you don't want to do it. Do it. Go ahead, I dare you." I order the stranger. "Step up there and give me your best Leo." I swing my arm in the direction of the front, and he follows my arm.

"All right, I will." He leans over the railing, and he's so tall, I'm scared he's going to fall and I pull him back. "Seriously?" He asks me.

"Sorry. I'm a worrier."

He steps back up and puts his arms out. "I'm on top of the world!" he shouts, and even with the roar of the wind, I can hear people behind us on deck laughing. He turns around with a grin. There is never an available man anywhere in a twenty-mile vicinity until you're married or decide you're never going to be. Then, they're like ants, marching through life, determined as the one they follow. "Come up here," he shouts.

I walk up the slight slope to the tip of the ship. I put my arms out and he puts his out. "We're the king of the world!" we shout and laugh like the freaks we are.

I shake my head. "You make a good Leo."

"And you are a fabulous Winslet. Is this your first cruise?" He puts his hand out and I grab it and he pulls me back to the bow.

"Second, but I was with my husband the first time, and I think it was before Leo and Kate."

"Ah, divorced?"

"He died."

"I'm sorry."

"I pushed him over the rail on that last cruise." I look at him in all seriousness and his smile evaporates.

"Seriously?"

"Stroke." I shrug.

"Ah. That's a relief." He steps toward the deck chairs just in case. "You have a sick sense of humor."

"I do, but I need one. It keeps me sane."

"Ah, this is sanity," he quips. "Where you from?"

"Bel Air. A little condo, not the mansions," I clarify.

"Brentwood," he says. "I live in a guesthouse. Not the mansions."

"Like Kato Kaelin?"

"Sort of, only I pay rent and have a job, and my little old lady landlord wouldn't hurt a fly."

"I don't have a job. I used to sell men's suits." I shrug. "I got a degree in Art History. It was pretty useless, actually. I had a Mayan artist staying with me, and I didn't even get that, so it's more useless than I remember."

He nods. "I'm a landscape architect."

"Wow. That sounds like a real job."

"Don't I look like I have a real job?"

I shrug. "It's just most guys in L.A. tell you what their job is while they're waiting for their role."

"You an actress?"

"Not until a few minutes ago on the bow of this ship. I was a trophy wife."

He blinks quickly. "You admit it?"

"I didn't really know until it was too late. Now I'm proud of it. I was a good trophy wife and in the end, I think he would have taken me ugly."

"That does sound like a good trophy wife. Norm Beckham," he says officially as he thrust out his hand. He's dressed like a tourist. Bad silky, floral shirt and khaki shorts with a brown belt. Too tacky to believe a woman had any part in the outfit, so I take him to be single.

"Lindsay Brindle. Got any cruise tips?"

He nods. "Stay away from the casino and if you drink, do so slowly in Mexico and go with a friend."

"The voice of experience?"

"A guy's weekend I will regret for a very long time."

"So you like to cruise then?"

"I like to get away for four days and not cook a meal and come home rested. You can't beat the value. No one can call you—well, they can possibly, but I leave my cell phone at home."

"I'm here to find myself." It sounds more twisted as I say it aloud. "I brought my shrink along." I take out a self-help title from my bag.

"Yourself? Not a new boyfriend?" he asks with raised brow.

"You men think we're all out to trap you." I look him up and down. "You're safe."

"Is it the shirt?" he asks, fingering his collar.

"Partly. Partly because I really am not looking for a new husband, and if I were, I'd have to figure out what I was looking for. Hence, the reason I'm here looking for me."

"There she is!"

I look up to see Haley and Helena approaching. I squeal like a teenager, "What are you two doing here?"

"We're here to help you vacation. You don't want to do that alone," Haley exclaims.

"Or with strangers," Helena says, arms crossed in front of her.

"Helena, Haley, meet Norm Beckham, a landscape artist from Brentwood."

"Only a Brentwood guesthouse," he clarifies.

"You don't have to make yourself any less desirable. We're not here looking for men," Helena quips.

Norm, a blond man with significant stature, gives a questioning gaze toward Helena. How do you explain our gorgeous, Spock-like friend to a complete stranger? "She doesn't mean anything by that."

"No?"

"She's just stating the facts. Aren't you Helena?"

"Wasn't that obvious?" she asks.

"This has been enlightening. I think I'll be going now. You ladies have a lovely cruise," Norm says. "Lindsay, same bat channel to-

morrow morning, if you want to fly with me." He winks and saunters off.

"What was that about?" Haley asks me. "Don't you have a few
men to get rid of before you add more to your cache?"

"I don't have a cache, Haley."

"A litter then? What do you want to call it?"

"History. So what are you girls doing here?"

"We were worried about you. So we got a last minute room in
the bowel of the ship, with no window, and we thought that doesn't
matter—we'll stay in Lindsay's suite. So we're here."

"How did you get off work?"

"My boss is out of town. I told Lily she could cover for me, or
come on the cruise, but we needed to be here for you. We booked
our room as soon as we heard from Bette."

"So this morning on the phone? You were already on your way
here?"

"Yep. We were making sure you actually got on board before we
got stuck on this floating bar alone."

We share a group hug. "My homeys are here for me," I say, de-
lighted at the thought that for once, I am the needy one and everyone knows it. I'm terrible at being the needy one. "I'm here to plan
my life on an organizational flow chart. I brought markers."

"Whoopee! That sounds like an exciting vacation." Haley rolls
her eyes. "Why didn't you tell the girls you needed some life planning? What are the Trophy Wives good for, if not giving advice?"

God bless her. I know Haley's trying to be helpful, but these
flirtations with Jake and Ronnie, however life altering they may be,
are the only sign of life I've actually felt in a year. They're the only
things that made me realize my heart does still beat and that there
is hope that I won't be alone forever.

"Jane doesn't think I'm good enough for her son, and I'm fine with that. But you know, Jake's mother didn't think I was good enough for him, either, and Ron's mother was dead or she probably would have felt the same. So I figured maybe God needs to show me why the mothers of America think I'm such horrible wife material. I need clarity. I want to learn from my mistakes, you know? All of this had to happen for a reason." Haley nods.

"Isn't it obvious?" Helena says with that look of duh she's perfected. Granted, she could be talking about the origin of anything from shampoo to Aristotle's separation from Plato, and she'd give you the same expression.

"It's never obvious to me, Helena. Enlighten me, if you get it."

"Clearly, you have a mother issue you need to deal with. God says that sin will be visited to the fourth generation."

"So that's why mothers don't like me?" I ask.

"No, that's why you need people's mothers' approval. You don't have your own to contend with, so subconsciously, you're searching."

Haley gives Helena a look and slices her palm across her neck. I can't imagine why anyone bothers to try to shut Helena up. She never takes notice of anyone's reactions. It seems to empower her. Any kind of feedback at all seems to empower her.

"Not to mention that you were married to Jane's former husband, and there's the whole six degrees of separation thing."

I shake my head. "Six degrees?"

"It has been empirically measured that we are no further than six degrees, or steps if you will, from anyone here on earth. Hence, the small world theory and the reason you are a mere one degree from Jane. Therefore, if you were married to the same man. . . . Gosh, you know." Helena puts a finger to her temple. "I don't believe that's even one degree of separation. You're related. It's the equivalent of coming from a small, mountainous state and announcing you're about to marry your brother."

"It is not! Helena," Haley barks. "It's like this, Lindsay. Women don't like to share men. You have already shared Ron, and now you're asking Jane to share her son with you. Remember how Rachel and Leah didn't want to share? Same thing. She's crying out to you, 'Mine!'"

"You're both here to drive me crazy. Tell me the truth. You've got a straight jacket in your suitcase, and you're here to take me away so that no one has to deal with me at all. Isn't that right?" I look at them both, and they blink innocently. As if everything they've told me should make perfect sense, and I am the one who has completely lost touch with reality.

"Let's go find the first buffet, shall we?" Haley asks, laughing. She hangs on to me as we walk, balancing herself carefully on her sparkling new Keds. Haley is not the most stable when it comes to walking, and I'm sure the sway of the boat is doing nothing to help the situation.

But suddenly I'm struck by what Helena has told me. "It's like I'm dating my brother?" I ask Helena. "Really?"

"Mathematically speaking, yes."

"But we're bad at math, Helena, so it hardly matters," Haley says.

"Right. It hardly matters. I don't think Ronnie or his mother are speaking to me anyway." I swallow the emotions this brings up for me. I wish I could be the sensible girl who doesn't feel everything so deeply.

"Well, it's fine. You didn't know them two months ago, and you won't know them two months from now. They were bit players in your life, that's all. Just two walk-on roles."

I stop walking as I try and figure out why Haley's statement makes me angry. "Ronnie has the same protective nature Ron had, and I felt really safe in his arms. I felt like I could simply sit with him for hours, and we connected without words. That's what I loved about him."

"You didn't love anything about him," Haley reminds me. "You barely knew him. This was just a stressful time in life, and the two of you came together in grief. It's a beautiful thing really. So romantic, but hardly real."

"It was romantic, Haley. In a way I haven't experienced before, and I know this is partly because I can't have him in my life. I broke the only promise I made to his mother. I lied to him. His appearance in my life—well, it absolutely brought out the worst in me. There's no doubt. But on some level, I felt at my best with him, too."

Haley stops walking. "Did you say his appearance brought out the worst in you?"

"Crazy, isn't it?"

"Ridiculous," Helena confirms.

"I'm not so sure," Haley stammers. "I know you, Lindsay."

"You're lonely. He's lonely, it's a stressful time and BOOM!" Helena claps her hands together. "It's social combustion. Oh, can I have the key to put my stuff in your room? You can't believe how disgusting ours is. No window or anything, and Haley keeps bumping into the wall because she can't tell which way is up."

"Sure. Sure." I take out the key and hand it back to her. "Suite 8000."

We walk down the hallway, and Haley falls into the wall while we search for the buffet.

"I can't believe you came on a boat for me. You have trouble walking on dry land."

"I'm here because it's you in crisis this time. I'm so sorry again about your mom. I know you wanted to see her before something like this happened. I'm here for you, girl. I'm your tub of chocolate frosting."

"Aww." I stop and hug her. "You like me. You really like me." I give her my best Sally Field.

"You can make fun of me all you want, but I am so glad to have my best friend back. I worried that you were going to spend your life getting your hair done and calling me for shoe sales. It was so unlike you." She pauses for a moment. "Well, there's more to you than that. Let's agree on that much."

"There are worse kinds of lives." I grin at her. "Look at you, you're still wearing Keds! The same shoes you wore when you were five, only now they have rhinestones on them. Is it any wonder I must call you with shoe sales?"

"Listen, Lindsay, you have to think about your skill set. I used mine, and I never even went to college. You've got a degree. You're light-years ahead of me."

"But I never used it. I worked at Nordstrom's. I sold suits by flirting. It's not like that's a real skill."

"It is, but technically, it usually leads to illegal work, so we're going to have to find something else, but you keep avoiding that conversation. Remember when we talked about design . . . styling . . . the ministry? At some point, you have to make a choice."

"Hence the flow chart I brought."

"You've just gotten out of the habit of asking God what the right things are. You know in your heart. That man you were talking with up on deck?"

"Norm?"

"Norm." She rolls her eyes as though she hadn't heard his name the first time. "Do you know, Lindsay, the first time I met you, you flirted with a coffee barista half your age. Oh, you read him the riot act that nothing was going to happen, but do you realize your first language is flirting? It's your comfort zone."

"What are you talking about?"

"You have gotten by your whole life by flirting and being beautiful. But what happens when you're not? *If* you're not? What happens when you're Cherry and your chest is still thirty, but you're not?"

"Banish the thought from your head! Right now!" I stop walking and wag my finger at her, as if I'm Bette. "I never thought of myself as beautiful. I always thought I was high maintenance with decent results from lots of cash spent. Besides, after I married, I didn't flirt."

"You did. I'm sorry to tell you that you did. Ron never minded—he knew you were there to stay—but you *did* flirt when you were married."

"Well . . . so what? It was innocent." But I'll admit, it doesn't sound so innocent now coming out of her mouth. I run through the men in my life I may have flirted with while married to Ron, and I'm ashamed to admit how many names pop into my head. Gosh, I hate those kinds of women. And here I am one. "Does everyone else think that? Was I the kind of woman people kept their husbands from?"

She looks away.

"No, seriously. I wasn't that girl!" I give her this pleading look. "No one wants to be that girl. Why are you telling me this now?" First, Haley has the nerve to tell me I'm holed up in my condo like the old women with cats, and now, she claims I'm a shameless flirt. I know I came on this cruise for a little soul-searching, but perhaps I got more than I'd hoped for in her answers.

"You're asking why mothers don't like you, and I'm telling you. You don't look like you'll be faithful to these men to other women.

The Trophy Wives Club knows better, but you asked, and I'm your friend, so I'm telling you. It's hard for me to believe that Ronnie is anything more than your latest flirtation."

I feel my head fly back and forth as I shake my head. *It's not like that*, I want to tell her, but what can I say to prove my point, really? I suppose I am a flirt. It simply never meant anything to me, but now—now that she thinks Ronnie is just another conquest, that Jake is another notch on my lipstick case—now it's my reputation at stake.

"I can't believe this is coming from you, Haley. You, who fell in love with your husband's prenup attorney. How can you of all people question me?"

She holds up her palms, but soon has to use them to brace herself against the wall. "All I'm saying is there has to be more than possible romance in your life for me to believe you're ready. You have to go after something, and it should be something tangible. Even if it's the wrong career choice, you'll realize it before you get there—maybe it should just be something other than a man."

What else is there? I think to myself before understanding how on-target Haley is. It hurts me to hear her say the words, and I can see in her muddled expression, it pains her to say it. But she's right. Just like I was right about the empty frosting cans in her room. They were symbolic of her empty life. "That's why I came on this cruise though. To regroup and fix myself so I knew that I was ready."

"What would happen if you truly trusted Christ to be your husband?" She says this with all the soft passion of a television evangelist, and it sparks something ugly within me.

"You're going to preach at me? You, who is getting married in two months? You, who I rescued out of a ratty motel and told you all about Jesus? You're going to tell me about faith?"

"Yes, I am. Remember me, who had no value outside of Jay

Cutler, until he shoved me out the door and I had to figure it out? It's time. Life goes on."

But I'm still lost in the audacity of the situation. "You holed up in a ratty motel for eons and ate chocolate frosting until we came and got you, and you're going to preach at me."

"I never said I had all the answers. Only that I figured out my problem. I'm trying to help you move out of this rut. You have nothing to do every day. Doesn't that bother you? Worse yet, doesn't it get you into a lot of trouble?"

"I'm sad, Haley." I feel the sting of tears behind my nose. "I am. I'm sad, and I miss Ron, and I feel there's no one who will ever take his place, and I'll die alone and no one will care. No one but you girls will even come to my funeral."

"You are not going to die alone, Lindsay. It's time to think about a daily goal. That's all."

"I'm making a chart," I say to spark some encouragement.

"What do you want, Lindsay? I mean, really want? You can't find that answer on a chart."

"With colored markers," I add.

"Even with colored markers, Linds."

"I want someone to hold me like Ronnie did and make me feel safe. I want a home base."

"It can't be a person. Not a human. As you've seen, they could leave you."

"I just want to go back to what was comfortable. Is that so wrong?"

This conversation has my head swimming. I want what I can never have. I want to go backward, and here's the thing about life, it forces you to go forward. Every time you try to take a step back, some new wind swirls in and forces you ahead. It's like a big game of Chutes and Ladders. Instinctively, I want to go have fun and slide down to the place where I started, but God keeps pushing up those ladders, like an overwrought personal trainer.

"I wasn't flirting with Norm. He came up to me," I say to maintain a sense of dignity.

"You were Kate to his Leonardo. There is not a court of law in this country where you could prove your case."

"So what are you saying? If I don't get a job, you're going to disown me?"

"The Trophy Wives have all tried to tell you gently, but it's time to get more direct. You know when you came and rescued me from the motel. This is your floating motel. Ron is gone. I'm so sorry. He was a good man, and he loved you deeply, but you can't live your life in the past. You can't live your life flirting with every man to make yourself feel loved. It's time to get real."

I gaze at Haley in wonder. She went from being a dingbat trophy wife, and I'm sorry, but even us trophy wives have our caste system. She was the type who never questioned, who never rocked the boat until she was replaced. I worked hard to keep my mind sharp, to keep our relationship balanced.

"Who am I kidding? I'm a mess. Ron was the only person who ever accepted me as is, and the idea that Ronnie would do the same thing is nothing more than my own wishful thinking and not wanting to live in reality."

"That's not true, Lindsay. We all accept you. Bette, Lily, Helena in her offbeat way, and Penny and me. We accept and love you the way you are. We want you to move forward for you, but if you stay stuck in your pathetic, flirting status quo, you're still welcome."

I nod.

My eyes blink. "That's it. I'm angry." I look at Haley. "I'm angry at God because He took from me what I loved. The one man on earth who loved me, and I don't think I care to please Him anymore. Ron was my rock. My salvation. That's not right, Haley. What if He took Ron from me because I didn't love them in the right order?"

"God doesn't work like that, Lindsay."

"I know you're right, but that's why I am here. I don't care anymore. To trust in the unseen. That verse. Faith is being assured of what you cannot see. I don't think I can do that anymore."

"Lindsay, did you have something to drink?"

"No. I never did really put my trust in Jesus. I put my trust in Ron. And he died. What if it's my fault?"

"Lindsay, you know that you don't have the power to say who lives and dies, so what are you talking about?"

"God wants me to live without the safety net, and I need to see it beneath me."

"He's not asking you to do it alone, he's just saying not with Ron any longer. We're here for you." She rubs my shoulder, and I give her a hug.

"Thanks for coming, Haley. I know this is terrible timing for you."

"On the contrary. My mother can't reach me, and she can't nag me about the wedding. It's perfect timing."

We finally walk into the buffet, and I'm glad to get away from this painful conversation. Realizing your life is a mess and actually doing something about it are two entirely different realms. I'm going to deal with the one and allow myself to process the idea that I'm a flirt by nature. That's ugly.

Norm.

Jake.

Ronnie.

Only one face flashes through my mind, and it's definitely the most inconvenient of the three. Oh yes, I definitely need to learn to live alone and find my purpose. Clearly, it isn't flirting.

I look back at Haley and her happy glow while she fills her

plate with vegetables. Clearly, she's given up chocolate frosting until the wedding. I, on the other hand, am single with no prospects. Which wouldn't be a bad thing necessarily, except I've just been told I'm a flirt and mothers don't like me, and my intrigue with Ronnie was nothing more than a figment of my overactive imagination. And I haven't even started a flow chart. I am so *not* the king of the world.

Chapter 23

Jane

"S he's dead."

"She can't be. Are you quite certain?"

"She is." I sniffle. "She's dead." I stare into the phone wondering what Bette means, am I certain? I didn't take her pulse or anything! "The coroner came and got her a few minutes ago. They wrapped her in a sheet, slid her in a rubberized bag, zipped it up and took her away, like she was nothing more than yesterday's trash. It's been so traumatic for everyone in the complex. All of the women are out on the patio weeping. It's horribly depressing and solemn." I try to shake it off, but death here in L.A. isn't like Mexico. With all the plastic surgery and lack of aging, it almost has you believing the residents are going to skirt death.

"Stay there, I'll be over to get you soon. What about the cat?"

"The neighbors are going to care for them. There's three of them, and they're all going to take turns. Lindsay's going to be so upset when she gets home." I pace the room thinking about it. Lindsay plays tough, but I see her check on her neighbors all the time. The cats congregate at the doorstep in some sort of emergency meeting, unaware of what's going on, but fully capable of understanding their life will not go on as before. "At least when you're dead, you're not left to wonder what might have been."

"Jane, what a horrible thing to say."

"It was a horrible thing to say, but it's like *Dia de los Muertos, La Catrina* has come to call."

"Jane, you're not making any sense."

"In Mexico, we don't fear death, well, except for the *angelitos*, the little children. We celebrate it on the day of the dead, believe the *animas*, the souls, come back to nourish themselves for the afterlife. We feed them, as well as ourselves. There is no feeling of celebration here. It's dark. Somber and frightening." I feel a chill run up my spine and look down to see Kuku at my feet.

"Is there anything I can do for the ladies there? They're so frail, most of them. I'll stop by the bakery on my way and give them some nourishment. I'll be there in a few minutes."

"They're pulling together." I slide the curtain open and peer out—just like they usually do to Lindsay. "They're planning the cat schedule and contacting the next of kin. Apparently, she's outlived most everyone, but someone thinks she has a cousin or a sister somewhere in town. They're doing fine, very practical in the matter."

Truly, they're weeping, and they haven't stopped since someone brought her dinner and found her on her porch. The scream is what woke me from my own black nap.

"Death is such an odd experience. It brings about reactions you never expect and hits people in ways you never imagined. I think perhaps we celebrate in Mexico rather than face the painful realities."

"You're talking about Ron, I presume."

How does she know these things? I didn't think I was, but when she says it, I realize his death is an experience that I never took the time to grieve. I simply went into business mode and did what needed to be done—especially since he'd been dead for a good year before I got word. I never stopped and thought about the man, and regardless of what my endpoint with him was, there's an extremely complicated middle.

"Maybe I am. Death brings with it so many questions about life." Davis, for instance. How many times I could have simply told him that I loved him. He sat across the room from me reading his paper and he'd smile up at me. *I love you.* How hard would it have been for me to say those three little words? Or I could have told him how I appreciated his always being there while I gallivanted all over the country, leading tours and teaching art in some forsaken land. I'd follow the path of my art someplace, and come home to a warm fire on a cool desert night. Or a glass of wine set out with a fresh salmon feast to celebrate my arrival. I took it all for granted, what he did for me every day. What is wrong with me?

"Someone else's death always reminds us of the mess we have made of our own lives." I tell Bette.

"It always reminds me that I'm glad this earth isn't the end."

I'm not sure how to process that. I mean, I'm all for spiritual fulfillment and believing in your truth, but how does one really have that kind of assurance? I mean, she doesn't know where Cherry's soul is anymore than I do. I know that her body looked pretty lifeless, and it's hard to believe there's more that went somewhere else.

"Don't feel like you need to run over here every time my life goes awry, Bette. I've leaned on you enough, and you need to spend some time with that man of yours. You don't want him running off."

"He's in Minneapolis on business, so you needn't worry about him. The Trophy Wives who aren't on the cruise are going out for dinner. You'll come with us and get away from the macabre scene. It will do your heart good."

"Why on earth do you call yourselves the Trophy Wives? It's so demeaning. Especially since most of you aren't married any longer." Her silence lets me know I did indeed say that aloud. Finally, Bette speaks again.

"There's a Bible verse about running for the eternal goal. 'I press on toward the goal to win the prize for which God has called me heavenward in Christ Jesus.' We're looking to eternity—the eternal prize—rather than dwelling on the mess we've made of things here."

"Uh-huh," I say, sorry I asked. I didn't know I'd get a sermon.

I have a headache. "Thanks for the invitation, but I think I should be here. I'll let you know tomorrow how the women are doing. Do you think I should call Lindsay? Or let her enjoy the cruise?"

"She'll find out soon enough when she gets home. Let's give her the rest she needs. But there's no sense in you being there without Lindsay home. We're going out for a little fun, and we'd love to have you, especially if you plan to leave soon."

"I don't want to intrude again." And really, I don't want any more Scripture verses thrown at me. I've done everything wrong according to Bette. I live in mortal sin, and I didn't even do that right. "I think I'll just take a nap on the couch and wake up late and paint."

"Nonsense. There's always room for one more with us. Lily worked today, even though it's Saturday, so she's ready to be out, and Penny gets a night away from her twins, so she'll be turning out the lights at the restaurant. There's life in us yet, wouldn't you

say? There's nothing you can do there at the condo now, so I'll be
arriving soon."

I feel guilty for all the people who have come to my rescue over
the years. I've spent my entire life thinking of myself as independent, when in fact, that was never true. I used people probably to
the point that I wrung them out like a sponge by simply not considering them. All the niceties and trinkets given to me, while I went
about my business and acted like the innocent bystander about returning invitations. My patio was always open. My courtyard free
to anyone who dared to venture onto it, but when did I ever make
a point of inviting people to share a meal with me? That was all
Davis, and he allowed me to take credit for having the *casa fiesta*,
the party house that was all him, every time.

"Bette"—I swallow and force the words before I lose my nerve—
"I need you to do me a favor."

"You name it."

"I need you to call Mexico for me. There's a man who isn't taking
my calls, and I *need* to talk to him." I don't even try to keep the desperation out of my voice. Chances are, he will know it's from me regardless with the area and country code. "I need to apologize before
it's too late." Honestly, I think if Davis turned me down flat, I would
understand, but I don't want him to go like Ron did—without him
realizing I did understand what he did for me. I did appreciate his
efforts. "Maybe if I call from your cell number and ask for him—"

"Certainly. I'm right around the corner. In the meantime, you
relax. Maybe paint a little to calm your nerves." Bette clicks her cell
phone shut, and I continue to walk back and forth, with Kuku at
my feet.

I feel tight and anxious. Seriously? What broke him? I gave
Davis his freedom. Don't most men want that? To be left alone to
change the channel as many times as they like, and eat deep-fried

things without nagging? I never nagged him. I allowed him to be all the man he wanted to be. I didn't babysit him or treat him with disrespect. We had an agreement. We were both free to go at any time. We were together because we wanted to be. Not because of some worthless piece of paper or empty promise. We were there by choice.

And he left by choice.

I fall back onto the sofa and repeat that to myself. Davis left by choice. He wanted more from me than I was willing to give. Just like Ron wanted from me, back in the day. Who am I to keep him against his will?

The doorbell rings, and I hesitate before answering. The somber mood of the outdoors is more than I can bear presently. I want to push the darkness back more than they can understand.

Life is bitter. Filled with rejection and remorse, and no one probably knows it better than these old women with their lonely existences and misery as they wait for their lives to end.

I open the door to face more rejection. It's Mitch. My heart begins to thump and the dizziness returns. I grab at my heart and let out a weathered sigh. "What is it, Mitch?"

"I wanted to thank you. Thank you for raising a son any father would be proud of. You did good, Janey."

I look around him, wondering what he is really here for, but he follows my eyes and then our gazes rest upon each other again. "He was good all by himself, Mitch. I simply fed him."

"The best we had to offer, huh?" He smiles, shaking his head in disbelief. I know how he feels. Ronnie will do that to a parent—fill them with false pride.

"He's certainly proof of good coming from horrible circumstances."

"I've seen a lot of proof of God in my years, Janey, but he's the best one of them. So I came to say thank you. We made our mistakes, but not everything turns out badly." He thrust out his hand toward me.

"You're welcome." I try to keep the question mark off the end of my comment, but it's hard for me to believe with all Mitch has been through, he doesn't have more animosity toward me, the system, his brother. There's so much more to say, and yet neither one of us seems to need to say another word.

"You have a good life, you hear?"

"You too, Mitch."

Before he leaves, he turns back, with his finger in the air. Underneath the lines that cloud his face, the dark ruddy complexion that has overshadowed the pale tone of his youth and light green eyes . . . underneath, I see the man I loved as a young woman. He *was* a good man, and searching his eyes now, I can see my son in them, and it's there I find my compassion.

He turns and brings his hand to my cheek, and I close my eyes against his touch. That touch takes me back thirty-odd years when I was a young girl filled with romantic dreams and pride in having the captain of the football team as my personal chauffeur. I've avoided the truth to protect myself, but I need to hear it now.

"Tell me what happened that night, Mitch. I want to hear it from you."

"Ron ran, Janey. I didn't. He always was the smart one. I was the jock who thought I could handle anything. I guess we found out for certain who had brains and who had brawn."

"I know who had compassion," I tell him.

"Maybe I should have run, but I've thought about this for thirty-six years, and I know I'd make the same decision today that I did then. I wanted to save my little brother. He had such a hard life with my father."

"You all did what you could, Mitch. Maybe it's time you had some compassion for yourself."

His eyes look up slowly and his gaze meets mine. He simply nods.

"Tommy was mentally ill." I touch him on the shoulder.

"I believe so. Yes."

"He needed help."

"Yes."

"Saving him wasn't possible. He was committing suicide."

His eyes flash. After all these years, he still doesn't believe it.

"He didn't mean to shoot the cop. I think he wanted the cop to shoot him."

Mitch's face twists in a knotted expression, and years of anguish are drawn on his forehead. He tries to hold back, but his emotion bursts out of him in angry, tormented tears. I reach for him, and he falls into my arms. I pat his back and feel his body shaking. It can't be possible he never thought of it. I told him years ago that Tommy was sick. Abuse, drug use, his brothers rescuing him from every trial imaginable while his parents ignored them. It was apparent to everyone on the block what Tommy would become.

"I was so angry at you, Mitch. You sacrificed me. You sacrificed Ronnie for your brother."

He pulls away, but he leans back into my shoulder nodding. "You're right. You were right."

"I married your brother to get back at you." This is the first time I've ever admitted the treason I committed and it stuns me . . . but not Mitch.

"I know. He would have been good to you. He always did love you from afar."

The fact that I wasn't an innocent victim in all this resonates with me—like it did a few minutes ago as I realized Davis didn't abandon me without reason. I am not the pillar of righteousness I pretended to be. Not then, and not now.

"You were willing to give me up for your brothers. Doesn't that say anything to you?"

"No. You don't understand, Janey. A man's brothers. They're his life."

"And his son isn't?" I hear the screech in my voice, and it's foreign to me. This isn't what I want to say to Mitch. I want him to admit he threw me to the lions, but he's not ever going to do that. How else could he justify all those years in jail unless he'd been there for his brother?

"It's over. Right? It's over."

I nod.

Mitch grabs my hand. "You live a beautiful life, Jane, you hear me?"

"I will. You too. You take care of yourself, Mitch."

He nods as he saunters off past all the chaos in the hall. "It's just you and me, Kuku. From here on out."

"Not quite."

I look up and cannot believe my eyes.

"Davis!" I rush into his arms and hug him so tightly, I feel I might squeeze the very life from him.

"Well, for a sickly old girl, you still got quite the grip. I think Ronnie's been lying to me about you being sick."

"Davis." I kiss his entire face everywhere I can plant my lips. "Davis, oh, how I missed you. Davis, marry me! Marry me!"

"I do believe I have the wrong house." He searches around me, his dark chocolate eyes creased in their familiar smile. "I'm looking for Jane. She looks like you, but she doesn't act anything like you. She's against public displays of affection, and I do believe she may be allergic to intimacy."

I shake my head. "She does believe in PDA now. By George, she does now. We're a family again, Kuku!" I allow Davis to hold me in his arms for a long time, relishing the warmth of his embrace and wondering how I ever missed the beauty of such moments before. They're what made life matter.

Davis lowers himself to one knee, but not without extensive groaning. He clears his throat and pulls out a velvet box from his pocket. "Not quite a family yet."

"Davis, what are you doing? Get up from there. You're not going to be able to get back up and then we're both going to be laid up. What good will that do us?"

"I'll get back up. I'm from the old school. This is my job. Jane, you are a pure delight to my soul, but I'll not be your kept man anymore. It's time you made an honest man of me. Will you finally marry me?"

I slide down to my knees and face him on the floor. "These tiles hurt."

"Answer the question."

"Davis, nothing would make me happier than to be your bride."

"And you're going to marry me in the church. We're going to do this right."

"I don't think the church will let us in."

"We'll go to confession. We'll own up to what we did."

"You sure God's ready for that?"

"*Hoy mismo.* He'd better be."

The door opens and Bette is standing on the porch. "Oh, heavens, I'm so sorry!" she says as she sees us in this ridiculous position.

"No, wait, Bette! I'm getting married!" I look at Davis. "Everyone's trying to feed me because I passed out because of the diabetes." I look up again to Bette. "Davis cooks for me normally. I get lost in my art and forget, and then I have to grab something fast so

I don't pass out. Well, Bette, don't just stand there, come get us two old folks up from this painful position."

With a mighty heave, the three of us fall over into a laughing mound, and Kuku takes the moment to climb to the top of the heap.

Ronnie has met his father. The world has not crumbled, and he does not hate me. Coming clean is exactly what my life needed.

I feel a warmth seize me, and my whole being feels drenched with love and compassion.

Chapter 24

Lindsay

Only ten days on dry land, and I have yet to start my color-coded life chart. Instead, I'm in a giant Pepto-Bismol ad. Thick, pink liquid flows freely and I clutch my stomach. *I think I'm going to be sick*. All of this overwhelming, goody-gumdrop romance and pixie-dust sparkle surrounds me. The idea that Hamilton Lowe is capable of this kind of response from a woman, much less my best friend, is cause for serious concern.

I mean, I flirt on a cruise ship, and everyone gets up in arms with all this deep concern; but Haley can have a wedding shower that resembles a *Quinceañera*, and everyone's good with that. It's nothing more than a quirk. What must one do to have a serious deficiency in taste known as a quirk? Lily, one of the most practical women I know, seems like the proper person for such a question.

I lift my arms to point out the putrid pink color surrounding us.

"Why is it a quirk when Haley falls for her ex-husband's lawyer, but it's a crime of passion when I flirt on a cruise ship?"

Lily exhales, rolling her eyes. "Would you get on with it already? Your best friend has a fifteen-year-old's taste. Is this a problem for you?"

"Clearly it is a problem for me, or I wouldn't bring it up."

"It's not your shower. You have no choice but to get over it. And speaking of taste, you were flirting with a man in a Hawaiian shirt and khaki pants, so you're clearly *not* the arbiter of taste."

I purse my lips.

"Lindsay, I have to give you props," Lily says. "I can't believe you did this all by yourself. It's gorgeous." Looking over the patio, it is gorgeous, albeit extremely pink. From the powder-pink rosebuds to the Hello Kitty pink napkins, with pink crystals and sparkles sprinkled over the table. It screams Haley's name. "You did a fabulous job all by yourself."

"I wanted it to be right, and I knew a professional party planner would screw something up, trying to make it tasteful." I look to Lily. "No offense to Haley, of course."

"Naturally."

"The perfect shower is the necessary precursor to the perfect wedding, which I want to be the highlight of L.A.'s marital season."

"Naturally," Lily says again. To a trophy wife, all of this is unnecessary information.

What I don't mention is how this shower is a celebration for new beginnings all around. It's my last party in this Pacific Palisades's mansion, and my last technical duty in my role as Ron's trophy wife. After today, this part of my history stays in the past where it, no doubt, belongs. "It's my last party here."

Lily puts an arm around me. "You won't miss it, Lindsay. You threw some great parties here, but you're capable of that no matter where you are. This was a phase of life; it's over now. Open up your heart to something better from God." She moves a place card on the table.

"Excuse me, what are you doing?"

"You had me next to Bette. I don't want to hear about how much I work. I'm not in the mood. I've got too much work to do."

"You do realize the hypocrisy in that statement. Maybe you do work too much. Did you ever think of that?" I move the card back. I don't want to hear about how I should have come home after the cruise instead of spending my last few days here with my first love—my bathtub.

As if reading my mind, Lily asks me the question I dread from Bette. "Lindsay, why haven't you gone home?"

"I just haven't wanted to face Jane and her son. All right? That's all I want to say about it."

"It's your house, Lindsay. You have to go home at some point." I hear Haley's voice and turn on my heel to see her dressed in a frothy pink halter dress with a sequined neckline.

"Obviously. The house goes on the market this week, so you needn't worry about me staying." I look at the house and specifically my bathroom window. It's funny how an entire mansion could be scrunched into one fiberglass tub, and I'd be content. "You're not supposed to be here, Haley. This is your shower. Bette was supposed to pick you up, and we were all going to greet you. You ruined the moment."

Haley peers at every detail on the table, brushing her fingers over the place cards, and her eyes water against the sunlight. Haley turns and wraps me in a bear hug. "Oh my gosh, this is so perfect! I can't believe you did all this by yourself! You really should do this for a living."

"That's what I told her," Lily says.

"Come in the house with me before people get here. Bette wanted me to tell you something before the shower. Jane offered to tell you, but you never went home." She puts her arm around me and peers back at Lily. "We'll talk at work tomorrow."

Lily shrugs and pops a pink candied almond in her mouth. "Sure. Whatever."

The breeze is starting to kick up, and I'm worried about the place cards. But the look on Haley's face tells me I'd better follow. It's not often my beloved, sequined friend gets so serious. We walk into the family room, and sit in front of the fireplace. My stomach twists as I think about the last time I sat on this sofa, but I'm not sharing that. Definitely don't want to hear the flirting sermon again.

Haley sits down, kicks off her practical heels and curls her feet underneath her. "So . . . are you going to tell me why you didn't go home after the cruise?"

"I came home to Jane still living in the house, so I brought my suitcase here instead and decided to stay until today." I shrug. "It's my last chance in this house. I fell in love here, and now that I know why mothers dislike me, I figured why put Jane through the turmoil of being around me?"

"With the house or the man?"

"Both, I suppose. Tomorrow, the house will go on the market and I'll return home like nothing happened."

"The reason Jane is still at the condo." Haley inhales. "The reason she stayed is because Cherry died while we were on our cruise, and she thought she should be the one to tell you."

My smile fades. "No! People like Cherry don't die." I'm incredulous. Within me, I honestly thought that Cherry would outlive us all. The news is like a blow to my gut.

"I'm afraid so."

"She was only eighty," I say. "That's not that old, and she had so much fight in her, I just assumed she'd live past me."

"She was actually ninety-three."

I can't help it—in the midst of my grief this makes me giggle right out loud. "I hope that doesn't get put in her obituary. She would have had a cow!"

"The neighbors wrote it. I brought a copy with me." She opens her clutch pocketbook and brings out the newspaper.

I nod as I wipe the tears from my cheek. In a way, I've become numb to death. "The older I get, the more I feel like it's frightening to get close to someone, for fear they'll die on me."

She puts her hand on my shoulder. "There's no getting around death, but you've experienced so much of it lately. I knew this would be hard for you before the shower, but I didn't think we should keep it from you any longer."

"I should have gone home. Jane is someone I'm going to have to face. I've got to stop running from my problems."

Haley nods.

"I can't believe Cherry's gone."

We both giggle, and then I sniffle. "I'm really going to miss her." The idea of Cherry, a mainstay at my complex, not being there when I get home makes me feel ever more lonely. It makes my desire to redo her condominium seem petty and heartless. "I wanted to fix up her condo. Why didn't I just go over there and buy her a new screen door, Haley?"

"She wouldn't have let you put it on."

"I'm a terrible person."

"You're not. You were focused on the business aspect of the complex, and the fact is, she did make that place an eyesore. Gosh, those funky plants she had out front were enough to send anyone back to 1957."

"Cherry made me laugh. She challenged me. Why didn't I tell her that?"

"We just don't know these things, but there's no sense in regrets."

"That's the point, isn't it? We don't know, so we can't take for granted. I talked to her right before I left. She was fine."

"You may not miss her quite as much as you think."

"What do you mean by that?" Cruelty is not in Haley's repertoire.

"According to all the neighbors, Cherry left her condominium to you."

"To me? Why would she do that?" I groan and drop my face in my hands. "That makes me feel even worse! Why didn't I take more time? Half the time, all I thought about was how I wanted to kick her cat off my porch and feel the satisfaction. I'm hateful!"

"She said she knew you wanted to bring the complex to its former glory and why not start with hers."

"Stop, you're going to ruin my makeup." I pat my eye with the back of my wrist.

"Before you get too choked up. It was Cherry. Let's not forget that."

"What does that mean?" Truly, I'm afraid to ask.

"It means she also left you three cats. They're all seventeen years old, so she didn't expect them to live long, but—"

"Three cats? I hate cats!"

"She said they liked you. The neighbors were disappointed. They're good cats, apparently, and they all volunteered to take them."

"How does a good cat differ from a bad cat?"

"I suppose you'll find out."

"See, this is my luck. Ronnie inherits this house. I inherit Cherry's." But it's an honor. I know it is. It makes me miserable that Cherry had no one to leave the condo to except for me. "I don't want to be lonely like her, Haley."

"You won't be, but that doesn't mean you have to flirt with everyone that crosses your path as potential, either."

"So I guess I'm going to be designing after all, huh?"

Lily walks in. I wipe my tears again, sniffle, and sit up on the couch.

"Are the guests arriving?" I ask her.

"No, there's someone here to see you, Lindsay."

I stand up and look out the window. My heart jumps at the sight of Ronnie, but as the girls catch my enthusiasm, I tone it down immediately. "It's Ronnie," I say casually. "He's probably here to ensure I don't ruin the house before it goes on the market Tuesday. The realtor tour is tomorrow, so he's probably nervous. Excuse me, won't you?"

Nervous? No one could possibly be more nervous than me at the moment. With calculated thought, I take slow, deliberate steps out onto the patio, and I measure my words in a formal tone. "Is everything all right?"

He smiles, and it's as though it's in slow motion. His green eyes glisten under the late morning sun, and my heart feels as if it's glowing. I'm E.T. and I want to go home. Stay home, and break into a Neil Diamond tune.

I feel myself pulled back by a firm hand, and Haley spins me around to give me her mother look. "With the way he's looking at you, you need to be careful. This is all fresh, and you're very sensitive right now."

"All right, Mother."

As I get closer to Ronnie, all caution is thrown into the Santa Ana winds, and I can't keep any part of my face from participating in my smile. "I missed you."

"I missed you."

"Are you still mad at me?"

"No." He's wearing a pair of worn-out jeans with the sexiest hole in the knee.

"Is there a reason you're not looking at me?" he asks.

Deep breath. "Yes."

"Is there anything I can do to change that? I was looking forward to seeing those blue eyes."

I can't help it. I stare up at him, and every moment of his kiss on the beach comes streaming through my brain. "I went on a cruise," I say with Helena-like conviction.

"I heard. Any particular reason for the sudden vacation?"

"I needed to get away. It seems I made everyone in my house angry."

"She loves you, Lindsay. My mom's all bark."

"She doesn't love me where her son is involved, that's for certain."

"She will. She'll warm up to the idea."

"Do you mean it?" I look at him imploringly, wondering if he means we do, indeed, have a future, or that his mother will get used to the fact that we had an attraction once.

"You're wrong, you know. You said I didn't have an emotional attachment to the house like you did, but I had one of the best days of my life in this house, and if I had a few million on my teacher's salary, those kids at my Mexican school would be in for more trouble, so I guess God knows my heart after all."

"Don't." I shake my head. "Don't tease me, Ron. Haley says I'm a flirt, so you can't trust me. I might have ended up snuggling with anyone that night, according to my friends. It seems I might be a tad bit desperate."

"You're going to tell me that in front of the fireplace, that was just flirting? If that's flirting, I don't think I could handle the hard stuff. We'd better stick with that and . . ." He walks toward me, placing his palm on my cheek. "If you think I'm foolish enough to believe that night could have happened with anyone, you don't know yourself very well. Self-awareness is key in Greek wisdom. Know thyself."

"Now you're sounding like Helena. What are you saying?"

"Come to Mexico with my mission team for the summer. Find out if this is real, or if we're victims of what God has for us."

"Victims?" I laugh.

"Maybe that wasn't the best word to use."

"I have three cats to take care of now."

He raises his brow. "You're a smart girl, you'll figure it out. Think about my offer. I feel I need to prove this relationship to you, as well as my mother. The trip is chaperoned with plenty of people who know me and what I stand for. Give me a chance to prove our meeting was more than happenstance. That's all I ask. Just a chance for you to see your true self, engaging in the world."

I nod, as I gaze dreamily into his eyes. "I'll come. I don't know how, but I'll come."

"Have you ever been on a mission?"

I shake my head. "Other than for the perfect pair of shoes? Never."

Everything happens for a reason. I just hope this hasn't happened to prove how incredibly ill-prepared I am for the mission field. Looking into Ronnie's eyes, though, I have to say, the chance to be with him is enough. I am officially back to life.

Epilogue

Lindsay

Haley's wedding day is perfect. The sun is shining, the sky has never looked more blue, and Haley sparkles without the help of beading or Svarovski crystals—though her gown is embellished well with both.

Her gown is a satin halter with full skirt and the bodice covered in seed pearls and crystal beading, but it's the back that makes it Haley's dress. It's a lace-up corset that covers a subtle fuchsia (if fuchsia can be subtle, she's found a way to do it) cathedral-length train with old-fashioned, fabric-covered buttons all the way to the floor. On top of the fuchsia, there is a bodice band of silver beading that makes the gown seem Victorian.

Naturally, our dresses are fuchsia, but I have never been happier to be in a bridesmaid gown, tacky or otherwise, than for my best friend Haley. Bette's gown is more mother-of-the-bride, but still hot pink. I suppose it's a good thing Bette is a tiny woman. Her own wedding will be coming up soon, and I imagine it will be nothing like this one, but a joy nonetheless.

"Haley, it's probably a good thing you didn't marry Gavin. I don't know what he would have thought of this dress. Pink, my goodness, what this L.A. lifestyle has brought to you!"

"Stop it, Mom. You sound like Lindsay. This is who I am."

"Yes, Mrs. Adams, even L.A. won't take credit for Haley's taste." I wink at her. "I'm kidding. It's a beautiful dress, Haley. I could have never picked a better one for you. The glow on your face is unmistakable. I daresay you're in love." I pull at my gown, which is strapless. The fuchsia is just an added bonus, but maybe that's what friendship is all about—you give a little of yourself up so that someone else can refine you and make you that much better, and they, in turn, do the same for you.

All of my Trophy Wives have improved me. Bette's made me realize I'm made of more mettle than I thought; Haley taught me that my looks were nothing more than temporary and God had more important things to do with me. Lily taught me that I'm an entrepreneur by nature and a good manager in both design and the occasional lunch for whiny, fat men in bad suits. Penny taught me I have a long way to go before I'm ready for children rather than cats, and Helena showed me that when all else fails, blurt out the truth.

"Is it true that Jane's getting married in Mexico?" Helena asks me.

"Next month in her local, Catholic church. The priest has been trying to marry them for years."

"Focus, Lindsay. Haley's just about ready to walk the aisle," Bette chastises. I run to my favorite bride and adjust her train and check her lipstick, and then I hand her the bouquet of pink roses.

"My stomach is churning. I'm so nervous for you, Haley."

"I'm not nervous at all. I have been waiting for this day far too long."

"He's a good man, Haley. I pray you make each other's dreams come true."

"We're certainly going to try."

The wedding coordinator from the church appears and says, "One minute!"

Haley turns to face me, her flawless skin the very picture of a Disney princess come to life. "Don't let my pink side flip over and show the white underneath, all right? I want everyone to see this silver beading."

"Crystal and bead patrol. I'm on it."

"Don't think we all don't know you've been seeing Ronnie, either," Haley adds. "We're the Trophy Wives. Nothing gets past us. When Jake got married, did we leave you in the dark? Heck no, we told you he finally got up the guts to marry that poor girl. But Lord love her, I pray she'll be all right in that family."

"Don't think about that, Haley. It's bad luck. Purge your mind. Purge your mind." I move my hand like I have a washcloth. "Clean?"

"Clean. I believe you, Lindsay."

"You believe me about what?"

"It's more than a flirtation. Ronnie looks at you the way a man in love looks at a woman, and you look at him like he could lift the world if he wanted to. Naturally, it's inconvenient. Love usually is."

"I'll tell you a little secret," I whisper. "I think he probably could lift the world. He's got the kind of faith that can move mountains."

Haley's vote of confidence fills me with joy. The bridal march begins, and we all fall into line like bright, pink ducklings. Ham-

ilton's jaw goes slack as he sees Haley, and I don't think there's a
woman alive who wouldn't covet that expression on their man's
face. I peek around her, and I notice he gets teary. Hamilton Lowe
is teary. Wonders never cease. I didn't know lawyers actually possessed these emotions, but if anyone could provoke them, Haley
could.

Ronnie is toward the front of the church in one of the pews
beside his mother. At the sight of him, I am in eighth grade again,
feeling the surge of emotion when a guy walks across the gym in
front of the entire school and asks you for your first slow dance.
That is what Ron Brindle Jr. does to my heart. And who says it's so
inconvenient? I won't have to change my name if things work out.

Jane's given up the battle over her son. I suppose she found the
wars waged in her life were useless in the end, so why prolong
this one? Ronnie takes after his mother in that way—he has a very
strong will all of his own accord.

The truth always rises like cream to the surface—no matter how
long you try to push it down under a milky film of lies.

Jane and I pass a knowing smile to each other. We Trophy Wives
converted her to Jesus and she, in turn, converted me . . . to a cat
lover. The women at the condo complex are going to care for my
three while I leave for Mexico for the wedding and our mission
trip. I've been told to bring good walking shoes, and I'm going to do
that—just as soon as I find out what they are. I am very attentive to
the pink on Haley's gown throughout the entire ceremony. I even
help her back to the altar for pictures.

"Lindsay, it's okay. You don't have to be quite that diligent."

"No?" I look up innocently.

"No."

"Beautiful wedding." Ronnie appears beside me, and I bask in his smile. He secretly takes my hand for a brief moment, and I feel flushed by his very touch.

"I think everyone's onto us." I grab his hand publicly and pull it to my waist. "We don't have to pretend anymore."

"It's been fun, though. I'll miss it. My mother probably ratted us out."

"She was worried I was seeing someone who wasn't you. She's exactly like me in that she thinks there could be no one else out there. But she couldn't figure out who I would spend so much time with who didn't bother to get me at the door."

"That stoop of yours is like Grand Central Station. Never know who you might run into there. But not picking you up at the door." He drops his head, shaking it. "You think a guy would be raised better than that, wouldn't you?"

I giggle. "So it's official. We're dating, and the Trophy Wives know it. Which mean our romance is now for public consumption."

"So we can dance at the reception. Maybe we can sneak to the backroom and cop a kiss."

I slap his shoulder. "You're a missionary boy, now. Don't forget that."

"No, I wouldn't. Besides, my mother is burning holes in your back right now. If you're not planning on treating me right, you'd better let her know right up front." He whispers this into my ear, and the tickling makes me laugh like a schoolgirl.

"Pictures! Pictures everyone! Bridal party I need you right here." The photographer points to a place in front of the altar.

"I have to go now. I'll see you at the hotel for the reception." I look to Jane who watches her son with level eyes and a knowing gaze. "She would do anything for you, Ronnie. You do realize that."

He walks me into the picture. "I do."

"Even give you the one thing she thought wouldn't be good for you."

"She's sacrificed her entire life for me. Now it's my turn to pay it forward. I plan to let one woman in my life know I'd sacrifice anything for her."

"I've already given up good shoes. Is there more sacrifice on my side?"

He grins. "That's all. For now, anyway."

I run to the top of the stairs and throw out my arms. "I'm the king of the world!" I say with a spin.

And I won't be there alone.

Because sometimes God takes our worst fears and turns them into beautiful dreams come true. Ultimately, He knows when it's time to get back into life.

Dear Reader:

Have you ever noticed that God brings annoying people into your life? Not just annoying people, but the same kind of annoying people! Over and over again! It's taken me awhile, but I've come not to resent those people, but to try to see what lesson that God has for me to learn. It's clearly something I have trouble learning, or I wouldn't keep going through the same trials! My prayer for you, Dear Reader, is that you take all the lessons God has for you and try to find your place in His Will—especially when you want to run the other direction.

Sometimes you hear the most horrifying stories of people's pasts and yet they can thank God after coming through those trials because they grew as people. They learned a lesson that God allowed them to pass on by comforting others. Granted, maybe not while passing through the lesson, but definitely later.

With Love,

Kristin Billerbeck

Praise be to the God and Father of our Lord Jesus Christ, the Father of compassion and the God of all comfort, who comforts us in all our troubles, so that we can comfort those in any trouble with the comfort we ourselves have received from God.

—2 CORINTHIANS 1:3

Discussion Questions

1. Lindsay is known as the woman who has it all together, who is able to handle life, but it turns out she was better at handling other people's lives. Have you ever felt like you lost your own rudder?

2. It sometimes feels like God seems to pile things on when life is tough. Lindsay is still mourning her husband and figuring out her own life, when Haley's wedding crops up with a myriad of chores. Have you ever had to put aside grieving to help the living? If so, how did it work out?

3. Jane has managed to spend most of her life avoiding intimacy since making mistakes when she was younger. Have you ever had a hard time forgiving yourself and moving on? How did you ultimately handle getting unstuck?

4. Have you ever used avoiding a decision rather than make any decision at all? Did you notice that in itself was a decision? How did it turn out?

5. Jane's avoidance of her feelings hurt a lot of people. Did you have a hard time identifying with her?

6. Lindsay also needed to move on from long-ago mistakes. What does it do to your faith when you hold on to old hurts?

7. Jane had a hard time forgiving people from her past and she held a grudge and took it out on a man who loved her dearly (Davis). Was there a time you took out your anger on an innocent? How did you move past it?

8. Do you think all people are capable of change? Did you think Mitch had changed?

9. Lindsay fights a relationship with Ronnie. Have you ever done that only to find it was inevitable?

10. Although Cherry had an abrupt way of seeing things, she was trying to help Lindsay to move on. Have you ever had someone tell you the right thing in the wrong way?

KRISTIN BILLERBECK, one of the first Christian chick-lit authors, has been featured in the *New York Times*, *USA Today*, the *Atlanta Journal Constitution*, and *World Magazine* for her work. She also appeared on the *Today* show for her award-winning book, *What a Girl Wants*. Kristin has been married for fifteen years and has four children. She makes her home in California.

Introducing

AVON

INSPIRE

Celebrate the grace and power of Love

Discover Avon Inspire, a new imprint from Avon Books. Avon Inspire is Avon's line of uplifting women's fiction that focuses on what matters most: family, community, faith, and love. These are entertaining novels Christian readers can trust, with storylines that will be welcome to readers of any faith background. Rest assured, each book will have enough excitement and intrigue to keep readers riveted to the end and breathlessly awaiting the next installment.

Look for more riveting historical and contemporary fiction to come from beloved authors Lori Copeland, Kristin Billerbeck, Tracey Bateman, Linda Windsor, Lyn Cote, DiAnn Mills, and more!